The Horror That Represents You

The Horror That Represents You

An Anthology Edited by S.D. Vassallo

Brigids Gate PRESS

The Horror That Represents You

Copyright 2024 © Brigids Gate Press

Individual works are copyright © 2024 by their respective authors and used by permission.

These stories are works of fiction. All of the characters, organizations, and events portrayed in the fictional stories are either products of the author's imagination or are used fictitiously. Any resemblance to actual events or locales or persons, living or dead, is entirely coincidental.

All rights reserved. No part of this publication may be reproduced in any form or by any means without the express written permission of the publisher, except in the case of brief excerpts in critical reviews or articles.

Edited by S.D. Vassallo

Proofed and formatted by Stephanie Ellis

Cover illustration and design by Alison Flannery

www.AlisonFlannery.com

First Edition: December 2024

ISBN (paperback): 978-1-963355-12-3
ISBN (ebook): 978-1-963355-11-6
Library of Congress Control Number: 2024943464

BRIGIDS GATE PRESS
Overland Park, Kansas
www.brigidsgatepress.com

Printed in the United States of America

Dedicated to all fans of dark stories, and the horrors that represent you

Content Warnings

The Craving: extreme gore

Khotoum: body horror

Folie à Deux: cutting

This Side of the Moment: child death, anxiety, intrusive thoughts, grief

In the Darkness We Dig: religious imagery, dental or oral trauma, body horror, anxiety, hallucinations, emotional abuse, self-harm, violence

Two Heads, One Body: suicidal ideation, anxiety, murder, possession

One Star, Would Not Recommend: ableism, fatphobia, misogyny, body horror, references to mental health concerns including disordered eating

Skin: none

Why I Wear the Mask: gore, violence

Blood and Dust: death

Something Blue: domestic abuse, sexual assault, self-inflicted harm

It Calls at Nightfall: none

The Grandmothers That We Leave Behind: elderly neglect/abuse, medical procedures, terminal illness, dysfunctional family, bigotry

The Visitor: stalking, harassment

A Lesson in Obsolescence: misogyny, amputation, paralyzation

Low Contact: death, bodily harm, homophobic language

The Last Train: suicide

Mad Lullaby: forced hospitalization/treatment, restraints

Someone Who's Not Me: homophobia, domestic violence

Just Lucky: none

Monster Spray, Monster's Prey: harm to a child

Wire Laurel: BDSM, dubious consent, sexual assault

Adrift in the Salish Sea: none

Contents

Acknowledgements	1
Introduction by Stephanie Ellis	3
The Craving by Vivian Kasley	7
Khotoum by Sridhar Shankar	19
Folie à Deux by Koji A. Dae	25
This Side of the Moment by Megan M. Davies-Ostrom	33
In the Darkness, We Dig by Nicole M. Wolverton	45
Two Heads, One Body by Scott J. Moses	55
One Star, Would Not Recommend by Anya Leigh Josephs	63
Skin by KC Grifant	71
Why I Wear the Mask by Samuel McQuail	79
Blood and Dust by Fred Furtado	83
Something Blue by Anna Fitzgerald Healy	93
It Calls At Night by Samantha Lokai	101

THE GRANDMOTHERS THAT WE LEAVE BEHIND by Christine Lucas	109
THE VISITOR by Hiro Finn Hoshino	121
A LESSON IN OBSOLESCENCE by Christopher O'Halloran	131
LOW CONTACT by Simo Srinivas	141
THE LAST TRAIN by Jen Mierisch	151
MAD LULLABY by Ray Pantle	163
SOMEONE WHO'S NOT ME by Micah Castle	173
JUST LUCKY by Patricia Miller	191
MONSTER SPRAY, MONSTER'S PREY by Sheila Massie	205
WIRE LAUREL by Stephanie Parent	207
ADRIFT IN THE SALISH SEA by Bebe Bayliss	221
LAGNIAPPE	229
THE NATURE OF ME by Linda D. Addison	231
ABOUT THE AUTHORS	233
ABOUT THE EDITOR	241
ABOUT THE ARTIST	243
MORE FROM BRIGIDS GATE PRESS	245

Acknowledgements

Thank you to Stephanie Ellis who, as always, has been a tremendous help with the editing, assembling, formatting, and all other aspects of putting together an anthology.

Thanks to all of the authors whose stories appear in this anthology. Your passion and talent shine in these dark tales.

Thank you to Alison Flannery, who provided the amazing cover art for this book. Welcome to the Brigids Gate Press family!

Thank you to Alex Woodroe and Lauren T. Davila.

And thank you to all our readers. These stories are for you—may they keep you company on many a stormy night, as you sit in your favorite comfortable chair before the fireplace, with creaks and groans and the occasional strange noise sounding in the house.

S.D. Vassallo
from the wide windswept prairies

INTRODUCTION

by Stephanie Ellis

"When I grow up, I want to be ..." is something the majority of us have said as children. Encouraged to consider joyous, extravagant, nothing-is-impossible possibilities, a young child's imagination and ambition is nurtured to dream and hope and believe. But children grow up and in those formative years changes occur. Lessons received from school, parents, and society give weight to the *type* of person they might become: kind, caring, ambitious, hardworking. And 'don't' becomes a commonly heard word. Now, the child begins to measure themselves against their peers: Am I smart enough? Am I as pretty? Am I good enough?

At this point, doubts arise—what has been taught seems to be a lie. They read Roald Dahl's *The Twits*, see the line 'If you have good thoughts they will shine out of your face like sunbeams and you will always look lovely,' and gaze in the mirror. Good thoughts do not stop the cruelty of the playground, and the realization dawns that the most beautiful face can hide a monster and the ugliest can hide a beautiful soul.

Advance a few more years, tweens and teens. Eyes become even more open to a society of double-standards, of shallowness and hypocrisy. The journey of self-discovery, of finding yourself in terms of sexuality, belief, and ambition, can bring with it horrendous conflict when what you 'are' doesn't fit with what those around you want you to 'be.'

A person is never shaped in a vacuum but is a product of family, of society, of rules, regulations and expectations. Conform or Defy? Break the mold imposed? Whichever path is taken, pain is often the result.

The Horror that Represents You is a wonderfully thought-provoking collection. Within its pages are stories which I guarantee will immediately connect with the reader, perhaps on a societal level, or maybe more personally, but they *will* connect. These tales offer a mirror in which we find ourselves reflected—and it is not always a pretty sight.

Vivian Kasley's "The Craving," births a monstrous metaphor for the pain and tyranny that is a woman's reproductive system; the sheer trauma it induces is portrayed in visceral detail. Another female perspective is given in "Skin" by K.C. Grifant, where a woman's body is seen as something which is free for others to touch, comment on, or worse ... An experience normally dealt with by the building of mental walls but here, a more drastic solution materializes.

"One Star Would not Recommend" by Anya Leigh Josephs takes the idea of being not just 'seen' but 'judged' in truly creative fashion as reviews are inflicted upon an individual body from the perspective of visiting aliens. Here is the shallowness of current society laid bare. Please note that contrary to the title, this is indeed a five-star tale!

Got a stalker? "The Visitor" by Hiro Finn Hoshino describes one woman's attempts to gather evidence in order to prove he exists. On what planet should a person be told by police to 'Come back if anything actually happens.'? A throwaway comment which forces the victim into dangerous territory.

"Two Heads, One Body," by Scott J. Moses and "This Side of the Moment," by Megan M. Davies-Ostrom, both consider the power of 'what-ifs' and how allowing this thought to dominate, regardless of reality, can cause torment beyond imagining. How many of us have been frozen by a 'what-if' scenario?

Christopher O'Halloran's "A Lesson in Obsolescence," is a clever take on the idea of the distortion of reality. Here are the consequences of an AI world taken to its logical conclusion. And speaking of society, its 24/7 nature is explored in "Mad Lullaby" by Ray Pantle which turns the concept of sleep upside down.

"Low Contact" by Simo Srinivas with its humorous tone compares with the air of sadness cloaking Micah Castle's moving "Someone Who's Not Me," as both explore what one would do to find love, whilst Samuel McQuail's "Why I Wear the Mask" portrays the wearing of an actual mask as necessary for survival in a post-apocalyptic world.

Molds are broken or recast in order to survive and continue to do so, this time under the impact of cultural influences in "The Grandmothers that We Leave Behind" by Christine Lucas. In the days of migration, so many are expected to cast off their heritage in order to fit in to their new world, to bury the past, leaving us all the poorer for it.

"It Calls at Nightfall" by Samantha Lokai brings Caribbean folklore into the mix with a story of creatures lurking in the darkness to snare a wandering child. Whilst "Monster Spray, Monster's Prey" by Sheila Massie conveys those years of growing up, of painful self-discovery in so few words, the shift from a mother's child to independence.

Challenging the convention of 1950s womanhood and marriage hits hard in "Something Blue" by Ann Fitzgerald Healy. I will admit to cheering Lizzie along as she cast off those 'shackles'!

"In the Darkness we Dig" by Nicole M. Wolverton is another exploring the downward spiral of wedded life as doubts set in when strange discoveries are made in the couple's new home.

Stephanie Parent's "Wire Laurel" is a brutal read of a woman in pain, where two different pairs of hands touch her skin, one that hurts, one that heals. This is the story of a journey to freedom.

Communication, it's lack or even miscommunication, is something which drives "Folie à Deux" by Koji A. Dae where metaphors cleverly add a disturbing dimension to a couple's relationship. *Be careful what you say …*

Remember I mentioned a parent's expectations earlier? That children are encouraged to dream and aspire? Beat that child down with enough 'not good enoughs' and you get "Adrift in the Salish Sea" by Bebe Bayliss with its sociopathic Jack bringing his dreams of being a scientist to macabre reality.

The horror of environmental disaster, as a result of deforestation or the dumping of nuclear waste, is touched upon in "Blood and Dust" by Fred Furtado and "Khotoum" by Sridhar Shankar. Even worse is that these are preventable horrors.

"The Last Train" by Jen Mierisch is a fable illustrating how self-absorption and lack of empathy in an individual can come back to haunt them. Such traits are further explored in "Just Lucky" by Patricia Miller where an art collector's greed and selfishness leads to obsession.

I could have gone into more detail about each story, but it is for them to tell their tale, not me. Every tale carries a truth within, what that truth may be to a reader will vary from individual to individual but the ultimate truth is inescapable, that if you hide a part of yourself or try to become what you are not, then your world becomes darker, heavier to bear—creating the opportunity for a monster to appear. And when you see those monsters, what do you do?

To paraphrase Martin Luther King: "Our lives begin to end the day we become silent about the things that matter."

It is time for the silence to end. Don't let the monsters walk.

The Craving

by Vivian Kasley

"A female's body is as fascinating as an unexplored cavern or the deep dark depths of the sea. No matter how much we've explored them, we sometimes find things we never knew existed," Kurt said, tracing his meaty calloused fingers across my smooth bare thigh. He'd come back to my apartment, hoping to get know me a little better.

I'd become bored. The sex had been mediocre. Nothing to write home about. And he kept blathering on and on, like someone who'd cooked dinner for the first time and couldn't shut the fuck up about it. It didn't matter that we'd fucked, my stomach still rumbled and growled, and an insatiable hunger gnarled at my insides. I rolled onto my side, rested my face on my hand, and murmured, "And sometimes you find things you wish you hadn't. Things that shouldn't have been found at all."

Kurt chuckled. "Oh, do tell me more, Anita, my little minx. What sorts of things might I not want to find?"

I moved swiftly and straddled Kurt. "Let me show you," I hissed. And that was the end of Blathering Kurt.

Maybe I was born with the Craving and it was always there, dormant inside me, waiting to grow. Or maybe it'd entered through some bad sushi or an alien spore from another galaxy that I'd inhaled up my nose like some sort of cosmic pollen. I'm not really sure. What I do know, is that it began when I was fourteen, not long after I started my first period. I had wanted my period so bad! I'd see my friends in the school bathroom, proudly displaying their pad or tampon in their hand like a badge of honor before they entered the stall and envy would saturate my bloodless soul. I'd smile at them and nod in understanding. As far as they knew, I'd had my period for two whole years already, like most of them had. Eighth grade is the pits for girls as it is, but if you're an eighth-grade girl who's chock-full of unshed uterine lining, you might as well light your own dumpster fire.

It started with bad cramps on a Saturday morning. Being lactose intolerant, I thought it was from the cereal milk I downed after my bowl of Fruity Pebbles. I tried to shit, leaning forward to ease the terrible ache, pushing and straining, but nothing happened. When I'd wiped, there was a rusty brown streak on the toilet paper, but for whatever reason it didn't register at first. Then the cramps got worse, bad enough for me to roll around on my bedroom floor while clutching my abdomen and lower back. Besides the cramps, there was what felt like the tip of a hot poker being pushed behind my belly button trying to pierce its way through. When I cried out, my mother rushed into my room. She helped me up off the floor, and then we ended up in the ER.

"Has your daughter ever experienced a menstrual cycle like this before," the doctor asked my mother.

"She's never had her, uh, her *period* as far as I know. This would be her first," my mother replied in a hushed tone, as if the word period was a forbidden word that if spoken out loud would unleash the apocalypse.

I cried then. My first period and it had sent me to the ER. I felt like such a big dumb baby. Anyway, I was sent home and told to take ibuprofen and use a warm compress for my cramps. The follow up with a gynecologist led to me finding out I had a tilted uterus and possible endometriosis. Because our insurance sucked ass and didn't cover me getting a laparoscopy to find out for sure, I was put on birth control to help suppress my menstruation and control the pain. As far as my father was concerned—well, he wasn't. He lived in another state with another family, and my uterus wasn't his concern according to my mother.

The birth control helped and so did the NSAIDS, but nearly a year into my monthly shed, I began to experience a new symptom. An intense craving. Not for pizza, or ice cream, or chocolate and pickles, but for blood. Pure unadulterated blood! The more metallic and saltier, the better. This grossed me out because I barely even ate meat. My mother told me to calm down, that it probably wasn't actual blood I was craving but iron. She said my recent bloodwork had showed that I was mildly anemic and that during my period I lost even more iron. My body was telling me what it needed, she'd said. So, I started taking vitamins and ate foods high in iron right before my cycle. But despite the vitamins, iron-rich foods, birth control, stretches, heating pads, and pain meds, the cravings, the cramps, the hot poker to the back of my navel returned with a vengeance.

I was home alone when it happened. It was spring break and my mom had to work. I'd already canceled the beach trip I was supposed to go on with friends, because I'd gotten my period earlier than expected and it was heavy—we're talking *seep through your pants when you do a little dance* heavy. Nausea swam around my stomach and blood clots like chunks of liver slipped out of me whenever I used the toilet. The cramps were next level. They were the type of cramps that stole your appetite and crippled you as they dug their cruel hooks for fingers through your uterus, digging and digging until they burrowed deep enough to reach into your lower back and jab at your upper thighs.

I'd already taken four extra strength Advil, tried yoga, and had a hot bath, but nothing eased the pain that had made itself at home. I dropped the beach towel I'd wrapped around my wet body and stared at my weirdo belly button in the floor-length mirror. It'd always been odd looking, like the topknot of a Sumo orange. I poked at it with my finger, then winced at the pain it caused. I poked again, and screamed when the hot poker began to force its way out. Like a Fourth of July snake that'd been lit, the form from my belly button grew outward until it was able to do the type of dance snakes do when they're being charmed. My breath caught in my throat and dizziness sprinkled a bevy of stars over my eyes.

I fell backward and remained glued to the floor with my eyes squeezed shut. I tried to regain my composure, breathing deeply in and out, telling myself it hadn't been real. But then the thing that was attached to me began going apeshit. I opened my eyes and saw its body—it was honey beige like my own skin—shoot upward, then sideways, wriggling in a frenzy as it tried to figure out where it was. It pulled up the meat of my stomach as it moved and I stifled my scream by biting into my knuckles. Its pink forked tongue darted forth and tasted the air, then it opened its mouth into a gape, showing me its rows upon rows of needle-sharp curved teeth. When I attempted to sit up, it whipped its body toward me so that its eyeless head was erect and level with my face. The moment the forked tongue tasted the tip of my nose, I passed out.

When I awoke, my abdomen throbbed. I stayed lying flat, and rubbed my hand over the burning flesh of my topknot. It was tender. I made myself get up, using the bed to steady my legs, and then forced myself to look down. There was blood, but it was a small amount, and it was already congealing around the perimeter of my navel, like clumps of red jam. The debate to call my mom raged in my head for almost an hour. How in the hell do you tell anyone something like that? Well, I didn't. I needed to clear my head, so I took a walk, which, depending on how you look at it, was both a good and bad idea.

Our neighborhood was quiet. The kind of residential street where hardly anyone is home during the day and, if they are, you hardly ever see them. I walked with my head down, deep in thought. What'd happened was beyond fucked up and no matter how hard I tried, there was no rationalizing it. Sure, the doctor had told me I probably had endometriosis, but last time I checked, that had nothing to do with what had just happened to me!

Or maybe it did. Maybe the medical community didn't really understand the condition and there were always serpents growing inside the wombs of some women: scarring us as they grew larger and wrapped around our innards, causing great pain as they searched for a way to come out for air. I was certain it had to be the root of my problems. What I wasn't certain of, was how I was supposed to deal with it. But like my mother had said, my body would tell me what it needed. And just a few streets later, that's exactly what it did.

On a tree-lined road with very few houses, I'd stopped to grab some shade from the fire of the afternoon sun that'd begun to singe my scalp. Several squirrels chattered at me from the branches of the giant sprawling oak I'd chosen to stand under.

"Shut up, you rats," I said. They ignored me and a few skittered down the length of the tree, flicking their tails and squawking at me to scram. I stepped back a bit and studied their dark little eyes.

"Kuk. Kuk. Qua. Qua," they shouted at me, over and over.

I stood my ground. Then one of the more daring squirrels came closer still, stretching its curious twitching nose close enough for me to touch, and the thing inside of me wasted no time. It burst from beneath my shirt and struck like lightening. I fell backward and bit into my knuckles again to stop from screaming. The squirrel squealed in its mouth for only a moment, then went mostly limp, its tiny feet jerking now and again. The thing used its teeth like a steak knife to saw a hole into the squirrel's plump belly before worming its head inside. In the background, the tree came alive with a chorus of squawking as the other terrified tree rats watched their friend being eaten alive. I didn't move a muscle and watched in stunned horror as it slurped up the organs and blood from the squirrel. It didn't stop until it had eviscerated it.

There was nothing left but fur, flaps of skin, and bones. It had removed itself and slowly sunk back into the enclosure of my belly button, coiling itself away somewhere inside me. I whimpered and looked down at the dark stain it had made on my yellow shirt and then threw up. Nothing that'd happened had made any sense and I was sure I'd lost my fucking mind. I paced back and forth on the sidewalk, choking on the bile that kept rising in my throat and swallowing gulps of air. When I thought I could walk home without fainting, I did. Back at the house, I collapsed onto the couch and slept until my mother shook me awake.

It was almost six o'clock in the evening. I'd slept for over four hours. My mother asked if I was all right and I nodded. Funny enough, it was mostly true. Other than the mild throbbing around my mid-section, I did feel fine. The horrible cramps were gone, and my headache too. But most noticeable was the missing craving for blood. It had subsided and I felt better than I had in months. *The squirrel!* I sprang from the couch and frowned. My body had taken what it needed. And apparently what it needed was that fucking tree rat.

As time went on, I got used to the thing inside me. I'd even named it: the Craving. I'd decided to keep it to myself because telling anyone could lead to unsavory paths and I didn't want to become a living oddity, traveling around as a member of a circus sideshow. In my head I heard a greasy carnival barker, "*Uuuuuup next! The aaaaaamazing AAAAA-Niiiiiita! Watch as she murders this mouse using only her belly button!*"

I figured if none of the doctors I went to had noticed it during my exams—and my blood work was good—then maybe it wasn't that big of a deal. I mean, sure, I'd begun to actively hunt and eat live animals, but so what? Besides, it wasn't me doing it, it was the Craving, and it was doing what my body needed it to do. *Tomayto, tomahto*, right? If none of this makes sense to you, don't worry, it didn't to me either. I was just happy to not feel like hot death every twenty-eight days and was willing to do whatever was necessary to keep it that way.

College proved difficult because it's not easy to hide hunting and eating animals using your inner serpent when living in a dorm. I managed though.

Mostly stray cats and other small critters during evening jogs, and by then I'd learned how to keep my clothing from becoming soiled with blood. The problems began shortly after college, when I ate my first human. It was a mistake. I hadn't meant to, but the Craving was strong, and by the time I realized what was happening it was too late. It had already bit into the man's throat.

    I'd met Mark on Tinder. He was just my type. Tall, dark, and handsome. He had a smile like the sun it hurt to look at. His body was hard and lean, and the smell of his pheromones was intoxicating: like earth and salt mixed with the sizzling fat from a well-marbled steak swimming in herbed butter in a cast-iron skillet. He'd made me feel things deep in the pit of my stomach and loins. A hunger unmatched by any other hunger I'd ever felt. Like a fool, I'd mistook that hunger for sexual desire and went back to Mark's place. He carried me into his bedroom and pushed my long brown hair away from my face. His lips brushed my ear as he whispered the naughty things he was going to do to me, and he planted kisses down my neck causing my vagina to throb with its own heartbeat. By the time he ripped off my little black dress and trailed his warm tongue down my stomach, the Craving had launched.

    Mark's screams didn't last long. I tried to pull it free from his throat, but the Craving was latched on. Paralysis would set in and then it would saw its way into his abdomen and slurp up the blood and organs inside. I tried getting the fuck out of there, I did, but the Craving used all of its might to stop me. I sat in shock on the edge of that beautiful man's bed and wept. I don't know how long it took; I just know that when it was through, I felt it slink its malodourous slick body back into mine and all I could do was stare at the baggy shell of the man who used to be Mark.

    I wish I could say I'd stopped after Mark, but after him I'd felt incredible, better than ever, and Tinder was a hot and juicy buffet. I'd gotten good at getting rid of the bodies, too. Suck 'em dry, then bag the bones and skin suits and chuck 'em into any ol' body of water. I felt invincible, but I knew I had to make a choice.

    I'd have to go to my OBGYN and find out my options. I wouldn't tell the doc what the Craving was, but I'd tell him I was having problems with pain again and how I believed my endometriosis was getting worse. I'd ask if my womb could be removed. I still took the pill for contraception, but I hadn't needed NSAIDS or heating pads in years. It was only if I refrained from eating that the problems returned, and I'd been eating non-stop. And that, well, that was the *real* problem.

My appointment with the doc was the following week. I'd my mind made up—the Craving had to go. It was a nuisance. A terror. I'd given up the idea of having children, so a hysterectomy didn't seem like a big deal. I wasn't sure if removing my goods would stop it, but I damn well was going to try.

The doctor sent me for an ultrasound, both vaginal and uterine. I had blood work, and all that fancy jazz. I fully expected to be informed by a room full of serious-faced doctors of the freak of nature living in my womb at my next appointment, but instead I was told everything looked smashing. I had the tilted uterus(duh) and some small fibroids, but other than that, nothing to worry about. I sat there with my mouth hung open, confused as hell. How did they not see it? And what about my endometriosis? The doc explained that I might've been misdiagnosed all those years ago.

He went on to inform me that more than likely it was my tilted uterus and proneness to fibroids that caused all the problems during my menstrual cycle. He was going to put me on a different birth control and write me a prescription for pain meds to be taken as needed. Well, there went the idea of having a hysterectomy. My insurance would never pay for it without a good excuse; it'd be considered elective and I'd have to pay out of pocket, 'cause, ya know, I'm a twenty-two-year-old woman and I don't know my own body or what I want. What a bunch of stupid bullshit. When the doctor said if I could I should wait until menopause because it would shrink my fibroids, the burning sensation behind my navel felt like a blazing torch and I had to flee the office before the doc became my next victim.

The Craving had won. It had somehow figured out how to hide. The only other thing I could think of was to try and get rid of it myself. But how? What if I fed it poisoned gerbil meat? Or what if I cut its head off when it came out to feed? I didn't know if either of those actions would harm me in the process, but I didn't care. I needed to call my mom and make sure she was all right in case of my demise. I'd hate to leave her without saying goodbye.

"Mom?" I swallowed the melancholy lump in my throat.

"Who else would it be?" my mom snorted into the phone.

"Oh, I don't know. Snoop Doggy Dog? Look, Ma, I just wanted to see how you were doing, and tell you I love you."

"Anita, what's up? You never call me out of the blue just to say I love you. Are you okay?"

"I'm good. I just haven't seen you in a while, that's all. With the new job and my new apartment—"

"Don't forget the revolving door of boyfriends."

"Gee, thanks, Mom."

"Well, it's true. Look, anyway, I get why you do what you do."

"Y-you do?"

"Yeah. I've been dating a lot myself and I've decided men suck. None of them are worth a damn. They're all like your father. Selfish and arrogant. The sex isn't even worth it. That's what those bunny-eared dildos are for!"

"Moooom!" I laughed despite the tears in my eyes.

"Anita, I'm not telling you how to live your life, but be true to yourself and never settle. Remember to please yourself first because nobody else will."

"Noted. Well, this was a good talk. I hope to visit soon."

"Whenever you're able. Are you sure you're okay?"

"Yeah, yeah. Just the same old monthly BS. Hormones and such."

"Alright, well, if you need me, you know where I'm at. I love you, sweets."

"I love you too, Mom. And …" I choked up and had to take a breath before finishing. "Goodbye."

For some reason, that phone call changed my mind. Maybe Mom was right? Maybe I should please myself first. I figured if there was a God, then they made me the way I was for a reason. And God didn't make mistakes, right? Fuck it. I'd keep my uterus and the Craving. I would just be very, very, careful about who and what I ate. If I could do that, then I could live happily ever after.

Fast forward almost five years. In between dumpster cats and pet store rodents, Blathering Kurt had been something like my one hundred and thirty-second human victim. All was well. I was about to turn twenty-seven and was in fantastic shape, my job was going great, and I bought my first house and filled it with an abundance of trinkets and other inanimate objects. The only thing missing was a partner to share it all with, but I also wanted something else. A child. I didn't think I'd ever want one of those. I used to tell myself I hated kids to convince myself that I wasn't missing out, but turns out I was lying to myself and my heart ached.

I told my boss I needed to go away for a while to settle some personal business. I had so many unused vacation days I knew it wouldn't be a problem. The plan was for me to shack up at home, sorta like a little staycation. I'd been abstaining all month, keeping the little hungry fucker from getting what it wanted. I needed to see what would happen.

The week before my period, I had the worst cramps I'd had since before that first tree rat, and I rolled around naked on the cold kitchen tile in agony. It didn't matter that I'd eaten raw steak, a container of chicken livers, or drank an entire glass of pig blood. It wanted what it had become accustomed to. The fresh hot fear in the blood and organs of the living when they were being eaten alive. It resented me for treating it like a scavenger and burst from my navel like a lance. Even though it hurt, I'd started to laugh.

Sweat poured from every part of my body as I struggled to stand up. I was still laughing like a maniac as I searched for the sharpest knife I could find. The Craving hissed and tried to strike at me, but I wasn't afraid of it. I knew it wouldn't hurt me—it needed me. "Fuck you," I spat at it. Then I took hold of its wriggling body and pinned it down on the counter. It tried to retreat back to its humble abode, making my stomach meat ripple like mad as it fought me. Tears flooded my vision as I lifted the knife in midair. This was it. The moment of truth. Could I do it? Could I sever what had been a part of me for so long?

I brought the blade of the knife down hard. Then I did it again and again and again until all the blood and sweat loosened my grip on the knife's handle. Pieces of the Craving jerked about the counter and blood spurted from the wriggling four-inch stump still connected to my belly button like a living umbilical cord. The Craving's head was on the floor, and its mouth unhinged, opening and closing in a flurry, desperate to clutch onto the last seconds of its miserable life. Something came over me then and I stomped on it with my bare foot. Pain shot up my leg when its fangs pierced my heel, but I ignored it and stomped until there was nothing left but a gory splat.

The remaining issue was the bit still connected to me. I wiped my hands and then the knife on a dish towel. I looked down at the stump and poked it. It moved in protest. "That's it, this is my body," I rasped. "You hear me? Mine. I'd rather die trying to get rid of you than live with you anymore. It was fun while it lasted you ugly fucker."

I leaned against the counter and sliced into the stump carefully, treating it like it was a delicate cucumber. I cut away rounds until the blade came too close to the topknot of my navel. The nub bled, not as bad as the first cuts, but a steady stream of blood poured down my legs onto the floor until I was standing in a dark red puddle. All the adrenaline I'd garnered before vanished and an unspeakable pain, raw and fierce, took control. I fell to my knees and shrieked until familiar stars danced around my head, and then everything went black.

When I came to, I started to shiver. I needed a hot shower. I could clean up the mess later. Pain still echoed though my body and every part of me throbbed. I limped to the bathroom, careful not to put too much pressure on my wounded foot. The gnarled nub still seeped but was starting to coagulate. I rinsed away the blood from my skin as best I could, then patted my myself dry and threw on a loose-fitting nightshirt. All I wanted was to go to sleep, so that's what I did.

In the morning, I felt groggy and sick, like I'd drunk too many shots of tequila the night before. My head ached along with my bones and joints, and my crusted nub throbbed like hell, but I had to clean up my mess. I stuck my head under the bathroom faucet and guzzled water until I choked, then shuffled to the kitchen like the living dead.

The slaughtered bits of the Craving looked like dried hunks of beef and smelled like sun-baked rotting carcass. I gagged as I pried them from the tile and countertop and chucked them into the trash. It took a lot of effort to get rid of all the blood splatter but I managed. When I felt everything was clean enough, I decided I needed to eat. Hunger pangs kicked at my empty stomach. I made myself two peanut butter and fluff sandwiches, then drank two full glasses of lemonade. Satisfied, I went and sat on the couch and fell asleep within seconds.

In two weeks' time, my dried scabby nubbin fell off, and to my surprise, all that was left behind was my ugly Sumo orange topknot. As I neared my next cycle, I prepared myself by drinking lots of water, eating healthy, and doing yoga. What I wasn't expecting, were the familiar cravings. The lust for blood and iron-rich organs came back with a vengeance. I felt ravenous and rabid like I could viciously attack anything that had a pulse. Thank goodness for my stocked freezer. I ate packages of ground beef, gnawed on beef hearts, and swallowed chunks of calf's liver, but in the end, it was no use.

My body knew what it wanted. There was no burning poker behind my navel, though, so I was perplexed as to why I still had such strong desires. Was I addicted? Was it all in my head and I was a murdering lunatic the whole time? The week of my period was an excruciating battle, one that made me continuously check my savings account and decide to finally demand a complete hysterectomy.

The doctor came in and shook my hand, then he sat down on his swivel chair. He pushed his glasses up on his nose, knitted together his graying caterpillar eyebrows, and read over my chart. My legs dangled over the edge of the cold metal slab and the paper sheet under me stuck to my ass and crinkled anytime I moved. It didn't matter how many times I had a pelvic exam: I was always a nervous wreck. I agreed with my mother to have another exam before ripping out my goods. I'd have to do it anyway.

A few minutes later, a nurse came in and stood against the counter as the doctor asked me to lay back and put my feet in the stirrups. My breasts were kneaded for lumps and then came the cold goop-covered fingers being inserted into my vagina. He felt around, pressed on my abdomen, then felt some more. He did the pap, pulled off his gloves and threw them away, then rolled back in his chair and looked over his glasses at me.

"Well, Ms. Talulawitz, I did feel a mass of some kind on your uterus and it is tender. You complained of pelvic pain, yes?"

"Yes. I've always had horrible pain during my periods, since I was fourteen. This is why I want a hysterectomy. I need it gone."

"I see. Well, something is definitely going on. It could be a cyst, a large fibroid … or something else. I understand what it is you want, but before we proceed, I need to do an ultrasound and some bloodwork. I'd also like to wait for your pap to come back. Then we can go from there."

"Why? Why can't I just have the hysterectomy? I've got the money."

"I'm not saying you can't have one; however, it's important that you have more information before doing so. If it were something like endometriosis, for instance, a hysterectomy might not get rid of the problem. It's a life-altering surgery as you are aware and might be medically unnecessary. Such a thing can put you needlessly at risk. A hysterectomy is the right choice for some, but a less-invasive alternative may be the better choice for you. I want to make sure what's best before we go further."

"Well, when you put it that way ..." Of course, I knew he was right and was grateful for his candor, but I was scared of what they might find. Something was still lingering, causing the mass he felt and the tenderness I felt. I was so tired of being afraid.

My pap ended up being normal, but the bloodwork revealed I was anemic again and the ultrasound revealed I had some sort of egg-shaped mass attached to my uterus. The doctor said it wasn't exactly solid so he didn't think it was a tumor—but they weren't sure. They'd need to remove it and analyze it. He showed me the grainy pictures of the egg thing and tears sprang to my eyes. I started to sob, and the doctor and nurse tried to console me, telling me it'd be all right. Seeing it was like an immediate jolt to my heart. I knew what it was; I just knew. They scheduled an appointment for me to have it removed, but I knew, even as I nodded my head and blew my nose, that it was an appointment I'd never show up for.

Upon leaving the doctor's that day, I went straight to the local pet store. Judge me all you want, I don't care. I savored the fuzzy little morsels. A feeling of ease swam through my body and filled my heart with joy. I wasn't doing it for myself, I was doing it for the thing inside me. Maybe it wasn't human, but it was still a baby—my baby. The Craving must've laid the egg before I murdered her or maybe she did it in desperation while I murdered her. It never occurred to me that she could do it at all. I was in awe and planned on doing what I could to keep it safe.

Six weeks later, it happened. I got my period and fragments of leathery-looking white egg flowed out along with my blood. I knew it. I'd been right! I cried out and cradled my aching womb like a doting mother. Soon, it would singe the back of my navel, letting me know it was hungry. It'd grow bigger and need bigger things to eat, and I'd do whatever I could to nurture it and keep it happy. If you're wondering why I'd go through this, wondering why I'd risk everything to care for an unexplainable thing that grew inside me, I'll tell you why. Because that's what mothers fucking do.

Khotoum

by Sridhar Shankar

September 10, 2012

Day 3: I have to confess, I'm getting worried. Not a lot, but …

The phone is useless, because as expected, there's no signal here. I tried keeping it off to save juice. It probably tried too hard to find a signal and got worn out. Well, there's only so much Candy Crush I can play, and it's not like I can call anyone. And yet I was down to 10% battery when I turned it off.

Pretty sure that someone from the board will worry and get a search going. After all, I am the CEO of the company, even if it's a small tech startup. Wally might be the first to sound the alarm since he calls me every morning with my schedule and such, and I never miss his call. I guess, at a conservative estimate, I'll be out of here by tonight or tomorrow at the outside.

Meanwhile, I've figured out the directions—the sun rises right in front of me, across from the endless ocean, so that's clearly east, and it sets behind me, so that's west. North is to my left and so on. I've walked along the coast on this side, moving South. As far as I can see, it's a clean beach: coarse sand with lots of small shells. They're mostly crushed into small pieces—I don't see any large or intact ones. Clearly wave action at work, erosion and all that. After about half a mile, there's a dense but low forest. It comes on suddenly, as though there's a perimeter beyond which vegetation is not supposed to grow. The trees are short and twisted like bonsai—only larger. Gnarly is the best word to describe them. The tallest trees are barely at waist height, but I still cannot see a great distance owing to the density of the foliage, and, of course, the gradient.

It's hard to tell how big the island is, but for the first two days I was so hopeful I'd be rescued that I didn't even explore. Just walked up and down the beach and sheltered in the shallow cave of the rock face that rises from the back of the beach.

I thought the air would be clean here, the great outdoors and all that (hard to get more outdoors and farther from civilization), but no such luck. There's a strange vinegary-sulfurous smell here, kind of like you get at some hot springs, but a little sweetness thrown in.

Luckily, I had some food, rations from the lifeboat, bags of nuts, protein bars, other dense calorie packaged foods that taste like cardboard, and of course, water, but it's all running low. Tomorrow, I'll explore the island. Perhaps there are fruit trees, game. I don't see evidence of big animals here.

I'm alone on this island, I think.

September 13, 2012

Day 6: It took me four hours to walk, then wade, and climb around the island. After the beach ends, there's the forest that grows up to the water's edge, so I waded for a bit, worried there might be snakes slithering in the dense undergrowth, so I put off exploring the forest until later. After a bit, a sparse pebbly area appeared, then a slight rocky hill. I discovered a pond, a depression really, but filled with fresh water, rain water. I filled my half-gallon bottle and tasted it. A slight unpleasant taste but not bad on the whole. It's a bit of a trek to get there, but I ain't complaining. I figure the water will last me a day at least, and then I can return. I might look around for a larger reservoir, but, for now, this will have to do.

Nothing from Wally. I guess it's taking them a while to search the area.

September 20

I'm not alone here. The feeling has been growing over the last few days, although I have walked around the island and avoided the jungle in the middle. My body is going through changes, from living rough, I suppose. I'm weak, no solid food. My skin feels rough, wrinkly, leathery.

9/29

Earthy. That's how earthworms taste even after I wash them in sea water. Icky! I know. I didn't want to, but there was no food. When building my shelter, I picked up a rock, and there they were.

Kind of like a bunch of wriggly noodles. Quite filling. Some fat, some thin and two-headed. Maybe not earthworms. Some other worm?

Oct 4

I have to hide them from Khotoum. He … it lives in the forest, I know. I have seen it creeping toward my shelter at night. Beware. Gotta tell Bally. Walleye.

7/10

Strange thing I noticed today. No birds here. But there's a lot of protein. Worms and grubs under rocks. Have to keep my stash safe from Khotoum, though.
Another strange thing. No fish in the sea nearby.

10

Khotoum visited last night. He says there's nothing to fear from him. He's been on this island for a long while. His face is squashed from the top down, and he has only one eye in the center of his forehead. No hair. A pretzel he is, and wrinkled like a raisin. He walks on all fours like a dog but with a limp.
He showed me where to find oysters. Not really oysters, they're some kind of weird shellfish. That's all you can find around this island.
I think I'll share my grubs and worms with him. Maybe when I leave this island, I can take him with me, keep him as a pet … maybe.

October?

Khotoum showed me the center of the island. There's nothing but blistered, bare earth for about a hundred yards. Like a volcano crater, except without the crater. No vegetation at all. Or grubs or worms. Could it be a nuclear bomb site? Can't imagine how I missed it on my explorations. Just beyond the devastated area, the trees are misshapen, gnarly, short. Shorter even than on the beach.

Dt:

Khots is becoming good friend. So, maybe not a pet, perhaps a companion? His feet are like thin branches, falling off.

It's easier to walk on all fours like Khots. Nose closer to ground, easier to find grubs, worms and things. We're so close together, I don't even notice his weird one-eyed face or his crooked, razor-like teeth. I have to make do with my knife.

I think Kho is stealing from my stash. Watch him careful. I did. He has a second eye. Just below his cheek. Smaller than forehead eye. Sneaky.

I caught Kho looking at me strange. Like he wonders what I taste like. I have to make plan.

I not remember. My teeth into his leg.

K not moving at all.

K blood green. I ate him. Piece by piece, over many days, all of him. Even the bones. Some parts rotted. Better than earthworms.

Is that chop-chop bird?

"What's the matter with this one?"

"Well, doc, it's classified." The navy man shifted his weight from one foot to the other.

The doc stared him in the eye.

The navy man practically squirmed, his face turning red. He was the first to break eye contact. He sighed. The doctor was a navy man, too, and outranked him.

"You see, sir, this man was marooned after his yacht went down. He ended up on a dump site for ... we think a couple of months, sir."

"Dump site? For what?"

"Sir?"

"The dump. What was it? Nuclear waste? What?"

"Mixed bag, sir. Some nuclear waste. Some experimental chemical warfare gas. The details are in the file. They buried containment units, but apparently some of them leaked ..."

They turned to the viewing window. The man once known as Victor Benedict, playboy millionaire, CEO of a billion-dollar tech startup company, lay contorted on the military cot, in restraints. His eyes were wild, staring blankly into space. A patchy beard darkened his chin and cheeks. Above the level of his brow, his skull seemed misshapen, squashed. His skin looked greenish, ridged, and thickened into coarse folds. He bore no resemblance to the face on his driver's license.

"He says there was a creature with him."

"Another survivor?"

"Could be," said the navy man. "But it appears the other one was there before. Could be another shipwreck survivor, or maybe some larger animal."

"And what happened to … it, well, him?"

"It seems he ate it … him."

"He said?"

"No sir, he doesn't talk. Just grunts and makes noises. A journal …"

He held out a tattered notebook.

A fly buzzed in the room on the other side of the glass. The men watched as Victor snaked out his tongue, long and limber, quick as a whiplash.

He chewed.

Folie à Deux

by Koji A. Dae

Jamie and me totally u-hauled it. Classic lesbians. Not that either of us are lesbians. I'm bi. She's pan. Whatever. We're still two women who plummeted into love and moved in together with a crash-bang. I'm talking one date, two days. In all honesty, it was longer. She just doesn't know it took months for her to notice me, while I was pining away for her like a whimpering puppy. She's a dancer. Total spark of light at parties. Always surrounded by an adoring flock of … we'll call them friends. Me? I'm just a poet. Quiet nose-in-a-book type. I didn't stand a chance of catching her attention. Until, by some goddess-type miracle, I did.

I went to Felix's *'Can't miss it, babes. Everyone will be there'* rager because he mentioned Jamie might come. Luckily for antisocial me, Felix's party ended up more like a kickback. He drank his embarrassment in vodka while the music stayed low and people chatted. Not surrounded by her usual entourage, even Jamie seemed approachable. Her ponytail was down, her hair a messy halo around her face. Less makeup? I moved closer. No makeup. Just a natural flush and a smattering of freckles I'd never noticed. Her lips were still like cherries, but unripened, ready to be watched instead of eaten.

She noticed me when I happened to be laughing, mouth open, head back. Like it was nothing, she came over and said, "Hi, you're Felix's friend, right?"

My heart totally skipped a beat. Like, something from a book. Poetry, even. My poetic response? Some kind of grunt and mumble.

Then, somehow, we were two drinks down and snuggled up on a sofa, her long arms around my plump belly and our foreheads nearly touching. The wine had purpled her lips and I so wanted to kiss it away. We leaned in at the same time. Smack. Stars and all that. Perfection.

We fucked in Felix's room, him passed out on the floor. After, while rummaging the kitchen for snacks, we found these stupid stick-on tattoos. Hearts with snakes wrapped around them. She put one on her left arm and its partner on my right. Satiated and feeling silly, we returned to the party and spent the rest of the night telling everyone we were married, didn't they like our matching tats?

I expected to wake up wrapped around her, squeezing her like that serpent we had worshipped the night before. But my bed was empty. I groaned and sat up. It wasn't my bed. Felix's. Still empty, though. I reached out, as if I might find her in the rumpled sheets. She wasn't there. All she left me with was a nasty headache, a stupid tattoo, and murky memories of what was probably the best night of my life.

I padded to Felix's bathroom, and stepped into the shower, hoping the steam would clear away the aching hollow I always get after I drink—but hey, for once I had an excuse. For a night she was mine, and she just left me there.

The water washed away the majority of the after-party funk seeping from my skin, but didn't get rid of my embarrassment or that damned tattoo. Even after scrubbing, it remained bright as a blood drop. I turned off the water, wrapped a towel around myself, and went through Felix's bathroom cupboard. No baby oil. No alcohol. Nothing. For such a fashionable guy, he was totally lacking in the hygiene department. In the living room I poured vodka into a napkin and tried to rub the tattoo off, but it didn't even smudge.

Well, damn it.

I found Felix's phone near his nightstand, unlocked it, and scrolled for Jamie's number. She'd totally think it was a pathetic excuse to call her, but I had to know how she'd gotten her tat off.

Her voice was groggy. Shit. I hadn't even thought that she might not be awake yet. Now I felt doubly stupid. But I tried to keep my tone disinterested. "Hey, yeah, just wondering what you used to get that fake tattoo off."

"Fake ..." She giggled. Then groaned. I bit my lip. Both sounds were adorable. "I mean, soap and water?"

"I tried that. Alcohol too. Damned thing won't come off."

"Hang on." There were some muffled bumps and thuds, then the unmistakable sound of water running. Longer. Longer. I waited. Then, "Well, shit."

"Yours won't come off either?" I stared at the splotch of color. It had the fade of a real tattoo, as if we had lived a lifetime in that night.

"Are you free? We have to figure this out."

When we met up, both wearing dark sunglasses, she said she was happy I called. Happy. About me. She hadn't known whether or not she should stay, so left when I fell asleep. Was hoping I'd call.

We scrubbed and tried all kinds of solvents, even pouring bleach over our skin. It itched and irritated, but didn't remove the tattoo. If it wasn't for her carefree attitude, I might have freaked out. Gone to the hospital. Got Felix involved. These weren't normal. But she took it in stride, and I wanted to match my step to hers. That night we were both back at her apartment, and a week later, that's where I was living with the love of my life and a strange stick-on tattoo that wouldn't come off.

The tattoos became part of our meet-cute story. All our friends—shared now—thought we must've gotten them inked when we got together. But we didn't. They just stayed. Sometimes, lying in the early morning sunshine, refusing to leave our nest of a bed, we'd spend more time tracing the tattoos than navels or nipples.

"Magic," Jamie insisted. "The universe demanded we be together."

The thing about Jamie is she believed the universe had our best interest at heart. Call me a cynic, but the universe as I knew it was at best a neutral party. Years of nihilistic depression made me guess there was something sinister lurking beneath our shiny concept of fate.

Every adorable couple has an issue. Ours was communication. As someone who spoke in movement and another who spoke in metaphor, we couldn't sort an honest word between the two of us. In the spaces between the grunts and groans of passion—which grew longer as the year went on—we danced this strange mimicry of emotion. She couldn't say, "I love you." I said it so much it meant nothing.

Then that trickster of a universe revealed its true intentions. We had a fight. I can't even remember what it was about, but it ended with me calling her a bitch and slamming the door. I fully meant to stay away for the night, but Felix had a lover over and I didn't have anywhere else to go. With teeth still aching from too much clenching, I returned to her apartment. It was ours when things were good, but just hers when we fought.

An eerie silence filled the entryway, accompanied by an out-of-place stillness.

"Jamie?" I scratched my arm nervously, and that's when I noticed the pulsing of the tattoo. It was warm. Alive. A second heart, beating slowly in my arm, recycling my blood as its own.

Stop it. No sense drifting into hysterics. I called out for Jamie again.

A muffled whine answered. Moving closer to the bedroom door, I heard a soft scratching. Long nails on the tiled floor. That whimper again. I swallowed a gulp of sour bile, took a breath, and opened the door.

A puppy bounded out of the room, wrapping itself through my legs, its tail thumping into me.

"Hey." I bent and scratched between its ears. They were the big floppy kind. Cute, soft. Light brown. Maybe it was some sort of beagle or something? The more pressing question was how this dog got into our apartment. Still crouched next to it, I looked around as if its owner might be thieving our second-hand television. But there was no one but me and this puppy. "How'd you get here?"

More whimpering and nuzzling. The dog licked my hand, its tongue wet and warm. It's nose found my tattoo. The cold of it set off a burning, as if the tattoo was searing into me. I yanked my arm away, hissing at the sensation and glaring at the dog. In the bathroom I ran it under cold water, biting my lip and watching the animal from the corner of my eye. The water hissed as it rolled off my skin. The dog continued tripping me, and I nudged it away over and over until the pain in my arm subsided.

Cautiously, I knelt in front of it. It licked my cheeks. My forehead. No pain as long as it stayed away from the tattoo. I stroked its fur and asked, "What the fuck is going on?"

It didn't have any answers. I closed my eyes, pressed my forehead against its soft fur, and willed the world to make sense. In the chilled bathroom, my arm burning, holding a strange puppy, the whimpering turned into crying. The fur turned to skin. The puppy expanded into a familiar, long shape. Jamie was in my arms, with no sign of the puppy.

I kissed her salty cheeks. Her trembling lips.

"Babes," she cried into my neck.

I shushed her. "It's okay now."

And it was okay for a while. We thought … I don't know what we thought. That we imagined it? That we had shared in some delusion? Better to pretend it hadn't happened. But after that night, the pulsing of the tattoos continued. What had once been a flat symbol on my body turned into a soft lump, always warm as if some infection was growing beneath my skin. Jamie's tat echoed mine, swelling and turning purple around the edges. We traced them in the dark, but never mentioned them during the day.

The next argument was closer to the heart of our problem. I spent the morning badgering her. "Tell me what you're feeling. I need to hear it."

She finally broke. "Why are words so damned important to you? You know how I feel."

"Do I? I don't know if you want tomorrow or forever or if you're bored and wish you left last month."

She rolled her eyes. "You say it over and over again. It's like you're trying to convince yourself. Doesn't inspire much confidence."

I turned away from her and stared out the window. The sky was gray and roiling, echoing my stomach. The damned itching was turning into a burn again, and I knew I should let the emotion go before we went too far. But I couldn't help myself. "I'm just trying to get you to say you love me."

Her voice turned cold. "You think you're so much better than me. That you can express all this emotion. But you're like a stone reflecting the sun, it never gets into you."

A chill started around the tattoo. My arm grew heavy. Then my shoulder. My chest. My legs wouldn't move. My neck felt precariously brittle and wouldn't turn. My mouth wouldn't open.

"Babes?" Jamie's hand was on me, but I couldn't move beneath it. "Babes!"

I ached to talk to her. To tell her what was going on. My heart slowed. My breath turned to slush in my lungs. I can't describe the pain of the transformation. Rocks don't have nerves or a brain to process sensation. But the death of feeling was like an infinite needle that didn't let up. Then I was gone, and it was too late for honesty.

Jamie told me I was a rock for three days. She didn't leave the apartment. Why didn't she call someone? Get some help? At least Felix ... but she had been distraught. Besides, all our friends had enough problems of their own. And who would believe this insanity we were sharing? I wouldn't. Not from the outside. Barely from the inside.

When my body came back to me, it was exhaustion and pain. I wept for hours. Jamie took me to the bathtub and gently rubbed heat back into my flesh. She moved my toes, and I cried. She bent my knees and whispered apologies. Her touch was tender, her guilt real. I sucked it up as the tattoo sucked up the movement of my blood.

"We can't ignore this," I told her once we were wrapped up in bed. "We need help."

"Who are we going to tell? No one will believe us."

We thought about going to therapy. Telling our friends.

She wrapped her arms tight around me. "You know what they'll say. That we need time apart. That we're not good for each other."

I bit my lip until it hurt.

"Babes, I love you. I don't want to lose you."

It was all I needed. All I wanted, at least. Tattoo and insanity be damned, the universe, too, if it was involved. She loved me.

That was enough for a few weeks. But it didn't stop the fights. Harsh words still flew from our mouths, and the tattoos picked up on them quicker, the results of our metaphors hovering in our apartment for longer periods. When I called her a harpy, she transformed into a crusty bird and covered our apartment in guano, snapping up raw meat from my hands for a week. Then she called me a leech, which was probably easier for her to take care of, but I felt the slime on my skin for a month after I turned back. I had to get creative hiding a donkey in our apartment when I called her an ass, and she had to put up with a week of dirty diapers after calling me a baby.

We had to do something. The most logical choice was to get rid of the tattoos.

"Do you think, like, a tattoo parlor that does removals?" she asked.

"One, they aren't real tattoos. Two, could either of us afford that?"

She tapped a random key on her keyboard—a habit that irritated me to my toes. "What about … I dunno, some kind of witch or something."

"A witch? You're just going to pop 'witch that removes cursed tattoos' into a search? Go ahead."

"Well, what do you think?" she snapped.

I didn't take her anger personally. We both knew what had to happen. I rubbed at the mark, and my heart sank to a deep, chilled place within me. One of us had to say it. "We need to cut them off."

As if responding to my threat, the itching and burning grew to a clawing and piercing. I sucked in a strong hiss of breath. Jamie moaned.

"Let's do it now," I said through clenched teeth.

She let me lead her to the kitchen and pull out the long chef's knife we had bought together. A quality instrument. It could slice through anything.

She shook her head. "No. No, babes. I can't do this."

The pain was spreading as an ache up my arm, as if tendrils were growing from the heart. "We have to. Now."

"We could … we could …" She lost her words to another wave of pain. "I'll go first."

"No. I can't watch." She thrust her arm out. "Me first."

I took a gulp of air and held the blade to the tenderness of her skin. "You sure?"

She nodded, but looked away. I pressed.

The knife sliced, first soft and easy. Pus leaked out, and I gagged but kept pushing. The knife met resistance, cutting through tough ropes. I sawed back and forth, pressing harder. Blood rushed into my ears, drowning out the screams she tried to hold in.

Then the blotch of ink was off, revealing wet muscle. Thick grayish ropes entwined through her flesh and around her bones. They pulsed slightly and retracted deeper into her arm. I pressed the kitchen towel over it and she sobbed.

I wanted to hold her, but I wasn't done yet. The pulsing in my own arm was growing stronger, as if I had been injected with some poison that sent leaden needles down to my fingertips and up to my shoulder.

I can't, I can't, I can't, I thought. But I looked down at her, curled into a fetal position, trusting me to follow wherever I had driven her. I picked up the knife again and plunged it hard against the tattoo. I couldn't be gentle. If I took my time, I would lose my nerve. The slicing into the skin didn't hurt as much as when I got to those tethering ropes. They screamed into my mind, echoing until I was somewhere else altogether. A void of darkness.

When I came to, I was on the kitchen floor, smeared with blood, curled around Jamie.

"Do you think it worked?" she asked.

"We could get in a fight, try to test it."

Her laughter was weak but beautiful. I didn't tell her that I still felt that pulsing. That I had seen the tendrils of a creature clinging to our bones. What was the point? There was nothing else we could do.

The wounds healed into a knot of scars that we kept covered. There was a certain amount of shame around the tattoos at that point. We never shared our meet-cute anymore. We didn't share much of anything. We just sort of drifted apart as if whatever had been holding us together had released us.

I caught myself looking at her while she slept or cooked or danced in the living room. I didn't want to be released. But the more I stared, the fainter she became, like the outline of a ghost.

She was the one who left. "Take the apartment. I just can't do this anymore."

I didn't want to be cruel, but my damn poetic mouth always demanded the last word. "It's fine. You're nothing to me, anyway."

I never heard from her again. Sometimes my arm still aches. Pulses. And I wonder what nothingness I sent her to.

This Side of the Moment

by Megan M. Davies-Ostrom

There are moments in life where things hang in the balance. Good or bad, success or failure, life or death. The scales could tip either way. The outcome isn't certain.

Usually, we're none the wiser. They come and go, our lives continue. Even when we do notice them, it's only once they've passed and we're left reeling in their wake.

Don't think too hard about it. That's my advice.

I know it's tempting, but it doesn't do to dwell on those moments or the grisly 'what-ifs' or wistful 'if-onlys' they leave behind. Thoughts like that have weight. They'll punch right through this world's fragile skin and show you the horror on the other side. Lose your balance and they'll take you with them. I should know.

The smell hit me as soon as I opened the door. Sweet, thick, and oily.

We'd gone to visit a friend. Our daughter, Maddy, had opted to stay home. At twelve she was, oddly enough, one of the few things I didn't worry about. Smart, kind—geeky and goofy with just the right amount of adolescent snark—she was a good kid.

But returning home to that smell? That made me nervous.

I shed my shoes and jacket in the hall. My "We're back," was as much a question as a greeting.

"Hey, Mom!" Maddy's voice was high with excitement. "Guess what? I'm making churros!"

I glanced at Peter. He raised his eyebrows and shrugged.

We trotted up the stairs, and the sweet, greasy smell got stronger as we went. In the kitchen, we found Maddy piping a batch of misshapen dough into a pot of bubbling oil.

On the gas stove.

Hot oil and open flame were a match made in house-fire heaven. My head filled with disasters, and my heart flipped into all-too-familiar hyperdrive. I wanted to scream and drag her away from the stove. Instead, I reminded myself I wasn't a helicopter parent and forced a smile.

"Wow." A good, non-committal word.

Peter was more eloquent. "Super impressive, Mads. That's a complicated recipe. They look great."

"Don't they?" Maddy scooped a few churros out of the pot and onto a plate. "I only put a bit of oil in the pot, 'cause I know it's dangerous. I'm being careful."

Then the smoke detector went off with an earsplitting wail.

Maddy jumped and whirled and the pot teetered on the element.

Peter grabbed a tea towel from the rail and flapped furiously under the sensor. "Get the fan and turn the heat down, Mads," he called. "The oil's too hot."

Eyes wide, Maddy switched on the vent fan and fumbled with the knobs.

The siren shrieking stopped. Peter fanned the alarm a few more times. "That thing," he panted, "our neighbours must hate us."

I had to walk away. I went to the living room, opened the window, and took a deep, shaky breath. The air was crisp and clear after the oily haze inside. I was shaking. My insides were guitar strings pulled too tight, humming and twanging and ready to break. I paced from living room to kitchen, back and forth, counting my breath. Breath in, pause, breath out; one. Breath in, pause, breath out; two.

I told people I was the kind of person who considered all the possibilities and planned accordingly. Being good at risk management sounded better than being anxious. But I was anxious. Little things got in my head and stuck there like a popcorn kernel in your teeth. I'd poke at them endlessly till those little things had big stories all their own, and I was in tears. *'Andy thoughts'* Peter called them.

Now I was thinking about the alarm. Maddy had jumped. It had scared her. But what if it had gone off before we'd gotten home? What would she have done without us there?

That night, I couldn't sleep. Peter was snoring within minutes, but the strings running through me were still tight and humming, and my mind was a mess. Nothing had happened, but it was everything that *could* have happened that scared me. What if we'd come home later? What if the alarm had gone off sooner? What if she'd been alone? Would she have turned off the flame? Would she have panicked? So many what-ifs.

Minutes became hours, and I twisted and turned. I was weighed down by worry, trapped and heavy while my mind ran and jittered. All those wild *lightspeed* thoughts had one focus; how easily things could have gone wrong. The what-ifs were a black hole and they drew me in.

It was subtle at first; a tug, a gentle pull on tired limbs. It drew me through rumpled sheets and into darkness. Stronger now, it was a current, a river, a riptide dragging me pell-mell through an endless night, till suddenly I was surrounded by light and images; a nauseous kaleidoscope, *this-is-your-life* on speed. Polaroid-photo moments and memories spun round me, countless tiny choices. I recognized them all. Like me, they were caught in the maelstrom, plunging toward the precipice. The black hole of what-if; a singularity—a moment—made entirely of chance and fate and a hundred little inconsequential things. Silly things. But on one side of that moment was the evening as it had played out—we came home, helped Maddy with the smoke detector, ate churros, and kissed our smiling daughter good night. And on the other side was smoke and flame and horror.

Teetering on that event horizon, looking down at both sides, I was filled with a sick, cold dread. It could have gone either way. Both had been equally likely, equally possible. I was hollow, gutted by that knowing.

And then I slipped, grasped for the edge, and tumbled down into the smoky darkness.

We drove home, chatting about nothing; the kind of inconsequential conversation that forms the bedrock of any relationship. I couldn't tell what was different. Maybe we'd stayed longer at Melissa's or stopped at the store on the way home. Maybe the smoke detector had gone off earlier, or Maddy had left the pot untended … or … or … or …

Who knew? Maybe those little things didn't matter at all. Maybe they were just part of some greater, singular *Moment* with a momentum all its own.

I watched, a passenger in my own mind, as we pulled onto our street and were stopped by a cordon of police cars, ambulances, and fire engines. Flames and flashing lights split the darkness, burning bright after-images on my eyes and making everything else darker by comparison.

Black and red.

Red flames, leaping high from the roof of our townhouse. Black smoke that billowed up to cloud a starless sky as firemen ran and shouted, aiming hoses and trying to save the homes on either side. Red embers, drifting on the faint breeze to settle on the dark glass of our windshield.

I threw open the door and leapt from the car. Pelted across the pavement, only to be caught up and held by uniformed arms, dragged back from heat so intense my tears evaporated, leaving lines of crusty salt on my cheeks.

"Maddy!" My voice was an unfamiliar thing, ragged and wild. "Let me go! My daughter's in there! She's in there!"

I fought the arms that held me, straining to reach the house, knowing all the while it was far too late. Peter was frozen in place beside me, staring wide-eyed into the roiling flames, both hands clasped over his mouth as if to hold back his horror. I couldn't, couldn't hold back any of it.

"Oh god! Oh god! Maddy! MADDY!"

When I woke the next morning, it was with the echo of screams in my ears. My cheeks were damp with tears.

I slept poorly that night, and the night after as well. The dreams were bad—a million variations on the theme of *'dead child with fire'*—but the daytime thoughts were worse. I couldn't get it out of my head. No matter where I was or what I was doing, my mind went to the 'what-ifs.' What if we'd stayed at Melissa's twenty minutes longer? What if we'd driven more slowly or gotten stuck in traffic? What if Maddy had put more oil in the pot, or turned the heat up higher, or tipped the pot onto the open gas flame when the smoke alarm went off? What if, what if, *what if.*

By the time Friday rolled around, I felt like I'd been run over by a Zamboni. When I got home from work, I told Peter I was still upset.

"No doubt." He shoved his empty lunch-tote into the cupboard above the fridge. "It was upsetting."

I slumped into my seat. Maddy had badminton practice and wasn't due home for at least half an hour.

"It's just ... I can't stop thinking about it. About that narrow line between okay and not okay and how close we came to the edge. We were lucky, Pete. Really lucky. There were so many ways it could have gone wrong."

"But it didn't." He crossed the room and gave me a hug. "She's fine."

"But it could have!"

Peter sat down and took my hand. "Could have and did are two different things. If we went through life worrying about everything that *could* have happened, we'd drive ourselves bonkers."

"I know."

When Maddy was four, she'd been in an accident with my parents. A sunny, sleepy afternoon and a panicked overcorrection had conspired to roll their car. No one was seriously hurt but it had been close.

I'd talked with my father about it later, and he'd said the same thing. "Sometimes bad things just happen. There's no reason why, or when, or to whom. There's nothing you can do to stay safe. And if you spend your life thinking about it, you'll never be happy again. You have to let it go."

"But this isn't like that, Pete. This is …" I struggled to find the right words. "This is like slicing open life and seeing its guts … how it all works."

Peter raised an eyebrow.

"It's like there are these moments where things could go one way or another. Where everything is balanced on a knife edge of … I don't know … luck? Random chance?" I spread my hands in frustration.

"Like a fork in the road. Go one way, everything's good. Go the other and it all goes wrong. But that moment before you step; that's what I'm talking about. Like a pivot point, a split second where everything is possible. I know we said we dodged a bullet, but these past few days, I don't feel like we completely got off. I feel … grazed, if that makes sense."

Peter wrapped me in his arms. "Of course it makes sense, Andy. It makes perfect sense. We had a scare. It's no wonder you're still thinking about what could have happened. I am too."

"But that's just it, Peter. I'm not just thinking about it. The dreams I've been having feel so real."

"I don't doubt it. But the Madster's okay, Andy. Everything's okay."

I nodded and let him kiss me on the forehead. I *knew* everything was okay … I just wished it *felt* okay.

The first flash came Sunday afternoon. One moment I was standing in the living room, half-watching a cheesy horror movie with Maddy and folding Peter's T-shirts, and the next moment I was standing in a hollow, empty space. It took me a moment to realize it was the same room. Weak sunlight filtered through gaping holes in the walls and ceiling, but everything was dark, charred black. Water dripped and puffs of grey ash drifted down around me, an early snowfall.

I turned in place with growing horror. Gone was the shelving unit with the flat-screen TV and movies. Gone were the paintings on the walls, the throw blankets, and the scatter of Maddy's homework. Where the couch had stood sat an unrecognizable lump of ash and four stubby metal legs. The stairs looked as if they'd been punched in by a giant fist. The room was a cold, filthy maze of charred beams and water-logged ash.

The kitchen was worse. It was just … gone. The fire had burned right through to the third floor, and the bedroom above had fallen in, burying everything in wreckage.

Amazing how hot and how fast it must have burned. How quickly it consumed my world. Even more amazing was what had survived. My briefcase, charred but whole, the leather bubbled and peeling. Beside it a single pen, untouched. Maddy's bed had come down across the counters and burned completely, leaving nothing but a charcoal shadow of itself. Her favourite stuffy, *Squidy McSquidface*, lay unharmed nearby, an incongruous flash of red in a sea of grey.

Against my will, I stumbled forward and picked up the toy. Stained, soaked, and stinking of smoke, the cephalopod looked at me with sad plastic eyes.

"What happened?" Tears rolled down my cheeks. "What changed?"

"Mom!" Maddy's voice punched me in the stomach and knocked the breath from my lungs. Maddy okay, Maddy alive!

I whirled and found myself back in the kitchen—my own, unburned kitchen—hands empty. Maddy was staring at me from the living room.

"Mom, are you okay?"

"I … uh." Was I okay? I wasn't sure. My heart was still drumming against my ribs, my cheeks were still wet with tears. But this was real, wasn't it? It had to be, because I was home, and everything was whole and fine, and Maddy was right here.

But still, faintly, I smelled smoke.

"Mom?" Maddy darted into the kitchen, took my arm, and led me to a chair. "Mom, you're scaring me. Who were you talking to?"

"I … I don't know, sweetie. I guess I zoned out for a bit. I must be more tired than I thought."

Maddy gave me a doubtful look. "Bullpucky. I'm going to get Dad."

By the time Maddy returned with Peter, I felt a little better. Or at least, a little less confused. I related what had happened in general terms. Just one glance at Maddy's worried face was enough keep the worst details quiet. I didn't want to scare her any more than I already had.

"What do you think?" I asked Peter, when my truncated story was done. "Sleepwalking, maybe? Lucid dreams? I haven't been sleeping well."

Peter looked concerned. "I don't know. You do look pretty rough. Are you still sleeping that badly?"

Peter always slept well. Even through the worst of my anxiety-fueled tossing and turning, he could get a solid eight hours.

"Yeah."

"I think you should go see the doctor, then."

I nodded. After what had just happened, I was too scared to argue.

I managed to get an appointment with Dr. Rosa for Thursday the following week. That was something akin to a miracle, given her booking system.

Between Monday and Thursday, I had five more flashes, each one worse than the last. The first and second both came while I was at home. When the first one hit, I was lying in bed, and I found myself in the same place in that other home, laying on a damp, cold mattress under a rib-cage of charred rafters. The smell of smoke and burnt plastic stuck to the insides of my nose and throat like paste and made me gag.

The second time I found myself pacing the length of the upstairs hall. Unlike my hall, this one was filled with shadows and ash and ended in a gaping hole where Maddy's room should have been. The last rays of sunlight shone through the missing back wall. I walked with horrified care, picking my way through the debris, stepping over the charcoal stripes of the balustrade. My hand trailed the scorched and crumbling drywall. Somehow the pictures I'd put up ten years ago were still there, hanging in their blackened frames. The photos were blistered and curled but I could make them out. Maddy's tiny feet; her baby hand, holding tight to my thumb; Maddy sleeping, her face wrinkled up in baby dreams. Maddy everywhere, except where she belonged ... in my arms.

The third and fourth hit me at work on the Wednesday. One moment I was at my desk, and the next I was back in that house again, standing in the downstairs hall. A thinner, shoddier Peter sat on the floor of the study with his back to me. I watched, dismayed, as he picked through the rubbish that surrounded him, sorting debris into piles to keep and discard. The 'discard' pile grew bigger and bigger while the 'keep' pile stayed small; a pathetic collection of odds and ends in a cardboard box. A red Christmas ornament (one of the Maddy-proof plastic ones we'd never gotten around to replacing); my old copy of *Pride and Prejudice*; one of Maddy's badminton medals.

When I came back to myself, tears streaming down my face, I hurried to the bathroom, hoping no one would see me on the way. The moment I locked the stall, it happened again. I was thrown back into that other world ... the burned world. The pale, imitation Peter was gone, leaving the small, sad box behind. Sitting cross-legged on the floor, I hugged the cardboard box to my chest and sobbed. So little left. How could anyone rebuild a life from so little?

After that, I called Peter at work and asked him to come get me.

"I'm worried, Andy," he said, as he drove me home.

I nodded, huddled in the passenger seat, unable to speak past the crushing pain in my chest. I knew that pain. It was grief, and I wondered how this world—the real world, the world where Maddy was alive and at school right now—could feel so much less real than the one I'd just left.

The last spell struck just after I parked the car in the lot outside Dr. Rosa's office. Peter had wanted to drive me, but I'd told him I'd be okay. In truth, I hadn't wanted him to come, hadn't wanted him to listen as I recounted my dreams and—what were they exactly? I didn't know. Hallucinations? Spells? There'd been a look in his eyes, the past few days. A look I recognized from other times, earlier in our marriage, when my *Andy thoughts* had gotten the better of me. Pity, fear, compassion, and frustration, all rolled up in one. He thought this was just my anxiety, and I didn't know how to explain that it wasn't. That it was something else entirely.

I was standing on the sidewalk across from a row of five town homes. The row was a gap-tooth smile now, the remains of our house a blackened stump between its taller neighbours. The units on either side had been badly damaged, and there was a dumpster in front of the leftmost. Repairs and renovation, I guessed. That was fast.

I crossed the street and walked to the orange snow fence that had been erected to keep people out of the ruins. I pressed my face to the cool plastic and let my fingers slide through the diamond holes. On the other side of the barrier sat a pile of soft toys, flowers, and rain-wilted cards and posters.

'Rest in Peace' and 'We miss you, Maddy,' they said. One, in handwriting I recognized as Maddy's best friend's, read 'I'll never forget.'

They'd found Maddy's remains in the kitchen, just a few feet from the stove. Within a minute of ignition, the firemen had said, the heat of the fire would have been enough to burn her airway and lungs, the poisonous gasses enough to knock her out. She was already unconscious, they'd promised, when the flashover came three-and-half minutes later, blowing out the windows in great balls of flame and setting everything in the room alight. She hadn't felt a thing, hadn't felt the flames that charred and blackened her skin or the heat that fractured her bones and twisted her limbs into a fighter's pose. Hadn't felt her death.

I slid to my knees against the fence, arms around my head. I gasped for breath between sobs. Gone! My daughter was gone! A world without that quirky humor, those eyes, or that smile didn't make sense. How could the world go on without Maddy in it?

When I came back to myself, I was still in my car. The muscles of my stomach were sore, and my throat was raw as if I'd been crying for hours.

I told Dr. Rosa about the insomnia, the dreams, and the flashes. She nodded and 'hmmed' but she didn't believe me. She gave me a few weeks off work, prescriptions for anti-anxiety and sleeping pills, and told me to get some rest.

Peter was a picture of helpless fury. "I don't understand how this can be happening. It was nothing! How can something so little make everything go wrong?"

"It wasn't nothing, Peter! God, I know it sounds silly—churros, right? But it could have been terrible. I've seen what it could have been. This isn't just Andy thoughts!" I was crying again. I couldn't help it; I was so tired.

"Have you ever had a dream where someone's died, and when you wake up, just for a moment, it still feels real, and it crushes you? Have you ever felt that? 'Cause that's what I'm feeling. Every time I wake up, every time I have one of these … things … I come back, and I know. I know in my heart our daughter is dead. And it's killing me, Pete!"

"Oh, god, Andy. I'm sorry. I shouldn't have yelled." He hugged me close. "I see you hurting, and I want to help, and I don't know how. I don't know what to do!"

I tried. I really did. I didn't go gently into the darkness. Meditation, mindfulness, yoga; I did everything I could think of to derail the dissolution. I went to a church, a synagogue, a psychic. I took Dr. Rosa's pills. I even pulled out my old cognitive therapy workbooks, but nothing worked. My increasingly frequent visits to the other world continued.

As I walked through that bleak and burned-out realm, I began to get a feel for the strange double life I was living. I was starting to understand what was happening. Slipping, sliding, plunging toward that singularity. Tumbling over the event horizon.

Peter and Maddy hovered, unable to help, unwilling to leave me alone. Maddy sat next to me on the couch in the evenings, curled against my side like a much younger child. I cherished every moment. I wanted to memorize every line of her face, the sound of her voice, the way she moved. I wanted to imprint each and every detail into my mind, tucking them away like stores for the famine, against that time when there would be no more Maddy left.

"I feel like we're losing you," Peter said, one Saturday, when Maddy was at badminton practice. "And I can't, I just can't. I can't do this on my own. You're my best friend, Andy. How am I supposed to do this without you? I know it was scary, and it was a close call, but that's all it was. You have to fight, Andy. For us, for me and Maddy. Please! Please let it go."

I turned off the TV and took Peter's hand between mine. I had to make him understand. After all, I was losing him too.

"It was a pivot point, Peter. Don't you see? It was a pivot point and somehow you and I ... we went different ways. In one world Maddy was fine. In another she wasn't. She died, Peter. Our daughter died!" The pain was back, that familiar weight on my heart. Tears crept down my cheeks.

"You've got to understand. There's a world where she died, and that's where I keep going. More and more each day. That night was a pivot point. There were two possible futures, and I'm getting dragged into the wrong one!"

Peter shook his head. "No. Don't you hear how crazy that sounds? You've worried and worried and worried until you've made it real for yourself. But it's not! It's not real."

He kissed me on the forehead. "Maddy's fine, Andy. I don't know how long it will take, or how many times I'll have to say it, but I'll keep saying it till you believe me. Maddy is fine."

I nodded miserably. I was slipping sideways again, back into that other world ... the one that felt real ... the one on the other side of the moment.

We're living in a condo paid for with the insurance money. I've been told it's nice, but I haven't really noticed. I'm back at work. So is Peter. Our days are quiet. We eat, we talk, we love, but everything is perfunctory. Our world is smoke and ash, and we are carbon shadows of ourselves.

Sometimes I wonder if there's another me. Did she slip the way I did? Did she tumble from this world into mine? From smoke and ash to sunshine and smiles? From death into life? If so, she has my Maddy, and I have her grief. I can't hate her for it, even though I'd like to. Two sides of a moment, and I'm stuck in the wrong one.

In the Darkness, We Dig

by Nicole M. Wolverton

The first tooth is buried in a faded plastic Jesus figurine. It's out in the garden. I'm digging a trench for the tomato plants Kevin bought at the Feed and Seed. My spade damn near decapitates the savior. I almost feel bad on account of being a lapsed Catholic—might as well not add insult to injury and all that. The church never did anything to me. Not really.

The tooth I find is yellowed and old-looking, wrapped up inside an old piece of green flannel. I hold the tooth up to the light. Three roots tangle down to rounded points. A human molar from the look of it.

"Hey, Kev," I call, squinting against the bright sunlight. A bead of sweat rolls down the side of my face. It's much hotter than it should be for May, and it's late for planting tomatoes.

"You thirsty?" he says from the back door of the house.

"No, no, nothing like that, but thanks. You ever heard of people burying a St. Joseph figure in the front yard to help sell a house?"

"Sure. Why, you find one? I didn't think it was supposed to be lucky buried in the backyard. Unless the old owners wanted to move out the back door, I guess." He scratches his patchy brown beard. He's trying to grow it in—he's handsome either way, clean shaven or scruffy. We've been married for less than two weeks, but I've known him for years.

"I didn't find a St. Joseph, but I did find a Jesus. Know anything about that?"

"Can't say that I do. Maybe it doesn't mean anything."

"There's a tooth in it. Like inside of the statue."

"Huh. Pretty weird." He takes the ten steps out to the little garden at a jog and looks over my shoulder. "Here—I'll throw it out for you." He squints at it. It almost sparkles in the light but in a way that reminds me of halitosis—it's a dingy, mossy yellow.

I yank off my gardening gloves and cradle the broken Jesus figurine in my sweaty palm. "I don't know. It feels like bad luck to toss a tooth in the garbage, don't you think? Like maybe it's someone's wish."

"You think a conjure lady lived in our quiet suburban neighborhood once upon a time, burying teeth in Jesus figurines to … I dunno, petition the forces of evil to kill off her husband?"

I shrug. I know he's trying to be funny, but it feels like a moment to be serious. "Hey, you don't know. Yeah, it sounds crazy, but … but what about him?" I waggle the Jesus in my hand. "There's got to be a rule about putting religious statues in the garbage, right? Like you're fated to bring down the wrath of some elder god on you over it. At the very least, it's got to be bad karma."

"Forces of evil. Elder god wrath. What've you be watching on the television lately, Gemma?" he teases. When I don't answer, he says, "Okay, okay. I've never heard of either thing—throwing out old teeth or broken religious icons—coming back to haunt a person, but luck and karma and fate—I don't know much about that except I was fated to marry you." He grins. "So what do you want to do—keep the Jesus? He's pretty beat up."

And he is—the robes are brown with dirt, and Jesus's plastic hair has chunks taken out, possibly from my spade. Inside the figurine, a couple of tiny bugs still sprint around in a panic. The flannel, still in my hand, suddenly feels dirty and tainted.

"No, you're right. I'm just being silly. Might as well get rid of everything. Is there a ritual or something that you have to do when disposing of a religious figurine, though? Like how you have to get rid of an American flag in a specific way?"

"Do you really care all that much?" He grins wider. We've had a million conversations about religion, mostly because my parents were so disturbed that we wouldn't let their priest conduct the ceremony in the church where I was confirmed as a child. Kevin didn't care either way, but I couldn't imagine saying our vows under the watchful eyes of a crucified man and his mother.

"Well, no, not really. I *don't* care." I rub my thumb against Jesus's nose and try not to think too hard. "It's superstitious, I know. Old habits die hard sometimes."

Kevin says, "Tell you what—I'll go google it. About tossing out a Jesus figurine and about getting rid of a tooth. Just to be on the safe side. And hey, if nothing else, maybe I'll put the tooth under your pillow tonight, see if the Tooth Fairy comes."

I shudder. "No, thanks. That just seems downright morbid to do when we don't have any kids yet. It's like tempting fate."

"Maybe we can look at it as practice for when we *do* have kids. Practice makes perfect." He takes the figurine from me after kissing the side of my head, and I keep digging, smiling to myself and touching the underside of my own teeth with my tongue.

It's Kevin who finds the second tooth. I'm sitting in the warmth of a weak morning sun on the front porch with the Sunday paper. Kevin's cutting back the overgrown azaleas that came with the house. Hot pink, they are, and the bushes are the approximate size of an elephant. They overtake the entire house. The roots are thick as legs too.

"How old do you think these shrubs are," he asks.

"The house is almost a hundred years old," I say, "but I doubt the azaleas are as old as that. Maybe if they were healthy, but these are all straggly. They're probably fifty years old, max."

"Feels like these roots go straight to the center of the Earth, so maybe you're wrong about that. Maybe they're too stubborn to die." He laughs, wipes the sweat off his forehead with the back of his hand, and goes back to it. Fifteen minutes later, he says, "Gemma?" His voice is puzzled.

"Yeah, babe."

"Can you ... look at this?"

I put down the paper and lean over the railing.

He holds a thick tangle of azalea roots—lifts them up toward me. "What does that look like to you?"

I bend down. The wood is light brown, caked with clumps of dark soil. At the junction of two roots is a bump: yellowish, almost the color of smoke-tinged skies. Shaped like a tooth.

"Maybe it's a disease—some kind of nodule."

"Suppose so, but feel it. It's smooth. I don't think that's wood."

"Weird." I touch the tip of my tongue to my incisors, almost as though checking that I haven't lost one. But no, all accounted for.

He chews on his lip for half a second before chuckling. "Guess it's a good thing we're getting rid of the azaleas for good. We've only got another day of vacation, and I want to finish this before going back to work."

We review the list of projects we've finished in the two weeks. The closing was a week before our wedding, and we moved in all of our things the day before our ceremony. It was Kev's idea to skip the honeymoon away in order to make a home together. The azaleas aren't the last project, but it would be the last before getting back to real life. I've wondered a few times if improvement projects have brought us closer, or if we would have been better off on the beach in some tropical paradise.

That night I dream azalea roots permeate the walls of the house and wind around my ankles and wrists. Yellow human molars grow along each woody root and bite down hard, grinding bone and muscle and tendon until my feet and hands drop to the floor, lifeless and bloodless.

I wake with a screech, clawing at myself, but it's only the sheets wrapped around my ankles and Kevin's hand on my wrist. Somehow, he sleeps through my thrashing, even when I ease away from him and out of bed, down the stairs. Just as the days have been too warm, the night air is too cold. My bathrobe isn't enough to stop the shivering, especially with the chilly, rough concrete of the front porch on the soles of my feet. The soil is still in rough shape after yanking out the azaleas, disturbed and crumbling over the steps. I kneel in the dirt, but it's not cold at all—rather, it's the temperature of tepid bath water. Kevin says he cut out enough of the azalea roots that the shrubs won't regrow, but I can't bear the thought of any remaining roots, tooth-shaped nodules or not. For the next two hours I dig until my fingers bleed. I find nothing but small bundles that resemble capillaries of pliant wood.

"What happened to you?" Kevin asks in the morning. He hugs me close and examines each of my hands, scraped raw at the fingertips, bloody around the nails.

I snatch myself away from him and hide my hands in the pockets of my shorts. I don't know why I'm compelled to hide what I've done. Maybe it feels like I've interfered with our project plans, almost like I've cheated on our goal to be done. "I had a nightmare and couldn't sleep—I don't know, figured I might as well be useful. What else was I going to do?"

"You didn't have to destroy your hands. You could have woken me up—I would have helped you get back to sleep … or given you a new pair of gloves, at least." He kisses me, a light peck. Almost perfunctory, like an old married couple, which is at once comforting and alarming. "Well, come on. The least I can do is make you breakfast."

I follow him to the kitchen, let him usher me into a chair at the dining table. He pulls a happy face while he takes two mugs from the cabinet and places them on the counter. I admire the lines of his back under his T-shirt as he unscrews the cap from the green canister where we store the coffee beans.

He freezes in place. "What the fuck?"

I stand and peer around his shoulder. He upends the canister. Discolored teeth—molars and incisors this time—splash over the countertop like a torrent of yellow bile, jangling like plucked piano keys. *Tink-tink-tink.* Dozens of teeth. Hundreds. They cascade over the edge, mixed in with the coffee beans, and bounce off the floor.

"Is this a joke?" He's no longer smiling, and neither am I.

"Where did they all come from?"

He turns to me abruptly. "Did you do this?"

"What are you talking about?"

"You were skulking around the house last night—is this what you were doing? The coffee beans are ruined."

"Skulking?" My arms go over gooseflesh. "And you're worried about your *coffee*? There are teeth in our canister, Kevin. And you think *I* did this?"

He shakes his head. "No, no. I'm sorry—I didn't mean it like that. It's just … this is so creepy. I thought maybe you were getting back at me for not taking you seriously about the figurine." He's squinting at the teeth spread over the counter, the floor. "Sorry. It just freaked me out, and I reacted."

I can't take my eyes off the teeth, either—or stop the shivers that overtake me. The color of them … a ceiling stained with cigarette smoke. Kevin's tone bothers me. The accusation does, too, but it's the way he said it. He doesn't trust me.

After an uncomfortably long silence, he brushes the piles of dingy teeth on the counter back into the canister and throws the canister and teeth in the trash. I sweep up the teeth scattered over the floor, trying not to retch, and do the same. We stare at each other until it's me who finally says, "Truce?"

Why do I have to be the adult in this relationship? *He* accused *me*. He should be begging me to forgive him.

His shoulders relax. "Truce. Sorry. Again, sorry—I just … if it wasn't you, and it definitely wasn't me, who was it? Maybe we should change the locks."

With just the slightest bit of resentment, I say, "Maybe I never locked up after coming in last night. It could be my fault."

He chews on his lip. "I guess."

My sense of outrage grows. He should be assuring me that it's not my fault, and I know I locked the door.

"But if someone broke in—or didn't break in, I guess …"

I try not to glare. I never thought our first fight as a married couple would be over something like mystery teeth.

He continues. "Maybe someone is watching our reaction. I don't know why someone would leave us a container full of teeth otherwise."

"To be fair, a random container of teeth in *any* situation isn't something you want to find in your house, planted there or not. But it's scary."

"Good point. But I'll go buy some new locks. Tomorrow. I'll go tomorrow on my way home from work."

I shiver and glance around the house. He's suddenly being a little too cavalier about all of this. First, he's convinced I'm somehow guilty, and now it's no big deal? He should go right now, but I don't say anything. We're newlyweds, after all. My mother's advice about marriage was to pick your battles. "And maybe one of those home security camera things when you go."

At three thirty the next morning, I stare at the front door. It sounds for all the world as though someone stands outside on our concrete steps, hurling pebbles—*tink-tink-tink*—but the new security camera that Kevin *did* finally buy the afternoon before shows nothing. It has to be pointing at the wrong angle. But even a glance through the window proves the front stairs empty of anyone and anything. There isn't a soul around, not even an early riser driving through the neighborhood. Not even a feral cat.

I sit cross-legged on the floor in front of the door. Part of me wonders if Kevin is playing a trick. Maybe he really did put teeth in the coffee bean jar, and gaslighting me is just an elaborate joke or some payback for a long-forgotten slight. It's not like him, not at all, but ... things have felt so different since we moved into the house, especially since finding the tooth in the backyard. It's as though someone turned the lights off, and we're stumbling around like we barely know each other. Tonight he turned over and went to sleep without even looking at me. Without even a routine, dry kiss on the cheek. We *are* like an old married couple, and now it's not as comforting. Not at all.

Every few minutes the sound comes again—another high-pitched *tink* that sputters off into silence. I imagine Kevin, sitting at the window upstairs, laughing like hell every time he tosses down a tooth or a rock or whatever he's throwing. I don't want to believe he's capable of such a thing, not my Kevin ... yet I can't think of anything else.

Where did he find such horrible teeth? It's as though he soaked them in a brew of old coffee and pus to make them extra disgusting, just for me.

Pick your battles. Pick your battles. Pick your battles. I can't get my mother's voice out of my head.

Finally, I can't stand my own curiosity—but by the time I make it upstairs and to our bedroom Kevin is sound asleep … or pretending to be. I stand at the end of the bed and watch for any signs that he's faking. And when, after an hour, he doesn't so much as move, I edge over to his side of the bed and lean down to hear his breathing. His beard has grown patchier in just a day's time. Even, steady, deep, with a slight hitch before he takes a new breath. His mouth hangs open, displaying his teeth in the bright moonlight. He's always had nice, straight, white teeth—I always say his smile is one of his nicest features. Now his teeth look yellowed. Almost tarnished.

His breath smells like oranges and decay.

I curve down closer, counting his teeth, squinting into the darkness of his mouth. Is he … missing a molar? I touch one of his bottom teeth, gently, so gently, with the tip of my nail. For a moment, something in him reaches toward me. It's just a quiver of something slick and wriggly, deep in his throat.

Kevin's eyes flutter open, and he screams. I rear back and trip over my foot. He lurches against the headboard, still yelling at top volume. I manage to catch myself against the wall, barely able to move from the force of Kevin's terrible gibbering. His eyes are wide and bulging. Now I yell, too—I yell his name.

He stops abruptly and switches on the bedside lamp. Our bedroom is an exploding star. "What are you doing?"

"Nothing. I mean … nothing. It didn't sound like you were breathing, so … I checked." The lie sounds less strange than the truth, but I don't know why I won't tell him about the teeth. About *his* teeth. The thing in his throat. It was probably just his tongue. I cower at the end of the bed and wring my hands together. I don't want to fight. This battle isn't one I want to pick.

"Don't ever do that again." His chest heaves, and he gulps. "You looked … I don't know, but it was like something out of my worst nightmare."

I am his worst nightmare? "Sorry. I—are you thirsty?"

"No. Just come back to bed. We both have to go back to work … in hours, at this point. Honeymoon's over." He shakes his head, turns out the light, and turns over, curls up.

I climb in next to him and flop around until I find a position that doesn't feel torturous in our strangely cold bed. My hand slips beneath the pillow and touches something hard as a kernel. I struggle to sit and open my fist.

There, shining yellow in the moonlight, is a fat, stained molar.

My mouth stretches wide into a silent scream. Something in me breaks. The bonds we've developed snap, as though they've been stretched overtaut. I am a woman, not a blameworthy thing—and he is lying to me. He waited until we were married, and now he's someone new. Tricked me into thinking I'd startled him tonight, and I will not have it.

I have picked my battle.

I lay in bed for hours, clutching that molar and poking at my own teeth with my tongue. Kevin pretends to sleep. I can feel him beside me, planning and scheming. Is this what our marriage will be like? Me, the scapegoat. Me, apologizing and making nice.

In the early morning murk, a figure stands at the foot of the bed, smiling. It looks exactly like me. A twin Gemma, complete with long, light brown hair, tangled from sleep. It's wearing my nightie, too—it's the kind of thing a woman might wear to run through a thick fog, like what's wafting through the open window right now and curling around the room, poking into corners and wrapping tendrils across my skin.

The other me at the end of the bed beckons and I follow. I match her steps exactly. She drops a trail of teeth like breadcrumbs—first down the hallway, then down the stairs, and then into the cellar. Kevin and I haven't done much work down here yet. We did things out of order—maybe we should have lived together and made this place a home first, then got married. Maybe then I would have seen him for who he is.

The dirty concrete floor bows down to a clogged French drain in the center, all framed by plain cinderblock walls. Flickering overhead tubes give the basement a dreamy glimmer, turning the green, pockmarked door in the corner almost black. I smile wider at myself, my other self, both in our long white nightgowns. Our teeth are long and thin, incisors pointed slightly too much. White. We have a slight gap between the two upper front teeth. Kevin says it's sexy, only now—it's hard to trust anything he says.

We touch the scarred door in the corner. Behind it, we sense something breathing, and I hear a faint *tink-tink-tink*. The other me pulls the door open and gestures toward the thick darkness. I cannot see much except through the faint glow of cellar lights permeating the gloom—but my feet are bare, hugging the earth. She hands me a spade, and I set to work, barehanded. The digging is hard, the dirt is packed solid here. But I find them—*I* find the teeth this time. They are nestled inside religious relics. Stacked into small containers. Loose in the soil. Stuck into roots.

We—my twin and I—we are not the ones who put them there.

There's not enough light, but they must be the color of the others—vomit yellow, cigarette-smoke yellow.

The other me has gone, leaving me alone in the dark. I gather the teeth and fill the pockets of my nightgown. When I can find no more in the ground, I find them elsewhere.

Tink-tink-tink. It only hurts for a moment.

With the morning sun shining slits through the stone of this tiny room, Kevin's footsteps sound on the basement stairs.

"Gemma?" he calls. "Are you down here?"

"In here." My voice sounds different now.

"What are you doing? You're going to be late for work."

I burst out of my little room and smile wide. He screams. Oh, how he screams. The sound is so loud and so long that the walls ring with the sound. I toss my teeth at him, one by one. He skips backward and falls onto the bottom steps.

"What did you do?" His eyes are wide, scrabbling up the stairs as I advance on him. Blood from my mouth splatters on the dirty concrete floor, making the most intriguing patterns. "Your teeth. Did you—did someone ... do this to you?" His voice is high and squeaky. He sounds different, too. Like a different man. Like a different husband.

I dip my brown-and-red-streaked hand into the pocket of my nightgown and hurl a collection of teeth straight at his face, and I laugh and laugh. I am weightless, my battle picked. The other Gemma joins me now, and we laugh together as Kevin turns and sprints up the stairs, screeching and crying.

She kisses me full on the lips, and I taste my own blood. We return to the little dirt room and shut the scarred door behind us. This is what *our* marriage will be like. We are here in the loamy darkness, alone at last, we and our teeth.

Two Heads, One Body

by Scott J. Moses

What's the point, if we all die in the end?

Her eyes peel open with the thought and, as the hissing engine within the crumpled hood whines, she comes to. She winces, lifting her throbbing head from the steering wheel, and through her muffled hearing, the horn ceases its distorted song. She leans back in the driver's seat, the red blues of the now-silent siren washing over the pines.

How can you be sure this isn't some shared dream? Your dream …?

Lethargy, like these thoughts she'd once medicated away, slides down her limbs and neck like an oblique sap, giving way to pain. She undoes her seatbelt and groans; knows she's broken a rib or two. Gritting her teeth, she releases the wheel, and gazes into the spider-webbed windshield for the memory overtaking her.

Overflowing with fear as she fled the house in the deputy's car. The twisted image of her husband's face emblazoned in her mind—those black, bleeding eyes. His bloodstained smile. How the cruiser jerked, fishtailing as she slammed the pedal to the floor, unaccustomed to the Charger's might, that wall of thick pines rushing to meet her.

So close, she thinks, and it comes in a torrent then. A malevolent, all-smothering wave closing in around her. The summer air stiffens, becomes hard to suck down. *Guilt.*

She remembers her father in the hospital those months ago. The chirping monitor signifying life, though for days he'd slumbered there comatose. Days where she'd dreaded the possibility of fulfilling his wish. When he'd filled out the state's Do Not Resuscitate form prior to surgery. How he'd turned to her, pointing to his scrawl on the form as if etched in stone. Had said what he had, still haunting her: *"To hell with the cheese, I just want out of the trap."* And they say the dead don't speak … but they do. See, they haunt your mind, take up residence there, rattling windows, knocking things awry.

She can almost hear him there next to her within the ruined police cruiser as she stares into the gnarled bark of the pine. *"To hell with the cheese, I just want out of the trap..."* Thing is, she *can* hear it. The words come alive in low, thrumming static from the sedan's speakers. She trembles, breath stuck, as the volume knob twists on its own, plays it back louder. The forest whispers, *"To hell with the cheese, I just want out of the trap,"* and before she knows it, she's screaming. She yanks the volume knob from its place. Her father's voice fading into the ether.

She sucks in the air and rests her shattered-glass mind on the headrest before pulling the door's handle, pushing it open with maximum effort. It whines before hitting a nearby trunk, unmolested by the accident. She's on her feet now, brushing the glass, dust, and debris from shirt, jeans, and jacket. The summer wind flows in its way and her legs grow weak. She steadies herself via car roof with a shaky hand, sees her father's chest rise and fall that last time after pulling the plug. She'd always regretted how distant she felt when she heard the machine powering down, a final exhalation preceding her father's own, but she'd been far away, removed from it all. As if her brain had placed a blanket between her and what was happening, merely overseeing herself letting him go in that bleach-drenched hospital.

It washes over her again: like she's filling with water, utterly submerged in that separation, as she becomes that numbed, disassociated self again. The pain lessens, and she bends into the sedan for the shotgun still in its place between where the officers normally sat. The deputy hadn't thought he'd need it; how wrong he'd been. She takes it in her numbed hands, pulls herself from the vehicle, and walks back up the dirt road from where she'd fled. Somewhere once called happiness, *home*. And though she's numb, floating, watching herself, she racks the shotgun. Feels the shell slip into place, a bit calmer for it, despite her rampant, throbbing heart.

Why go back if it always ends this way? If we're only meant to die.

The thoughts whisper to her as she walks up the dirt road. The pines glowering down at her from both sides of the makeshift gauntlet. She seizes a passing memory. She and Kevin driving this road that first time. Joy in their heads and hearts at the prospect of a lakeside purchase, their new lives in this top-down, summer-town right on the water's edge. *Paradise,* she'd thought.

Her lungs constrict, birthing a lump in her throat, as she rounds the off-kilter mailbox to the clearing that was once their front yard. The pier in the middle distance, ever watchful over the waters and what they might conceal. That wide, glistening pane, Atlas, supporting the horizon, threatening to swallow the moon and minute remnants of her life.

The house stands as it ever was. Tall and grey, two stories, shingles missing from the dilapidated roof they'd planned to fix—oh, the plans they'd had.

What's the point? The thoughts again. "Thoughts are thoughts," she replies, and notes the priest straddling the tallest branches of the weeping willow before their front door. Slumped there, limbs hanging betwixt the tree's many arms. A puppet tossed to storage, breathing deep into the branch beneath it. She looks to the shed nearest the pier, remembers lugging the containers of gasoline to the porch. Something questioned by the priest, but she couldn't take any—

"Ain't it great, babe?" Kevin's voice behind her. "Like we thought it'd be?"

She jerks to the willow's branches, to the tattered priest's stare.

He smiles wide before his features distort into pained fear. "Run! Get—"

His last words before taking that assisted dive. She clutches her rosary, the one given her by him before beginning what she thought might be the end of it all. *"Keep it with you, always,"* he'd said before they'd climbed the stairwell to what she hoped was still Kevin.

The priest laughs in ragged coughs, blood spilling from his lips. She exhales—*1 … 2 … 3 … 4*—notes the pair of red jugs by the still ajar front door and, gripping the shotgun close, she ascends the creaking steps of her once-dream. The rosary heavy around her protesting neck. Never minding the dead man's raw laughter atop the summer wind made cool.

The house slumbers as she walks across the hardwood, overstepping the toppled grandfather clock in the dark foyer. She stops before the stairwell, closes her eyes, listens for it dragging itself on the floor above.

Another memory: she and Kevin painting the foyer matte grey, paint all over the walls and one another. Of eating cold pizza that first night on the living room floor. They'd slept there on piles of blankets and pillows pulled from the gutted boxes in the bedrooms upstairs, overlooking the lake and moon in distorted white across its expanse. Holding one another, none the wiser; though later, she recalled the sourness of the air. The hot breath on her neck that first night as she spooned her love. As something dropped from the willow's branch outside. She'd figured the house was settling, that the scratching within the walls by her temples was a family of squirrels. They'd waived the inspection at their realtor's suggestion. The market was white-hot, after all.

Numb and enveloped, she turns to the sunroom down the thin hall to the deputy, too skeptical to wear a rosary. The last of the good ol' boy cops wrenched and pulled from himself so that the wall and flesh fused with one another. Like the remnants of something strewn, trying to crawl from the house's bowels while slowly devoured. The stiffened liquid stretching over his frozen-in-time scream. The jutting bones blotched crimson atop the once-matte grey.

You can't know for sure if it's all in your head. If—

She growls and has the forethought to disable the safety like her dad taught her those early mornings duck hunting a lifetime ago. The steps whine with her footfalls, each creaking board in off-tune, minor-key.

She reaches the final step, and her eyes graze the clawfoot tub in the adjacent bathroom. How she'd stood there naked, drenched in red like *Carrie* as the tub filled with bubbling crimson. How it had spilled over the side as she cried in Kevin's arms. *"What the hell? What the hell...?"* she'd said, and though Kevin's dead stare in the mirror had unsettled her, she hadn't known what she knew now—that he was gone. That the house, or the ones within it, had their claws deep in him. He was *theirs*, as the priest had said when she'd called him again the next morning after trying all night. The only priest in the whole church who'd taken her seriously, who agreed to come off the record. She remembered him saying something about *"All that red tape"* before the phone died in the receiver.

A sourness permeates the hall, and she tenses as the bedroom door creaks open, revealing the edge of the salt ring in the room's corner.

"Kiley? *Kiley*...?"

She stills at the words summoning honeyed images to her mind, and, breath held, breaches the threshold.

The rancid tang assaults her, forcing a dry heave from her already-raw lungs. Hand on the door frame, she notes the shattered bedroom window burst outward. Remembering how the house had performed its own exorcism, expelling the priest from its gullet with a guttural groan, the splintering of wood and glass. How she'd screamed as she managed to complete the salt enclosure, encasing her husband and those within him in the room's corner. A crooked portrait of the two of them at the Outer Banks still hangs above his congested form. His limbs in knots and fighting for dominance. A blasphemous cesspool of appendages twisted and bent against God's intention. The veins of his flesh bulging from within his now-pale skin, eyes pulled down to reveal the blood-specked pink. His head lurches upward.

"I love you," he says, and black brims over his lips and chin. "And I know you've probably heard that from someone before, but I do …"

The shotgun barrel taps the floor as she collapses with a wail from the tone of his words.

The very same where she realized she loved him on that rooftop bar in Philadelphia. How something had burst within her with the utterance, bled out until it had all it had to give. An infection, some invader, love.

"Let me see him," she says, her voice low, exhausted. "See he's still there. I need to …"

Kevin's twisted form slackens, and he stands upon his heels uncoiling himself, the shifting bones rolling along one another. He coughs blood through stained teeth clenched to cracking.

She stands, says, "Show me," and tosses the rosary through the shattered window's frame. Laughter roars amidst the willow's branches, as Kevin's face dawns, an amalgamation of relief then terror.

"Please …" Kevin screeches through cracked lips as his head rotates, shoulders shaking as his eyes blacken.

"Still with us …" it says, and walks Kevin to the salt's edge, but Kiley can't quite hear for the volume of the memory, of her and him on the drive back from the hospital after her father. What he'd said which spawned two days' silence between them.

"If that's ever me, you'd … well, I'd do it for you, K. I would." But that was the way of it with the men in her life. They'd hold her hand for too short a time before asking her to sever the tie. *"Heal me of this life,"* they'd say, as if she didn't have to go on with how it felt to remove someone she'd loved from the world.

The prostrate mess of her husband crawls to the salt's edge, twists his head up at her, tongue flicking the air, bloodshot, bulging eyes taking her in.

"Release us, whore … it is done …"

And her mind floods again.

Her hand's on the cord.

Her body weightless as she lifts the Remington. They scream in Kevin's voice as the buckshot eats through his torso, flinging him back to the wall. The burst of light and sound a storm of her making.

She fires again, staring at what she loves, what she hates. A being with two heads and one body, like her. An invaded soul with unwanted thoughts barraging their mind. Kevin gnashes his teeth, dragging his lifeless limbs with the one good arm left him.

"Hell waits for him, waits for—"

And she puts a slug through the part of his brain that first realized he loved her.

The walls sing the praise of his ruin, and as she steps back, the room exhales. These sounds and colors strange to her vision, she puts a hand to the wall. That sense of beginning again, here at the end. But she's well-practiced. She's burned down a life or two on occasion. She surveys her late husband, the ones within him, his fingers twitch.

No, she thinks. And the thought is hers.

The house burns. The roaring flames reflected in orange-yellow waves along the lake. She smiles, despite the tears, and lies in the grass. The heat of the blazing wood and stone on her skin in that otherwise still night. She turns to the coast, to the lightning bugs on the shore slipping in and out of existence like low-flying stars. Memory flows in a torrent.

Of crying at her six-year-old birthday because she would never be six again. How even at that young age she had felt time slipping through her tiny fingers.

Of collapsing ten years later in the shower, her chest tight, struggling to breathe. "How do you know this isn't all a dream?" the thought had asked. The onslaught paralyzing, a weight pinning her to the floor even as her dad pulled her up in his arms as she screamed with everything she was.

Of sitting in that therapist's office being told she wasn't alone, and that this illness, this constant attempt to find certainty in the unknowable, could be quelled, or at least dampened, and that recovery was possible. She'd read once that no man was an island, but in those days, she'd felt like her own planet. How her mind wouldn't let her get on with life, not until she solved the unsolvable. How she'd lay there in half-sleep, panicking on the existential dilemmas we're faced with as a species. All those 'what ifs,' like her brain had asked a question it shouldn't have, couldn't take back, and had to find an answer before she could experience any semblance of joy again. This half-life of not wanting to die, but not wanting to live either. A living ghost floating in this could-be dream. A sane person's insanity.

What if it was for nothing? the thought asks, ripping her upward, arms squeezing her knees as the tears swell and her stomach drops. She sits, every muscle clenched, the rushed weight of it all tunneling in like a storm.

Her world grown small. The need to act in every nerve, to rush into the blazing inferno to be *sure*, to do *something*, *anything*, to—

Something Kevin once said in her mind, *"You can't put out half a fire, Kiley."*

And though she can't remember the context—when, or why—she smiles, lies back again, controlling her breathing, loosening herself, riding the anxiety. The thoughts violent within her, yet unheeded through her tears.

She takes in the stars, and exhales with a count of four, remembering how she plucked shells on the coast when she and Kevin first met. How his smile warmed her in bristling fervor. How she'd felt in that dress. The salt air kissing her skin in that infatuated spark gone rampant.

They still have him. This was all for nothing …

The blinking fireflies, dozens of miniature lighthouses upon the ether.

"You might have flare ups," her therapist had said in that last session. *"In times of stress, you may notice the thoughts get loud again. Remember what you learned, Kiley …"*

She exhales through the barrage of *what ifs* flooding her mind, though she rides the fear now. Breathing in and out, thinking of Kevin free from the house's grasp on some other plane of existence. Of him burning eternal; they cackling over him.

He's engulfed, asking why …

She stares these thoughts in the face, and beneath the willow's rustling applause, says, "Maybe, maybe not."

One Star, Would Not Recommend

by Anya Leigh Josephs

Thank you so much for joining us here on Earth! After a few wonderful centuries here, our population has really started settling in and getting comfortable. We're excited to continue making this planet our own: all while blending in with the fascinating native human population!

Your job is simple: choose a body, stick with it as long as you can, keep it healthy, fit in with the humans, and help us find new potential hosts out there on Earth. You can stay as little or as much time as you want, but please remember that every reset process causes some wear and tear on the body, so try to choose a model you might stick with for a while. And don't forget to rate and review once you return it!

We have plenty of terrific bodies for you to inhabit, and we hope you'll find the perfect fit today. There are a lot of factors that go into choosing the perfect body for you, so don't pay too much attention to the overall rating! Instead, keep in mind: until the full conquest fleet arrives in about six thousand Earth years, we'll be living among the native population, so you'll want to blend in. Humans are a uniquely close-minded species, and they're unusually attuned to "flaws" in appearance. For reasons our sociologists are still working to understand, they're especially concerned with what sort of genitalia the body has, its hormonal makeup, and the color of its skin. Make sure you're aware of those stereotypes before you start using your body: supplemental materials about human cultural beliefs are available at the end of this guide.

But everyone needs something different from their body. The right one for you might be unusual, but we believe we can help you find the right vessel for your valuable work here on Earth. Take a look at the featured profile below as we work together to find the host that suits you best!

The Horror That Represents You

Lot number:	E145928
Model:	human
Sex:	indeterminate, see note 1 below
Age at acquisition:	twenty-eight
Date of acquisition:	41 days after first arrival on Earth
Total number of resets:	81
Total number of local days in use:	71,187
Former name:	Anya Leigh Josephs
Biological offspring:	none
Height:	64 inches
Weight:	253 lbs
Hair:	black
Eyes:	green
Skin:	pale
Known bugs:	several, all manageable. See below.

1) Abnormal brain chemistry (predisposed to periods of unusually low or high energy, as well as excessive worry and obsessive thoughts), treatable with medication derived from an element widely available on Earth.

2) Endocrine system malfunction (human term: polycystic ovarian syndrome) not responsive to treatment. Causes weight gain (see note[1]), abnormal hair growth patterns, blood sugar fluctuations.

3) History of neurological disease, in remission since prior to acquisition.

4) Susceptibility towards potentially fatal poisoning by common human foods (specifically a sensitivity to tree nuts—humans refer to this bug as an "allergy") and insect bites.

5) Sensitivity to prolonged sun exposure.

6) Poor eyesight, treatable with corrective lenses.

7) Disordered sexual development. See note[2].

---

[1] Humans also have peculiar ideas about acceptable body size.

[2] The dominant human culture is vastly different from the galactic norm in many ways, not least the reduction of the spectrum of both physiological sex and gender identity into "binary" poles. This body has an indeterminate physical sex, with XX chromosomes, internal genitalia, and a testosterone and androgen-dominant hormonal makeup. Make sure to check your model once you're installed: often, humans don't even know the full range of chromosomal and physical attributes that make up their own sex! Keeping up with this information is important for the longevity of your model, as well as blending in with the local human culture.

One Star, Would Not Recommend

Average user rating: 2.23 out of 5 stars
Available for reset and installation: immediately
Sample reviews from confirmed users:

Galbirth hng'nTzir gave this body TWO out of FIVE stars.
  I try to give every body a fair shake, so I'll be honest. This one had some pros, and some real cons.
Pros: *super*sensitive mechanisms. All the senses worked easily twice as well as your average body's. Except the eyes, but hey, that's easy to fix with lenses, or it'd be a simple surgery. Bet they could even do it before you move in. Great brain hardware, so lots of room for your mind to work (though watch out, the sensitivity can backfire on you here! Major overthinking issues).
Cons: mostly aesthetic, but that's a big deal when it comes to a body. Biggest glitch was probably weight retention. No matter how little you fueled it, it kept gaining weight. MAJOR issue, when it comes to today's standards! Also, facial hair growth, which is NOT what you look for in a female model IMHO. I know it seems like a minor thing to worry about, but it's a pain to carry all that fat around with you, and trying to restrict calorie intake is the WORST. Gives the body such bad headaches you can't think straight.
  Plus, at this stage in the planetary settlement you're still living beside humans. And they are REALLY judgey about body size! I know, I know, who cares what a primitive host species thinks … that is, unless you're trying to fit in among them.
  I wouldn't choose this body again, but I care more about looks than most people do, I think. Just make sure to think it over before you commit.

Rllyor rngn'bRath gave this body ONE out of FIVE stars.
  This stupid site won't let me leave NO STARS!!! Would leave NO STARS if I could. THIS BODY IS GARBAGE!!!!!!!!!!

Angshleee fjel'deKarr gave this body THREE out of FIVE stars.
  Apparently, this body doesn't conform to human aesthetic standards. I definitely got some strange looks, and sometimes worse. I didn't do much with it. I stopped removing the facial hair (which apparently isn't supposed to come on a female model, but who cares about that?) If you ask me, sentient beings aren't supposed to be made out of gross lumps of muscle and sinew and all sorts of nasty stuff, but I'm not a human! I just live here! I ate whatever I felt like (you won't catch me giving humans a lot of credit,

but potato chips? Delicious. Almost worth preserving their whole stupid society for). I shaved all the head hair off since it was balding anyway.

Turns out humans are super, super weird about that kind of thing! One time, I was trying to empty the bladder, and a couple of humans stopped me in the toilet before I could even wash the hands. One of them pinned my body to the wall, the other started shouting about how I didn't belong there and people like me were dangerous. Of course, I activated the Local Assistance Network right away, and the humans were tranquilized and recruited as hosts within a few minutes, no harm done to me, but it was scary!

I asked my Host Integration Coordinator and apparently it was because people couldn't tell which sex the body was? Before I downloaded into it, I was told that female bodies go into the "Women's Bathroom" and male bodies go into the "Men's Bathroom," for whatever strange reason, and so I did what I was told to do. But the HIC said humans can't see each other's sex chromosomes, they decide these things based on hair length and what color shirt its wearing and four dozen other things I can't be bothered to remember.

Anyway, I know I've gone way off track here. The body worked mostly fine, aesthetic glitches aside. Humans are weird. IDK.

Garlene garke'niEthr gave this body TWO out of FIVE stars.
At first it was fine, but there were some major pain issues after a while. Worst was the lower back. I know, I know, some low back pain is kinda inevitable if you want a bipedal body, but this kicked in so early! The body was barely thirty when I got it! Pretty sure it's supposed to hold up for at least a couple more years.

I guess I could have tried to fix it at home, but I'm not good with that kind of thing. My husband's a DIY-er, so he suggested yoga, but I just returned it and got a new model that I'm very happy with. It's male, and for some reason that's way easier, even though I honestly barely understand the difference.

Crosedt leh'poTkeirie gave this body FOUR out of FIVE stars.
I actually really liked this one? Normally when you're downloaded into a body it slows your thinking down a lot. We're just brains, right? Just thoughts and ideas and creativity. It's how we've taken over, like, 90% of the known universe without anyone really noticing. But once we get moved into bodies, it's like there's a bunch of debris just in the way, and your thoughts can't go as fast. I always find this super frustrating, and I'd spend more time in the matrix because of it if I wasn't needed for the invasion.

But this brain actually worked super well! It had some quirks, sure, but the processing speed was superfast, almost as fast as a proper silicon brain. For something made out of carbon and accidents, it's impressive.

Angasmar kor'anElili gave this body ONE out of FIVE stars.

Why don't they give bodies a proper testing before they let people have them? That's my question.

It's just a fact—not every body we acquire is good for distribution! Some should stay in the recruitment center forever, not be issued to unsuspecting people who are gonna have to deal with a crappy body that barely works!

Lots of other reviewers have pointed out the aesthetic and functional issues with this body, so I'm not gonna waste my time repeating what they've already said, but the worst thing to me was the GLITCHES. We're talking super weird stuff. Get bit by a mosquito? You've got a welt the size of a baseball. Smell something too strong? Migraine that lasts for days. Eat a cashew? Enjoy being on the market for a new body early, 'cause this one will try to up and die on you if you forget to ask what's in that curry.

This thing shouldn't ever have been given to decent people who just want a nice body to live in. I get that things are hard in the first phases of a new planetary settlement, but this one is honestly just unusable.

Stay away from this body!

Amilir ngi'dEakai gave this body FIVE out of FIVE stars.

Wow, what a lot of nasty reviews this body has! I used it during my relatively brief stay on Earth, and I really enjoyed it. But then, I'm probably a lot older than most of you young folks just coming out of storage, and I've been through a lot of bodies on a lot of different planets. So I know what to expect.

Yes, you're gonna deal with some aches and pains as it gets older. That happens with, hate to break it to you, every body that exists. Species doesn't matter. Whether you're a hyperintelligent two-legged ape or an underwater eel with a thirty-cell brain, you're gonna have to get used to the fact that having a corporeal form means experiencing physical discomfort. I know we don't have to put up with that sort of thing when we're just growing in the matrix, but as soon as you get a body of your own, whatever body it is, you'll have to adjust.

If you care about looks this isn't the one for you, but it seems a little silly that we're taking on human beauty standards, if you ask for my two cents on the matter! I mean, we're all just a collection of electrical impulses that get beamed into suits made out of meat.

I'd have it reset and keep using it if I were staying on Earth! But I'm headed back to namSKREEE to be with my kids in my old age, and leaving this body behind. We had some little hiccups along the way, but I think those of you that are on your first host world need to realize that's just what is going to happen. Don't complain so much. Take the time to appreciate how lucky you are to have a body!

Fujix abllex'saiYir gave this body ONE out of FIVE stars.

I know other reviewers have mentioned thus, but ugh, the FAT on this body! I assumed it was poor maintenance from the human original and put it on a diet. No luck. Okay, nutritional shakes only, very limited calories. It started glitching out like crazy, pounding pain in the head, trembling limbs, constant nausea, couldn't focus. Barely worked! And get this, didn't do a darn thing for the fat.

Could NOT get it down to what the human doctor said was a normal human range, no matter what I did. Doctor said it was probably some kind of inherent metabolic issue. Not uncommon in humans, apparently, but nothing they can do. WTF??? That seems completely unfair to me. Figured it might have been some weird human bias, so I called all the way home to talk to my regular primary care provider, and he says the metabolisms on these things can't be controlled. "Sometimes they just don't work right," he said. "You can learn to live with it. Who cares?"

Well, I do! Took it back for reset after that.

Carloc festri'deStej gave this body ONE out of FIVE stars.

Might not be this particular body's fault but humans are *so* nasty? It got a viral infection and all this horrible squishy green stuff started coming out of its nose. *Ew.* I'd rather go back into storage, thanks.

Sarleeen karis'efrIjen gave this body ONE out of FIVE stars.

Yeah, okay, this body doesn't look great, but that's not the big issue I have with it. The thing you really have to worry about is that there's some kind of glitch in the brain. This was my third human host. That's right, I was an early adopter. Here on Earth when there were only a couple hundred of us, totally undercover. Crazy times. I stayed at least twenty years in the others before returning them for reset and maintenance. With this body, I could only make it six months. It's a smart one, but that doesn't make up for the glitches. And I'm not talking about aesthetics or even some minor physical disability. I get it, not every machine can run perfectly.

But this one is full of problems that go way deeper than that. Its hormonal balances are all off, and the brain—though it can run wonderfully—can also fall to complete pieces for no reason.

Cries at the least little thing. Has days it just doesn't start right. You'll feel so sad you won't even be able to get out of bed, even if you've got something really important to do. Sometimes the body just starts freaking out over nothing, breathing hard and heart racing. And even once you've figured out what's wrong—pro tip, stay away from crowds and enclosed spaces—you still can't calm the thing down. It's seriously unpleasant to have a brain that malfunctions like that, especially when you're used to being one of us, not putting up with all these weird chemicals controlling your thoughts and feelings.

Which is why having the right host is SO important. People think it's just a suit you put on to walk around the world, but it's way more than that. Your host's brain chemistry is all still there! Its moods can turn into your moods! The host doesn't just become a blank slate, and with this one, there's some baggage no one should have to deal with. It's not like we're humans who are just stuck in whatever body they're born in. They just have to put up with pain or sickness or having a body other people are going to judge, whether they like it or not.

Luckily, we don't. And I can't imagine anyone with a choice would want to live in a body like this.

Skin

by KC Grifant

Marina had just found the perfect spot in Washington Park to crack open her book when two college-aged men staggered toward her, one in glasses and a hoodie and one with a mohawk in a white argyle sweater, both with glazed eyes.

And both itching their arms like addicts. Were those spots of blood showing through the arm of Mohawk's sweater?

Not today, she thought. *Not going to deal with it*. She stuffed her book in her tote and walked rapidly away. She had lived too long in the city—mugged twice, assaulted once, so far—to not be on guard. The first spring day had brought out the masses, and not another bench was free.

One guy leered at her, also scratching—did everyone have allergies? She ignored him, using her long-practiced trick of imagining a brick wall around her, fortifying her against the daily bombardment of stares and comments. She had been cursed (or *blessed*, as her cousins argued) with big curves. Often the glances were paired with tongues flicking over teeth and, once in a while, the trail of rough fingers over her bare shoulder or butt on the bus or in the street. *Part of living in a city*, everyone had told her when she complained. Her friends had urged her to flaunt her body, use it to get free drinks. But Marina didn't want to use it. She just wanted to be left alone.

She gave up on her outdoor reading plan and started home. As she walked, the skin along her arms prickled just thinking about the two guys. But it wasn't in her head. Her arms really were itching. She rolled up the sleeves of her sweatshirt to look, but the skin seemed smooth, normal. The itchiness felt like something crawling across her forearms, down to her calves and up behind her neck. She pictured a parade of invisible insects burrowing into the roots of her fine body hair.

Don't think about it, she told herself. Probably psychosomatic. Or allergies.

At home, ice and antihistamines didn't provide any relief. And, she realized once she scrolled her social streams, she wasn't the only one.

Everyone seemed to be afflicted by sunset.

All her friends. Strangers in dozens of countries. Countless pictures of faces and arms ravaged by nail marks and streams of desperate comments on home remedies and prescriptions. She called her doctor of course, even 911, but all lines were busy.

Experts marveled that a pathogen could spread that fast and told everyone to stay calm, stay home. No one was dying, no one was feverish. There was only the relentless itching.

Marina sat cross-legged in her apartment as midnight approached, trying to still her mind against the prickling that undulated across her body. It was worse along her arms, legs, and neck. Occasionally the itchiness flared along her belly, butt, ears. She resisted the urge to scratch, to peel off her skin to get at whatever seemed to embed itself under its surface.

The smell of pot drifted up from the apartment below her and she sat by the window trying to inhale it. Too bad she didn't have any valium. After some digging in her cosmetic bag, she unearthed an Ativan and quickly took it along with a measured shot of brandy.

She checked Facebook group messaging with her cousins, friends. Not loading. Internet was in and out and her cell service seemed to be spotty. At least she had electricity.

"We're all going to die!" A man's drunken voice slurred from outside. Laughter floated up before it cut abruptly. "Don't touch me, you're making it worse!" the woman, presumably his companion, hollered.

Marina shut the window and set a timer, five minutes, as she waited for the drugs to kick in. Every time the beeper went off, she allowed herself to scratch the worst spot through gloves, the schedule helping her to not go out of her mind. Between the timer, she imagined she was floating in cold ocean water, forcing herself to feel the bobbing waves until the itching receded. As the sensation subsided, uncomfortable but more manageable, something else caught her attention.

A whispering.

"What on earth?" Marina said to her empty apartment. She was surely delirious, this skin condition making her hear things.

But no. The whispering was a hiss in her head, words just out of reach. The sound moved from one ear to the other in ocean waves. Trying to reach her.

It wasn't until the Ativan kicked in and she was about to drift off to sleep when the whispering had coalesced enough to form words. She shuddered against the sensation of thousands of gazes piercing her.

Not scared?

Definitely delirious, she thought.

Feeling? Fear? The words persisted, skittering around her.

"Invaders," she whispered. It was the first word that popped into her head and seemed apt. She should feel panic, but her curiosity got the better of her. Whatever the voice was, it seemed tied to the itching. Maybe it could help her. Or maybe she was hallucinating.

Marina sat up in the dark room. She pressed together her palms, inflamed as if dipped in poison ivy sap. "What are you? Why are you doing this to us?"

The voice offered single words in response:

Grow. Produce. Consume. Live.

She woke up to an army of invisible worms writhing under her scalp. She moaned and yanked her hair back into a ponytail, but the sharp pain didn't relieve the itching. She stood, trying to ignore the microscopic needles prickling around her ankles and fanning up her calves.

Turning to her phone for a distraction didn't help. News loaded slowly but there it was: immediate lockdowns had led to riots that morning. Shots of broken store windows, people crying, people shouting, cars driving into sidewalks. She waited for a sense of horror to grab her as she watched the scenes unfold jerkily on her phone, but it was all too hard to believe. Even as her arms bled from scratching, she couldn't stop.

She hustled outside. People were masked, hooded, guarded, walking quickly for the most part. It was sunny, with a slight breeze. Normally a perfect day. The park, maybe, would help her relax.

As she walked, she scrolled for the number she knew she had to call, her stomach a knot of dread. She hadn't seen her mother in nearly two years, not since her cousin's birthday party—when Marina had confessed to her mother that her uncle had groped her earlier that day. Her mother had actually laughed, shoved her back out to the party and told her to apologize for "being dramatic."

She had pictured the brick wall around her a lot after that.

The call finally went through but to voicemail. As Marina hung up, a scream reverberated from the direction of the park. Glass shattered somewhere and two car alarms went off.

I thought I had more time.

Her mind ticked through the list of things she normally stocked up on during a disaster, natural or manmade. TP and milk. Bread and tampons. Cake mix and contact solution.

She hadn't had time for any of that and now, her heart pounding, she half-ran back to her apartment.

Only when she was inside, door slammed and with a chair in front of it for extra measure, did she breathe a little easier. *Thank goodness I'm on the second floor.* She peeked out the window. Some shouts still floated up, indistinct. An ambulance droning from the south.

She surveyed her fridge. Two days of leftovers, half a gallon of peach juice and tomatoes on the verge of turning to mush. The itchiness had killed her appetite at least; the most she could manage was chugging water.

Biowarfare, mass psychosis, news anchors and social screamed.

It was all happening too fast. She should feel more upset, but she was so tired, so sick of everything. Maybe it was better it was the end.

She picked up her phone again, ignoring chains of messages from friends that quickly devolved into panic before abruptly ending.

She texted her mother: okay?

Not read. No response. A pang shuddered through her but froze halfway when she spotted something on her forearm.

Translucent threads, like white hairs, rose a few inches from her hands and arms, barely visible. When she tried to touch one, her fingers passed right through.

"What is happening?" she whispered. *No point in panicking,* she told herself though her heart had quickened. At least it didn't hurt. She checked the mirror to see more of the threads lifting from her shoulders and neck. It was almost hypnotic.

Good, she thought. Whatever was happening to her body, it couldn't be any worse than the curves and bulges that had made her life miserable for so long.

Voices were next. Everyone was rendered mute that evening according to her slow social streams. She waited for videos of people gesturing silently, panicked, to load. Hastily done images and memes of how to quickly learn sign language popped up along with text-to-speech video instructions.

She sat at her tiny table and watched the threads grow thicker along her arm. She cleared her throat, tried again to talk but her neck felt thick, almost like it was clogged with fur. No pain, at least. Maybe, she mused, the threads were growing in everyone's vocal cords.

No matter, she'd get along without speaking. Living alone, she felt she sometimes went days without talking to someone else. Riding the subway in silence, avoiding eye contact, dead earbuds firmly planted in. She couldn't say she particularly minded; it was the first night in a long time she didn't hear any noise in her apartment.

The next day, the filaments waved from Marina's every pore, gentle as sea grass, as she ventured out.

The streets were quiet. Dozens of bodies had collapsed, still. From the limbs waved the same filaments, sometimes breaking off and floating upwards like ghosts of dandelion seeds.

Produce, Marina thought. But what were they producing?

She couldn't seem to drink enough so she headed to the supermarket. There, in the abandoned, reeking store, she downed half a gallon of water. The liquid sang to her, a thousand voices in perfect harmony. The cells in her throat swished like dry bristles, fingers grasping for more.

She hadn't eaten since the itching began. Her sense of smell and taste were scrambled. Like now, the outside air smelled like something she couldn't get enough of, some tendril of a long-forgotten childhood dessert she couldn't quite place but that filled her with longing.

Food, not so much.

The quiet wasn't bad, Marina mused, heading home with water jugs in either hand. She looked up, where filaments floated through the sky like ghosts of dandelion seeds, and asked the invaders a question in her mind:

Why me? Why am I still standing?

The invaders rustled, trying to pinpoint the words. She could feel them like a presence nearby, buzzing and energized, happy to communicate with her.

Metamorphosis, they said. *Some survive.*

She told them, *I welcome it. This world sucks. Believe it or not I've dealt with worse than this. Part of city living. Any living, really. You have to go numb.*

She thought of her mother one more time, the moments with occasional friends and cousins, irrelevant, lovely. All things must pass, must grow. She'd let them go, along with the rest of the world. Tears sprang through her eyes, piercing her numbness. It had been so long since she let herself cry.

In the morning her hair had fallen out, neatly, in a fan around her pillow. But the itching had subsided, at last.

"Thank God," Marina tried to say but her voice was still gone, her throat closing as soon as she tried to speak. And she felt heavy, too heavy, as though someone had wrapped half a dozen weighted blankets around her.

She looked down to see a thin gray layer coating most of her skin beneath her PJs, like a mud bath that had stayed on too long, baked hard in the sun. She worked a fingernail along a soft spot, still flesh-colored, on the back of her hand to get underneath a piece of the layer. Eventually she peeled off a chunk of the gray, the size of a quarter.

The exposed area of skin was covered in translucent squiggles that squirmed frantically at the exposure. She thought of worms under a turned rock, a nest of cockroaches suddenly uncovered.

If she had her voice she might've screamed. Instead, she swallowed and used the edge of a pen tip to touch one of the squiggles.

It curled like a worm and lifted one end. As though it had paused in whatever busy task it was doing to look up at her.

The whole patch began to itch more intensely than anything she had experienced so far. She grimaced.

The gray material, reminiscent of dried Elmer's glue, dissolved against her fingers. She left the rest alone and avoided the mirror.

New layers appeared like parchment: smooth, unbroken bands of gray, endless scabs. Eventually a piece of the gray would bubble up into a tiny orb, break off and float away, leaving something deeper and shining beneath it. From her window, she watched a parade of miniature silver balloons soar into the blue expanse above.

The next day, whatever was left of Marina's skin and the gray layer had completely drifted off. She was left with something deep and silvery and hard but flexible, like a car bumper, covering every inch of her.

A true exoskeleton, she thought. This was way better than the brick wall. Her senses seemed to be intact. She felt denser, clumsier, though cool and clean. No hunger. No itchiness. No pain. When she peered into the mirror, a blurred silver figure cocked its head back. She was safe. Protected.

She breathed out, relief washing over her.

The invaders seemed pleased too, for their reasons.

The streets had emptied of movement and sound. Bodies lay in piles of desiccated husks. Clusters of the filaments sprouted like white stalks from the corpses. She wasn't sure what had allowed her to survive while others succumbed to the filaments, but whispered a thanks to the invaders nonetheless.

Marina walked to Washington Park under the arc of the cerulean sky and chatter of birds. Occasionally a dog ran by, barking frantically. Delight—something she had nearly forgotten—and relaxation flooded through her as she sat on a bench beneath a tree, letting the sun warm her new skin.

Two gray beings like herself lumbered across the street, lost in their world. Marina lifted a hand to them. They waved back, jerky like a baby learning the motions, before continuing.

Other silver figures came and collected the clear stalks from the dead bodies, stalks which colonized and began to spring up in the parks and sidewalks and roofs. She assumed they could be used for something. She'd join them and explore the new growths eventually, find out what they were and what the invaders wanted next.

But today, she'd sit in peace and enjoy the sun.

Why I Wear the Mask

by Samuel McQuail

The cold porcelain mask stares up at me, its smooth surface twisted into a smile. Fake. That's the only way to describe its expression; broad billiard-ball eyes in sunken sockets and a grin too big for its own cheeks. Sometimes I grin back, as if maybe I can try to match it for once. As if I could ever look how they want me to.

It never works.

A cacophony thumps at the walls. Endless chaos that beats its way into my head all day and night. I can't sleep through the sudden shouts and the banshee wails. My own hollow eyes ache. A quick glance across the cramped space I call home reassures me that, yes, the windows and doors are locked and bolted. Seven for each. I can't be too careful; they always try to creep and crawl their way inside my spartan sanctuary. There's nothing to take here. Nothing, except for me.

I pull the mask over my face. A few, slow breaths steady myself as it grinds against my skin. Missing pupils let me peer through, and the world peers back. I tell myself over and over that it's a short trip. I've done it before and I can do it again. No food left, so I'll have to go eventually. The comforting weight of my backpack helps—it means I have a goal. That I have something I can do besides stew in my loneliness. But the mask presses insistently on my mind: what if today is the day I make a mistake?

I hurry through the locks, counting off each one. The numbers ground me—keep me moving forward despite my trembling. One goes to two, down to three, opening four … When I'm done, the door swings open, and I have no choice but to go. No choice but to slip into the dark corridor, carefully picking past debris and filth. Down the old metal steps whose clanking echoes around me. Out through the open foyer, between ruined decorative pillars sprouting rebar branches, and into the world.

They loom above me—ghoulish giants on spindly limbs clicking on concrete streets. Hunched backs, arms that reach to the ground, bones threatening to tear through thin, translucent skin. Serpentine necks crane above the crowds of monsters and snoop along underbellies. Always watching. Always sniffing and snarling and scrounging for something. Someone.

I wait for one to pass by me before stepping into the river of twisted bodies. The chittering, gurgling conversations reverberate between garish buildings that claw their way into a dead, grey sky. I've never seen another person in this city. Not alive, at least. The iron stench of blood lingers everywhere.

If I watch long enough, I can start to work out the differences between them. The patterns they scar themselves with or the blood they've drawn and dragged over their skin. Subtle shades in the thin strands of hair limply draped over their necks. The nonsensical patterns of head-tilting and talon-clicking. Slowing my pace lets me watch their rituals for a while longer, gives me time to try and puzzle out the curious dances.

I can't stare for too long. They hate that.

I snap back to reality too late. One of them drops its head down to my level. I skid to a stop. Hold back my scream as its face hovers inches from mine. The same impossible grin lined with yellowish teeth. The same billiard-ball eyes set in blackened sockets. It cocks its head past ninety degrees, neck cracking and wispy hair brushing the ground. Breathless, blood frozen in my veins, keeping my eyes firmly locked with its own. I want to look away: I want to look anywhere else but at those narrowing pupils. But then it'd know. All of them would.

It bobs its head four times and burbles. I do the same and wait.

Warbling, it pulls its head away and lumbers over and past me. I can't afford a sigh of relief—any break from the ritual alerts the rest. All I can do is swallow the lump in my throat and keep going. Keep looking forward.

An old skyscraper stands like a dead titan, its glass shattered and its guts bare. Around the lobby, the things gather, hauling lumps of flesh in their teeth and monstrous corpses in their claws. The weak, the sick, the old. And other creatures too; things I don't know of, nor care to. It doesn't matter once it's thrown into the pile. Rot, iron, and the reek of decay flood my senses with each breath. I swallow back bile as I inch closer. And the sound …

An orgy of gnashing teeth and the wet smack of lips that never stay closed. They take a single bite of splintering bone and discard the meat.

They gargle blood and water and the drippings of torn flesh. Their shrieking and chattering dig into my skull; the same way their claws crack through the head of one of their dead young.

One of them buries its head into the torn open stomach of another, chewing through guts and gore. I recognize the corpse: the pattern of scars torn into its neck and the pale shade of their hair. I almost feel pity for it. What small thing had it done to condemn itself? Bowed at the wrong time? Warbled when it should have clicked? Not that it matters now. It's just another thing to be chewed up.

I snatch the scraps that tumble to the floor and stuff them in my backpack. A thin plastic liner keeps the worst of the juices contained. It won't last for long, though. Maybe by the time I get back, preserve it, and stow it away in my lockboxes, I'll have the energy to make a meagre meal before I collapse into bed. Not likely, but the hope is something. Like a rush of warm air under imaginary wings.

The journey back is worse. Their eyes burn into my back, though I know they aren't watching. I've done it all right. I nodded and burbled and walked straight on without a click of interest from the things milling around me. The meat weighs me down, making each step sluggish. It's fine, I tell myself. It's fine. It's—

I trip. The mask slips.

It skips across the concrete as I crash to the ground. A dozen clicking conversations go silent. My heart stops and I try to pull myself to my feet before they come.

But it's too late; they're already on me. Screeching, screaming, howling! Talons rake across my skin, pulling me every way at once as they lift me into the air. They hook my lips and pull my mouth into a grin. I shout and struggle, pulling myself out of their grasp, barely landing on my feet. The swarm blocks out everything else—nothing but a storm of spindly limbs whirling and crashing against each other as they fight to snatch me up.

I barely get a step. A dozen hands dig into my backpack. A dozen more yank my arm behind me. Hot blood gushes out of my pricked skin. Tears bud in my eyes, my voice growing hoarse. They won't listen. They don't care. One shoves its foot into the small of my back and pulls my arm further and further. Bone cracks. Shoulder splits. Skin screams as it's stretched.

They snap and gnash in confusion. They don't understand. Why doesn't my arm bend? Why can't it stretch? No matter how much they tug and pull, no matter how much they break my bones, they don't understand why my arm can't be as long as theirs.

A brawl breaks out between them. I squirm out from the straps of my backpack and tumble to the floor. They rip through the fabric and shower me with the meat scraps within. I crawl and stumble and scream. Where is it? Did they smash it? Where is my mask?!

White porcelain shines between grey limbs. I lunge, smacking again into hard concrete and knocking the wind from my chest. My fingers brush the chipped surface. Clawed hands and feet stomp around me. Just a little … Yes!

I roll onto my back and pull the mask over my face.

They stop and stare. Raised limbs lower as their snarling faces snake down. Their eyes narrow as they scrutinise me, the ground, each other … where did it go? Where did that thing disappear to?

I pull myself up, and a hundred eyes burn my skin. I smile behind cracked porcelain, hoping to bring the impossible grin into my eyes. My shattered arm hangs limp by my side, twitching as I try to hold the shoulder straight. I pray they don't see the hot tears as they drip off my chin. I pray they don't see every wince and shudder as lances of pain bring me to the brink of screaming.

I pray that all they see is the mask.

BLOOD AND DUST

by Fred Furtado

The dust cloud swallowed our small town, turning day into night—the second midnight, as my grandmother called it. Ever since I could remember, life had been like that—covered in dust. Dust on our skin. Dust on the ground. Dust on the furniture. Dust on the plates. Dust on the food. Dust everywhere. And coughing. Allergies. Difficulty breathing and swallowing. There was so much dust in our mouths, we spat mud.

Sometimes, the adults cursed their fate, complaining the new crop would be as meager as the previous one, that the ground was paying back the abuse of countless years. Later, I understood. Soy plantations had spread throughout the countryside of Brazil. Every biome fell to these vast cultivated fields tended not only by powerful landowners, but also small farmers, like my parents, who just sought a better life. They ignored the warnings about global warming. For fifteen years, soy ruled. But that agricultural brutality couldn't last.

It began slowly. Rains diminished. Winds, on the other hand, gained intensity and soil changed into sand. We sowed soy, but reaped deserts. When I was two, the first major crop failure happened. Without the precious grain, farmers found themselves drowning in debt. The government could do little to help. Many ruined families abandoned their lands, moving to other regions in search of a new beginning. Those who stayed survived on hope.

"It will be better next year," my father always said. It never was.

The dust storms came soon after. The ghastly combination of strong winds, dry soil and no barriers gave birth to dust clouds several kilometers in size. They swept the land, covering everything with a blanket of fine particles able to penetrate the most secure nooks. The first came in the year of my fourth birthday and was followed by three others. As a five-year-old, I witnessed sixteen of them. The following year, there were thirty-seven. When I turned nine, my town had already been hit by one hundred and twenty-three storms. Most lasted only minutes, but some endured for hours, blotting out the sun and making even the night a darker shade of black. Despite this dreary existence, we carried on trying to find some happiness. It seemed impossible things could get any worse.

We were wrong.

A month after my ninth birthday, a huge dust storm took us by surprise. It was spotted on the horizon minutes before reaching town, and everyone rushed to find shelter. In the confusion, the Sampaios didn't notice their youngest son, Marquinhos, wasn't home. When they finally realized it, the dust cloud had already enveloped our town. Desperate, his father, José, ventured into the storm. He would have died, if not for his wife, Sílvia, who called us for help. My father went after José and miraculously found him passed out about twenty meters from our house. We cared for him until the end of the storm.

The next day, the townsfolk found Marquinhos's body. In addition to the sorrow, we children sensed an additional uneasiness among the adults. They only spoke of Marquinhos's death in hushed tones. Although each child could only pick up pieces of the conversations, together we were able to make sense of the whispering. According to the town doctor, our friend hadn't died of asphyxiation but of a great loss of blood, caused by a horrendous injury to his neck, similar to an animal bite. They believed a jaguar had done it, though no one could explain how it had survived the dust cloud.

This became our main topic of discussion and each one had their own theory about the tragedy. The one about a rabid jaguar lurking around town was popular, but other options included aliens, *chupacabras*, and murder "pure and simple." Further elaboration required consulting our source for "weird affairs," Indian Tonho. He was one of the workers who helped local farmers. When the crisis hit, Tonho survived moonlighting as a porter, woodworker, electrician and plumber. Loved by us, he was derided by the adults because of his drinking problem—he was never far away from a bottle of *cachaça*. Tonho was always kind and seemed to have a genuine pleasure in telling us stories, especially about the Apiaká whom he claimed were his people.

We sought Tonho two days after Marquinhos's death and found him recovering from a particularly long bender. His expression changed when we told him about our friend—a deep sadness came over him. He was silent for a while and then asked how it had happened. We told him and witnessed a second transformation: it was as if the alcohol evaporated completely, giving Tonho an appearance of resolve I had never observed on him. He stood up with uncommon drive and sent us home, leaving hurriedly in another direction. He left town that same day.

Two dust storms hit the town the following week. Although minor, they had a devastating effect on Sílvia's sanity—she was convinced she could hear her son calling from inside the furious dust cloud. José sought help from the doctor in vain. Our town was one of many that had arisen during the soy golden years. It was a square with a bank, a grocery store, a clinic, and a church surrounded by several houses. There was no psychiatrist or therapist. For these 'luxuries,' we needed to go to the capital. During the third storm after Marquinhos's death, while her husband was distracted, Sílvia ran off. Her bloodless body was found the next day with the same injury.

Fear consumed the townsfolk, unleashing a furious search for answers. In a rowdy meeting at the Civic Center, the adults decided we couldn't wait for the jaguar to devour us one by one. We needed to hunt the "monster," so a posse was formed to patrol the outskirts of the town. It found and killed the horror-inducing predator. The jaguar's body was exhibited at the Civic Center and smiles returned to everybody's lips. Even those who realized the downed jaguar was thin and malnourished, maybe even sick, preferred to believe the problem was over. I was one of them.

Five days later, we realized our mistake as a new storm blanketed the region. When it was over, my parents and I went to visit José and his now only daughter, Teresa. We arrived to find the door ajar and a thick layer of dust on the floor, showing the house had been left open during the storm. There was no trace of José or Teresa. Their bodies were found days later in the field, in the same state as the others. The brief respite for our sanity over, we looked for solace wherever we could: the church organized a *novena*; the mayor asked the capital (unsuccessfully) for police backup; the wise women worked on spells and prayers. The most desperate packed their bags and left.

At home, the situation wasn't any better. The Sampaios' property was the farthest from the town square; ours, the closest to theirs. Everything pointed to us being the next victims. My mom and dad discussed this privately to protect me, but I knew they were scared. I was, too, and started sleeping in their bed with them. Even then, sleep did not come easily, especially on stormy nights. The wind lashed our house and the noise, for my impressionable nine-year-old ears, resembled that of an animal scurrying along the walls and ceiling, looking for a way to enter and suffocate us. Or suck our blood.

My mom wanted to move away, but my dad refused to be expelled from his land by something he couldn't see or understand. He was convinced the new deaths were the work of another animal. "Maybe the jaguar had a companion," he told us with fake confidence. Still, I knew my dad understood with absolute clarity that we were experiencing something unnatural.

Two weeks passed without any more deaths. We woke up the next Sunday to a perfect morning. The cloudless sky was a deep blue. The usually unrelenting wind lay still. And best of all: not even a speck of dust in the air. I couldn't remember a day as beautiful, and even my parents struggled to recall a similar occurrence. That paradisiacal morning had a soothing effect, as if nature was assuring us things would improve.

To celebrate, my dad organized a picnic. He loaded our old car with provisions and we happily set off for a creek about four kilometers from the town square that was used as a beach. Others had had the same idea—the place was packed, music and laughter filling the air. Happiness had returned, it seemed.

Around one in the afternoon, my dad's cellphone rang, starting an electronic chorus of simultaneous rings from the other phones at the creek. Acquaintances and relatives from nearby towns were calling with the same message: go home immediately! The sunny day had hidden an event of biblical proportions—the formation of a gigantic dust storm that had sped towards us the whole morning. The descriptions from those on the other side of the line were filled with words like 'apocalyptic' and 'world-ending.' My dad paled, like everyone else who had received a call. It wasn't just the idea of being caught outside by the storm that tormented him, it was the fact there would be nothing between us and whatever lurked around town.

This reasoning and its nefarious conclusions sent all those that, until seconds before, were relaxing on the edge of the creek or bathing in its cool waters into a frenzy of activity. Everybody was picking up towels, baskets, and children, and shoving them unceremoniously inside their cars, not caring if the water would ruin the upholstery. They wanted to get out of there as fast as possible and be inside their homes before the darkness arrived. We were the first to leave and my dad drove as if there was no tomorrow—literally—forcing the old car to utopic speeds for its engine. Our frantic escape raised its own dust cloud, redoubling the anguish of those behind us.

When we neared the town, I saw the black wall on the horizon growing rapidly. An anxious feeling assaulted me, one that had been germinating since Marquinhos's death. My head tried to cope with an overwhelming fear made even more terrifying by the knowledge that my parents were as frightened as me.

Dad, an obsessively conscientious driver, parked the car haphazardly. The apocalypse of dark dust had already taken over the town square and the sand-loaded wind whipped us mercilessly throughout the few meters separating the car from the house. My father opened the front door and my mother threw herself inside carrying me in her arms. The door closed with a bang, and we were plunged into darkness, as if the sun had gone out. The deafening howl of the wind coming in through the open windows filled the living room. Dad turned on the light and we rushed to close everything. Afterwards, we crashed on the couch and hugged, tears rolling from my eyes and leaving tracks on my dust-covered face.

Exhausted, we might have slept, I'm not sure. When we moved again, a few hours had passed, but the storm continued as furious as before. Mom decided to cook and Dad walked into their bedroom to return with his hunting rifle. He looked at me and smiled awkwardly, a way of saying 'just in case.' The meal restored a certain air of normality and we even chatted about everyday affairs. We tried getting news from the outside, but the storm had consumed all electromagnetic waves in addition to light: TV, radio, internet, and cellphone were silent. Even the landline, which had faithfully resisted other storms, had surrendered to the absolute power of that antediluvian dust cloud.

Intent on cheering us up, my parents dug out one of our many board games. It was a brilliant idea. For an hour and a half, we forgot our problems—immersed in dice rolls, card swaps and meeple movements. It's the last happy memory I have of them and I treasure it deeply.

Things seemed to be improving, although the storm raged on. We thought of sleeping, hoping the cloud would have passed when we woke up. But something was bothering me: an additional noise besides the howl of the wind and the play of sand on the walls. It sounded as if someone had stuck a knife in the outside wall and now was dragging the blade across, carving the masonry. Intellectually, I couldn't parse the origin or nature of the noise, but my heart could. A cold feeling seized my body, while my eyes met Dad's—he knew it, too.

A loud crash came from the kitchen, where my mom was, then pounding against the door; a splintery explosion; and the opening of our home to the elemental fury. Mom screamed and we heard an inhuman grunt. Dad grabbed the rifle and ran to the kitchen while I remained paralyzed in the living room. This time, the cry came from him: a "no" expelled with all the strength of his lungs, followed by Mom's name. Two shots punctuated this. Noises of suffocation and breaking bones reached my ears.

Even overwhelmed by fear, my legs moved, but to the front door, not toward the kitchen. One. Two. Three steps. I could almost touch the doorknob. I wanted to touch it, turn it and run, but I had to know what had happened. Heart almost bursting through my chest, I turned around slowly and looked towards the kitchen. I was 'rewarded' by a gruesome vision. A man—I use this word loosely, because to this day, I don't know what he was, but his build seemed masculine—held the inert shapes of my parents. His skin was pitch black and covered with grooves that captured the fluorescent light, as if he were made of burnt wood (a strange and independent corner of my mind wondered why he wasn't covered in dust). His hands and feet ended in long, wicked claws, also black, and a desiccated tangle of black fibers crowned his head. The creature's right arm enveloped Mom and his head was submerged in her neck. The left arm held Dad's body, whose head hung in an unnatural way, only possible with a broken neck.

This horrific scene froze me again. I had to get away, to turn and run for the door, but my mind, shattered by the future implications of what I was witnessing, tried futilely to find ways in which I could help my parents. Lost in this whirlwind of uncertain plans and brutal horror, I realized that the creature appeared to be chewing or sucking Mom's neck. A scarlet drop escaped from where the black mouth met the brunette skin. It ran down the curve of the neck to get lost in the fabric of Mom's blouse, but was soon followed by equally crimson companions.

A moan escaped my lips and the creature opened his eyes. They were bright red, contrasting with the darkness of his body. They seemed like human eyes flooded by blood that had rebelled against its confinement in veins and arteries. They stared at me and I felt pierced by the intensity of the gaze, rich with the promise of torment. The implied threat in those eyes dissolved the glue that kept me planted in the room. With a speed that I could never repeat during the rest of my life, I turned and fled, diving into the dark maelstrom of dust. I ran aimlessly at first—my only intention was to distance myself from that thing—but even if I had had a destination in mind, I could have never reached it. The terror had erased any semblance of organization in my mind and I was unable to recall any geographical information that could be useful.

It was then that I saw the light, weak and elusive, so much so that I thought I was imagining it, but the glow became stronger from time to time. Still overcome by terror, I clung to that ghostly light as a castaway might a piece of driftwood. I ran towards it, certain the creature was a few steps behind me, ready to strike. I believed, however, that if I reached the light, I would be safe. It seemed like forever, but today I know it only took a few seconds to cross the distance. I collided hard with something and fell. Trying to recover my senses amid the whipping dust, I saw above me a black shape and the feeble hope in my soul fell into a deep dark pit. The creature had gotten to me. I screamed and turned around, trying to crawl away from the monster. I felt his hand grab my arm and pull me up, putting me face to face with him. Out of nowhere, the light came up again, illuminating his features. I realized his skin was not shriveled or as dark as the creature's. His eyes were brown, human. In fact, they were familiar. He pulled the damp cloth that covered his nose and mouth down, allowing my stunned brain to identify him as a dear friend.

Indian Tonho had returned. The unexpected wave of relief drove me to unconsciousness.

When I woke up, I was inside the Sampaios' house. Tonho had carried me there and broken a window so we could enter. He had covered the hole with cushions and curtains. A dresser and a couch pushed against the window completed the makeshift barrier. The flashlight he carried, the source of the light I had pursued, was on, allowing us to see each other. I noticed changes in my savior: his gaze had acquired purpose; his face had aged years over the weeks he had been away; and in his body, in which fat had ruled, muscles now staged a comeback. Every piece of skin that I could see was covered with tribal markings and Tonho wore several beaded necklaces and colorful feathers around his neck.

What caught my attention most was the spear. It was a one-meter-long wooden shaft that expanded into a leaf-shaped blade at the end, adding thirty more centimeters to the weapon. It appeared to have been carved whole from a single piece of wood. There were symbols along the shaft and blade, but I had no idea what they meant. Tonho held the spear near his body like it was his most valuable possession. He realized I was awake and looked at me. Knowing the questions that were going through my mind, he started talking.

"He is old; older than our grandparents or their grandparents; older than my people. He walked in the jungle when only the beasts were here. He lives in the night, in darkness, and hungers for blood. The more he eats, the more he wants. He slept for a long time, but when the days got shorter because of the dust, he awoke. He won't sleep again."

Thirty seconds. That was how long the explanation for that nightmare took. It was so surreal I didn't quite know how to react. But there would be no time to think about it. Something struck the door of the house with an enormous strength, causing the hinges to come off the wall. A second blow would easily smash the door. Tonho was already up and raised me with a quick motion.

"Get up!" he said, and I ran upstairs without thinking, while the door was destroyed. I went straight to Marquinhos's room and locked myself inside. I could hear fighting, even with the storm outside. Tonho screamed something incomprehensible and the noise stopped.

I remained still for a time, uncertain what to do. Finally, I peeked through the half-open door. My heart froze when I heard the creaking steps of the stairs—someone was coming up. I slammed the door and ran to the window. I had to use all of my strength to force it open and sneak out into the dust. After a second of hesitation, I jumped to the ground, convinced that at any moment the monster's black hand would appear out of nowhere and close on me. Although my landing wasn't the most graceful, at least I didn't sprain my ankle or break my leg. My first impulse was to brave the dust maelstrom again, but I couldn't abandon Tonho. I needed to know if he still lived.

Against all my instincts, I rounded back to the front door and to my horror saw Tonho lying on the ground, his spear resting over his body. The flashlight, still on, eerily lighting the room. I remember kneeling beside Tonho, shaking him and calling his name, only to see my hands covered in dusty blood that had gushed from the wound on his neck. The stairs creaked, drawing my attention and sinking me into despair. The creature had returned to the living room, instead of following me through the window. Ready to pounce, his red eyes were fixed on me. I screamed and stood up, taking a step back to escape the attack without losing sight of the monster. I tripped on Tonho's legs and fell over the spear's shaft at the same moment the creature jumped me. I closed my eyes and felt a powerful thump that took my breath away. The creature's body was over me, his putrid breath on my face. His roar left my ears ringing. My time had come.

The moment stretched and … I remained alive. I knew that because of the pain, anguish, and fear that riddled my body and mind. Cautiously, I opened one eye. I couldn't see straight, but the weight of the monster on me showed that he was still there. Strangely, though, he was getting lighter. I opened my other eye and tried to get out from under the creature. That's when I noticed Tonho's spear had pierced the being's chest. Before my eyes, the monster was turning into dust and blowing away in the wind. I scrambled away as fast as I could, while the creature became one with that accursed storm. In a matter of seconds, he disappeared and the spear fell again over Tonho's body.

The following events are a blur. I stumbled up the stairs to Marquinhos's room, where I was found the next day curled up with the spear. My rescuers took me to the hospital and later to my grandmother's house. Everyone wanted to know what had happened, but I couldn't talk. I fell into a depression, became almost catatonic. My nights were consumed by nightmares from which I woke up screaming. My grandmother saw fit to move to Rio. Years of therapy have helped in my recovery, but therapists always assumed the supernatural elements in my retelling were how my mind made sense of the tragedy, including the loss of my parents. After a while, I thought better to accept their version, at least publicly, and keep the truth to myself.

I became an anthropologist specializing in Native Brazilian culture, more specifically, obscure and forgotten myths of our indigenous peoples. I thought that if one monster was real, maybe others were, though I never found any evidence to back that up. There were no further deaths in my old town. Over the years, the government finally invested to repair the environmental damage and the dust storms decreased significantly. Today, few there remember the deaths. Those who do, blame the jaguars. I know better.

I still have the spear. Just in case.

Something Blue

by Anna Fitzgerald Healy

Something old—the lost feeling that clings to me like a last-season perfume. Stale and cloying, it trails my every movement. Something new—my bargain-basement wedding dress. The white chiffon cinches my waist and puffs up awkwardly on my shoulders. Something borrowed—my best friend's ex-boyfriend. Something blue—my tears, muddled with mascara, streaking down my face in the church bathroom.

"You're such a beautiful bride." Margaret rolls her eyes as she sits on the counter, smoking a Pall Mall. "Hun, if you don't stop crying soon, you're gonna look like a monster walking down that aisle." She shakes her head in disparagement as she taps ash into the sink.

"I'm not crying. The smoke is just getting in my eyes," I protest as I dab concealer under each eye, then dust powder across my face. With any luck, my veil will hide my puffy eyelids.

Margaret snorts. "Lizzie, you've made your bed, now you gotta lie in it."

It's June 5th, 1950, in Millinocket, Maine, and this is the happiest day of my life. Or at least that's what I tell myself as rice pours down over my head. It piles up on my glittery veil and gets stuck in my fake eyelashes as David pulls me to him.

"I'm the luckiest fella alive," he says with a sloppy kiss. His tongue is thick and slimy as it pokes into my mouth. I blush and try to pull away, but his strong arms hold me tight. Behind us, the forest swishes and sways in the wind, as if it's also considering being a runaway bride.

It could be hours or days later that we arrive in Florida, it's all one cringeworthy blur. I fidget as David hails our taxi from the airport. My white tweed blazer chafes my arms, my kitten heels pinch my toes, and my white pillbox hat keeps slipping down my forehead. David brushes his hand over my skirt and digs his fingers into my stockings, which only makes me cringe harder.

I never asked for this. David came on to me at a party, then my best friend walked in. I explained that nothing happened, but she assumed the worst and everyone else did too. I was *news* in Millinocket, with better ratings than the top radio drama. And it was all so scandalous, that everyone just sort of hoped it was true. Even my parents wouldn't listen when I swore up and down that my virtue was still (*very much!*) intact. So when David proposed with a smirk and a vile gleam in his eyes, I had no choice. As a country girl in 1950, my virginity was just about the one thing that I had going for me, so all I could say was, "Oh, gee, that sounds swell."

The yellow cab takes us to a pink motel on Clearwater Beach. The palm trees rustle lazily in the tropical breeze as sandpipers run along the sand dunes and alligators lurk beneath the boardwalk. Our balcony overlooks the Gulf of Mexico. The curtains billow through it as I try to smile. They tremble as David unzips my dress. They flutter in and out as he grabs me. This isn't exactly the 'happily ever after' that the fairy tales advertised.

'Honeymoon' doesn't seem like the right word for this. I don't enjoy it when the moon is high, and David is making lewd comments while sucking down drinks. There is no honey then—everything is bitter and sticky as stale beer. But I like when the sun is up, and David is sleeping it off. When I can lie on the beach and pretend that my doting husband does not exist.

I float in the shallows as the sun tattoos itself into my skin. The Gulf of Mexico wraps its soft arms around me and gives me a hug. It has also been humiliated and repressed. But somewhere, under the gentle tides and the tepid waves, it still has the heart of a wild thing. I guess we have that in common.

As we fly back to Maine, I clutch the armrest hoping that we don't fall out of the sky. I've always been an anxious flyer. As I twist my engagement ring around my finger, I wonder what the future holds. I detest my husband, and we've only been married for one week. Will 'domestic bliss' be just as euphoric as our honeymoon? Surely, between his work at the lumberyard, his nightly visits to the Big Moose Saloon, and his drunken hunting trips, David can't have *that* much time left to torment me. I wince when the ring cuts into my skin.

Something Blue

Big band music plays from the car radio as David's Chevrolet Bel-Air cruises up the I-95. I gaze up at the silhouette of Mount Katahdin as we turn onto Route 11. We're almost home.

The Appalachian Mountains rise above us, cradling our little town in their foothills. Millinocket is a tacky paradox, pairing conservative country bumpkins with ancient folklore. It's perched on the edge of the 100-Mile Wilderness, an aptly named stretch of backcountry that straddles the Canadian border. The virgin forest extends across the horizon, untouched and untamed, its virtue still (very much) intact.

Mount Katahdin has always creeped me out. The tallest peak in Maine is a fun romp in the woods, if fourteen hours of backbreaking inclines and mosquitos are your idea of a good time. Every year, hikers fall to their deaths from the sheer cliffs of the Knife Edge trail, as the wind whips around them. The Penobscot Tribe believed that an evil spirit named Pamola lurked on the summit. They threw sheep and goats off of the Knife Edge trail as blood sacrifices to him—which no doubt increased the forest's overall creep-appeal. Some say that when the wind is right, you can still hear the squeal of those confused sheep.

The sunset flames up in rusty red streaks to puddle over Katahdin and dye the mountains crimson. A sunset like this is a bad omen—Pamola must be hungry tonight. As we head north, the mist tiptoes in, diaphanous and sparkly as my Goodwill wedding veil. The big band sounds degenerate into throbbing static as the forest encloses us. But David doesn't seem to mind—his musical tastes must be just as refined as his romantic sensibilities.

Please, don't let us reach Millinocket, I pray to whoever might be listening. I've never dreaded anything more than getting out of this car and walking up to David's prefab home. Lying down in his dirty sheets sounds like a death sentence. I'd rather be thrown off of the Knife Edge with the other livestock, than let my husband paw me ever again.

The glare of oncoming headlights throws a garish spotlight on David's lecherous smile as he rips a hole in my stockings. And maybe it's the static blasting from the radio. Or maybe it's his revolting sneer. Or the sticky feeling of his fingers as they pinch my inner thigh. Or maybe it's just because this was my favorite pair of stockings, and now he's gone and ruined them—but something strange comes over me as we drive onto the old Brownsville Bridge.

My hand seems to move of its own accord. I watch my baby pink fingernails reach for the steering wheel, then yank hard to the right. And this time, we *do* fall out of the sky. We plummet into the Penobscot River. The *smash* of impact, followed by the satisfying *crack* of crumpled metal.

The Chevrolet Bel-Air folds into itself as water flies up around us and blood drips down my forehead.

David splutters as he grabs my shoulders. "You bitch, you've ruined my Chevy!"

As my eyes flicker from the steam rising out of the hood, then over at David's scowl, I repress a grin. *Good. He ruined something of mine (my life), so now I've ruined something of his (his ugly Chevrolet). It's not a fair trade, but it's better than nothing.*

David wades over to my door and pulls me out. Rage amplifies his brute strength as he pushes the sedan over to the embankment. "You're a dead girl, Lizzie." He glowers. "Now I need to get someone to fish my damned car out of the river. You're gonna wish that you died out here." He snatches the engagement ring from my finger, smiling as the band catches around my knuckle and draws blood. He sulks to himself as he stomps away over the Brownsville Bridge.

I sit on the riverbank and gaze sadly at my kitten heels. I was a fool to marry David. Our honeymoon was torture, but married life will be far worse. I suppose that I *could* run off into the 100-Mile Wilderness, but my tweed set isn't the most practical hiking attire. Or I could try drowning myself in the Penobscot River but that seems rather cliché. Then I imagine pushing the Bel-Air into the rapids, and sailing away from my troubles, until the current smashes us to bits.

Then I hear it: giggles. Gay and bright, the laughter intrudes upon my disaster fantasies. I peer toward the sound, then gape at a woman standing at the edge of the forest. Why is she dressed all in white? Is she on her honeymoon as well?

"Hello," I call out, but she doesn't seem to hear, so I repin my hat and scramble after her. My stupid kitten heels slip across the gravel as I race forward. Just when I've almost reached her, the mist rolls in to cloud my vision. I rub my eyes, but when I open them again my quarry is waiting for me at the next bend in the river.

We continue like that for a while: me following her, and her staying at arm's length. I'm not sure how much time passes while we play our game of follow-the-leader. But I don't mind, because every step away from David's Chevrolet Bel-Air feels like a step in the right direction. The walk calms me and my companion does too. The distant sound of her laughter drifts down the river. Gradually, my tears dry, and my breath slows. The clatter of my heels keeps time with the gurgle of the Penobscot River.

After about an hour, one of my kitten heels breaks off. I study my shoe for a long moment, then take off the second one and hurl them both into the river. I never liked them much, anyways. Up ahead, the woman in white waits patiently as I unhook my torn stockings from my girdle and toss them into the water as well. As I watch my stockings get sucked away by the rapids, I experience an unfamiliar feeling. What is that? Freedom?

My pillbox hat is next. It falls off of my head and gets caught under my dirty feet. I trample over it, then toss the muddy cap into the murky waves. I grin as it swishes away. Laughter from up ahead—the woman in white approves.

As the night wears on, my tweed set gets soaked with mist and heavy with mud. And I know it's unbecoming for a young bride, but I struggle out of my waterlogged blazer and unzip my stained skirt. Then I pull the bobby pins out of my hair to let it cascade down my shoulders. My skin glistens in the condensation as I stand on the riverbank in my white bra and panty girdle and throw my clothes into the river. The mud isn't cold beneath my bare feet, it's actually quite pleasant. And the night air isn't chilly against my skin, it actually feels refreshing.

I was always a nice girl. Prim and proper, with modesty my favorite fashion accessory. But as I watch my tweed suit swirl away into the depths of the Penobscot River, I experience a foreign sensation: power. An owl hoots, but I don't cower in shame because it feels good to take control of my own body. To own my own skin.

I wait for the sun to make its ascent, but daylight never comes. I wait for my legs to grow weary, but they stay strong. I wait for my limbs to start shaking with exhaustion, but I feel nothing. I try to outwalk my frustration. My fear of a life of Hamburger Helper and David's crude jokes. I walk until I can barely remember his name. Until I can hardly recall my own. I walk until my feet grow tough and callused, in desperate need of a pedicure. I walk until I forget what a pedicure is. I walk until my hair grows down to my waist, and the silence envelopes me. I walk until I become a part of it. I walk into the 100-Mile Wilderness, until I find one hundred miles of wilderness within myself.

The woman stops, and I stumble straight into her. I yelp with surprise as I come face to face with myself. My jaw drops as I take in my tiny mouth, wide eyes, and pale cheeks. She's me, but she's also *not* me. She's a different version of myself—one with pillbox hat, white tweed set, and kitten heels intact. She makes *such* a beautiful bride. Her smile is warm, but her gaze is cold. Her clothing is elegant, but her eyes are vicious. She's savage and relentless, a monster in her own right. Or maybe it isn't *her* who is the monster—but rather, the world that raised her. The man who forced himself on her. The parents who demanded she marry someone she hated.

The priest who officiated a loveless union. She had to become a monster to fit in.

I gaze at her in shock, and she looks back with amusement. Then she turns and points. I follow her line of sight to an old steel bridge. It takes me a moment to remember the name: *the Brownsville Bridge*. The bridge where I crashed (*what was his name, again? Oh, right,*) *David's* car. The bridge where he took my engagement ring. The bridge where he left me.

Why does that feel like such a long time ago?

A pair of headlights bob down Route 11, and I run forward. I wave my hands. I'm trying to help. Trying to warn them. The car slows down, and someone screams. They almost follow the same doomed trajectory as David's Chevrolet Bel-Air, but at the last moment they right themselves, and I feel a tingly sensation as the car drives straight through me.

As darkness falls, the tourists, loggers, and hikers flee from the backcountry of Northern Maine. They stop foresting and polluting, then speed back to civilization, as if afraid that nature might strike back. Then the mist prowls in, with me at its heels. As I walk through the 100-Mile Wilderness, I celebrate all that is feral within myself. I'm looking for unsuspecting motorists: truckers who have overstayed their welcome and travelers who took a wrong turn down the road less traveled. Sometimes they crash, and sometimes they don't. Obviously, it's better when they do. The locals stopped sacrificing their bleating livestock long ago, and the mountains are hungry. The forest is furious and the river is insatiable—Pamola isn't the only one who enjoys a midnight snack. These morsels pacify us for a moment, but always leave us wanting more. Attention must be paid to the old gods, like Pamola. And to the new ones ... like me.

I've heard about other women like me. Ladies in white who frequent roadways and lead travelers astray. Are they damsels in distress, demons in disguise, or the ghosts of pissed-off brides? No one seems to know. Sometimes the cars whisper about them as they skid past.

I have to wonder: why is man so scared of the things he can't tame? Why is the world so petrified of independent young women? Why does everyone insist on dressing us up in white, putting us on an altar, and sacrificing our freedom? Is it really all that different from the living sacrifices that took place here long ago? My current occupation—of leading motorists astray—simply feels like the natural progression. The mountains proposed, and I said "I do." Then I wrote our vows in blood and tossed the bouquet, to see whose life would be ruined next. Finally, I'm a real bride.

Something old—my white tweed traveling suit. No one dresses like that anymore. Something new—a pair of headlights drifting down the highway. Something borrowed—a scream from the driver. A gasp. A fresh feeling of terror and shock as the car skids past. As it hits me in the middle of the bridge. Something blue—the Penobscot River as it washes over the car and swallows them up.

It Calls At Night

by Samantha Lokai

Some things stay with us whether or not we want them to. Like the things that scare us, the ones that truly terrify. They burrow into the deepest, darkest corners of the mind. Some of us keep it hidden, while others wear it like armor. Either way, they become a part of us. I was ten the first time I felt that kind of fear. Back then, the summer holidays on the island were almost always the same. Except for one.

It was sometime in August, those jaded days when the novelty of school holidays was over and the heat had already worn me out. My terracotta skin, sunbaked to a deeper brown, told of endless days spent lying along the river bank. I was bored and restless and took it out on Mama most days. It was just the two of us in our big, old house.

The seclusion of our own land made the house grandiose in its presence. It stood two stories tall, with weather-worn walls veiled behind twinning vines, creeping along the veranda, down the stone steps and sprawling wildly into the front yard. It was naturally fenced with tumbling bougainvillea shrubs that teased passersby with its heart-shaped purple blossoms, and chastised wandering hands with its sharp poison-tipped thorns. Royal palm trees darkened by age towered on either side of a dirt path leading to the end of the estate where it was bounded by dense jungle. The house felt much too lavish for us, but according to Grandmama it had been in our family for generations. She had been devoted to it, proud that every inch of cut stone and blood-heart wood was built by the hands of our great-great-grandfather.

After my grandmother passed, the house had been a constant amid change. I had come to regard it as something of a second parent, a comforting presence when my mother couldn't be there. Supper times were less lonely with the lingering aromas of Mama's cooking in the kitchen, long after she had left for work. Nights would have been restless if it weren't for the solace of my bedroom while I waited for her to return. Each room with a job to do; it's what makes a house a home. Back then, it wasn't unusual to be left on your own while parents worked. Neighbours would look in on each other's children. It was the way things were in the old days, and we lived in a small unremarkable village where nothing ever happened. That was until one night.

I was brushing my hair in front of the old-fashioned mirror in my mother's room. Resigned to the advice of the women in my house, I applied coconut oil and aimed for one hundred brush strokes every night to tame my tangled curls. I hated mirrors but didn't mind this one. Perhaps it was the room's soft lighting that made it less harsh and the distraction of the ornate markings that made me judge myself less. During my final brush strokes, there was a disturbance outside. I thought it might be Ms. Rosita checking in on me but it was a little late for her to call by. If Grandmama was there, she would have blamed it on the house. Over the years we had grown used to the shadowy stirs, and eerie creaks and rasps. It's what old houses do.

I doubted whether I heard anything at all, then caught the sound again. It was a peculiar whooping call, neither human nor animal. I descended the staircase into the front hall and listened. The antique floor-standing grandfather clock towered in the corner and began chiming the hour ten minutes too early. It echoed throughout, emphasizing the lonely rooms within. On reflection, I have often wondered if it was the house trying to warn me.

"Ms. Rosita?" I called from behind the front door, but there was no answer.

The jungle was home to a mystifying assortment of wildlife and it wasn't uncommon for creatures to roam the estate under the cover of dark skies. It was quite possible it was the mating call of an animal I hadn't encountered before, or the macabre cry of an unfamiliar night bird. Halfway up the stairs I was brought to a sudden halt—drawn to an unspoken call. The hairs on the back of my neck stiffened and something stirred at the bottom of my stomach. This wasn't Ms. Rosita.

I edged down the stairs, took cover within shadows and avoided creaky floorboards until I reached the window in our living room. The curtains brushed against my bare legs and startled me. It was the time of year for spiders, although in the Caribbean it could be any of a variety of crawling things. The jolt of adrenaline gave me the courage to look outside. It was likely nothing and I exhaled with contempt for myself as I peeled back the curtain.

I expected to see the familiar stretch of yard, with a rusty wheelbarrow toppled next to the tyre swing, framed against inky swathes of wilderness. So when I saw someone standing motionless right there in the middle, it startled me. For a split second I wondered if it was a trick of shadows and moonlight. There were many times I thought I had seen things toward the jungle and I wasn't the only one from the stories I heard growing up. This time, I was sure. There was something out there—petite, draped in hessian sackcloth cropped above the knees, and with an oversized straw hat lowered over the face. It tilted its head toward me. My skin prickled with goosebumps and I flinched out of sight.

After a moment, I eased the curtain open again, but the path was empty. Confused, I scanned the banking to the jungle frantically, until something shifted in the corner of my eye. Directly across from the window, they appeared. It was too small to be an adult, but surely it wasn't a child on its own all the way out here this late at night? Unless they were lost and needed my help. I tried to get a better look, but their face was obscured. It was more than a little strange, this whole thing, and I needed to make sense of it, to appease the uneasiness brewing inside me. The only way to do that was to go outside and find out. They beckoned to me with a slow mesmeric hand motion.

Darkness overpowered the faint glow of our porch lamp and cicadas buzzed their high-pitched song. A cool night breeze jangled wind chimes, rustled leaves, and breathed life into swathes of murky silhouettes.

"H-hey, you lost?" I stepped forward. "What you doing all the way out here?"

They continued gesturing for me to come to them.

"You need help? Can't you talk?"

Annoyance got the better of me and I stormed down the cold stone steps barefooted. We should have been a few paces apart, but instead we were further away from each other and I hadn't seen them move.

"How did you—" I blinked and it happened again.

This time, they were all the way at the end of the path to the jungle. Unable to speak, the silence was soon broken with a dawdling call, like the magnified plinking of dripping water, and I knew for certain it was coming from that thing. Confusion turned into fear. Coldness wrapped around me, and I was suddenly aware of how exposed I was standing out there alone in the dark. This was not a child. I needed to get back inside the house but couldn't move. Instead, I stood there breathless like I had pedaled my bike up a hill. It vanished again and my heart pounded, knowing it could be anywhere. A piercing sting on my ankle broke my trance and I gasped in horror at a thick menacing trail of ants snaking along beside me. I brushed a few off my leg, and backed away toward the house, grateful to be moving my legs.

"Ophelia what you doing out here!"

"Mama!" I pummeled into her and pressed my face against the course fabric of her uniform, breathing in her perfume and the faint scent of hospital antiseptic.

"Ophie? Something happened? Why you out here catching cold?"

I pointed toward the jungle, but the thing was nowhere to be seen and to my bewilderment neither were the ants. My mother hurried me into the house and up the stairs to my bed. She was more guilty than annoyed, and the sooner she could erase the memory of finding me outside late at night the better. She hated leaving me by myself when she worked nights at the hospital. My attempts to explain what happened were brushed aside while she gave me a good telling off.

"You were sleepwalking is all, Ophie." She hushed.

I knew not to persist unless I wanted a second dose of scolding. It was late and Mama was exhausted from her shift. She paused at my bedroom doorway before switching of the light.

"Ophelia, you know you shouldn't be out there on your own at night."

Then Mama's whole way about her changed and she said something that made the hairs stand up on the back of my neck.

"When it calls you must never answer, and you should never ever go with it. You hear me, Ophie? You won't ever find your way back."

The next morning, my friends, Anisha and Jamal, stopped by. When I told them what I had seen the night before, they began talking over each other and firing questions. I barely got a word in or understood what they were saying.

"Shhh!" Anisha hissed at Jamal and covered his mouth with her palm. "Don't say it, dum-dum! You should never say it out loud! She lowered her voice, "Granny says, if you speak of it, you invite it."

I knew what Anisha meant. Stories of the unexplained, and beings that caused mischief and trepidation, were as much a part of our upbringing as the lessons we learned at school. Superstition was at the core of every household. Old folks loved sharing tales from *long time* and as kids we begged to hear them. We would gather on the porch at nightfall with roasted corn cobs and the smell of paraffin from lit flambeaus made from used glass bottles. Curious, excited, and frightened by the end too. My mother always cast it aside as *old talk* whenever I asked. She didn't want to scare me, but perhaps it was she who had been afraid—*if you speak it, you invite it.*

Anisha and Jamal were convinced my encounter hinted to the old folk tales we had heard of children lured deep into the jungle, under the charm of something we were too afraid to name. It made my blood run cold thinking about what might have happened to them after they were taken. Still, I wasn't ready to give in to this possibility just yet.

"That's what happened to Jo-Jo." Jamal sighed.

"Who is Jo-Jo?" I asked.

"He was a boy my mother went to school with. Granpa said Jo-Jo went out catching fireflies out in the bush one night and never came back." Jamal shook his head.

"They took him." Anisha sighed.

"Who took him?" I rolled my eyes.

"You mean *what* took him," Jamal muttered.

"If he went to school with your mother, it was a long time ago! There probably wasn't even a Jo-Jo! How come we never hear of children going missing nowadays? Your grandpa told you that to keep you from mischief, dummy."

"That doesn't mean some haven't come close. Like you, last night? Maybe we just don't hear about it because people are afraid to talk. Like Granny says—if you speak it, you invite it," Anisha whispered.

The three of us were quiet for a long while after that.

Later that evening, I was restless after my mother left for work. There had been no mention of the night before. Mama left me some tea steeped from soursop and bay leaves and Lord knows what else. By the whispers between Ms. Rosita and her that morning, I suspected there was something in there to ward off Jumbies too. My mother had an herbal concoction for everything. She told me it would help me sleep and I was under strict orders to drink it at suppertime.

After double-checking everything was locked, I settled into the rocking chair at the window to watch the sun make its descent. Twilight was when the wilderness came alive on the island. Wind whipped and whistled while trees swayed and whispered. The jungle continued to glow in parts long after the crimson and orange skies faded.

Fireflies twinkled like fallen stars caught in the trees. My grandmother used to say they were the spirits of people who had passed on, keeping watch over us. It was a comforting thought and I liked to think that maybe Grandmama was now one of those lights too. I rocked back and forth, eyes heavy, drifting to the memory of last night and Mama's words floating through my head in pieces. *Ophie—don't answer—stay away from the jungle at night—you'll never come back. Ophie ...*

Over and over her words repeated, lulling me to sleep.

I was in limbo between asleep and awake when a gentle breeze fluttered over my skin. Something felt amiss—the windows had been locked. I fought against the haziness in my head, struggling to wake fully until a burning tingle on my ankle urged my eyes open. I thought I had woken up into another dream. There I was, surrounded by inky darkness, the squelch of damp soil beneath my bare feet.

A full moon bathed the tree tops in pale, silvery light and the air was fragrant with ripe fruit and wet moss. Crickets and tree frogs joined an orchestra of wild night life, and beneath it my soft whimper as tears stung my eyes and fear crawled up my spine. A giant cotton tree loomed above me, its roots and branches mangled and grotesque. I was stunned by its presence and felt immediate dread, as would anyone who had stumbled upon one. No good ever came from the Jumbie tree as we called it, a well-known dwelling for malevolent spirits, and a bearer of bad luck.

Something was there with me, hidden in the shadows. I recoiled and backed up against the trunk, rough bark digging into my flesh. An icy chill stiffened every bone in my body upon hearing the familiar whooping call. The thing from the night before emerged, small with a bulging middle, long spindly limbs, and a cone-shaped hat with a wide brim slanted over the face. Remaining under the cover of darkness and keeping its face unseen, it attempted to lure me with hypnotic hand motions, its coyness suggesting something far more deceptive.

"No!" I shook my head, and averted my eyes.

It murmured strange hushed noises that unsettled me, forewarning a presence not of this world. With trembling hands, I grabbed a fallen tree branch and held it in front of me. The thing moved forward into a beam of moonlight and I shuddered with revulsion at what I saw. Faceless with a small mouth and fine pointy teeth, its legs were fixed back to front with its heels facing forward, and the knees twisted backwards. It spoke my name, mimicking my mother's familiar call. Hearing her voice come from this wretched creature sent shivers across my skin. My name echoed in chorus around me. There were more of them appearing out of nowhere. The tops of their hats glimmered under the moonlight as they gathered together and whispered taunts. I wailed with a guttural force and bawled for my mother.

I was transfixed by harrowing thoughts of what these wicked brutes might do to me and with every passing second my chance to escape was less possible. Then came the sharp stings on my feet again and I looked down to see an outpouring of ants, oozing like molasses out of a mound of earth. My mini saviors bit with urgency, hurrying me into motion, and I gained enough courage to hurl the stick at the thing in front of me and bolt off.

Disoriented and frantic, I ran through the jungle desperate to find my way back home. I had no idea which direction to go and paused to look around. I stifled my cries, closed my eyes and begged for a sign. The wind rushed around me and leaves rustled above, providing a melody of comfort. There was a shift in the air, a strengthening invisible energy, and when I opened my eyes, a single green glow whirled in front of me before darting forward. One by one, little dots of green lit up ahead and without hesitation I followed their lead.

Upon reaching the dirt path leading to our house the fireflies dispersed, swirling and disappearing back into the jungle. There were no lights on apart from the amber glow of the living room window and our front door was slightly ajar. It slammed shut behind me once I was inside as if the house had been impatiently waiting on my return. I checked every other door and window was locked before sinking into my bed with my mother's Bible clutched to my chest.

The morning after, my head was foggy and heavy like I had been sleeping for days. My memory was blurry and out of sequence until the image of what I had seen surfaced and jolted me fully awake. I bolted upright, heart pounding against my chest, and scrambled out of bed and into my mother's room. She was asleep and I wanted to throw my arms around her but decided not to wake her. Being near her was enough and I took comfort it was daylight.

I tried to piece together the night before, but I couldn't remember how I got to the jungle. The last thing I remembered was feeling drowsy and then I was somehow standing under the cotton tree. In the light of day it all seemed so distant, diluted by the morning sun. I wondered whether it had happened at all. That was until my mother mentioned the mud on the floor and I looked down at my dirty, scratched feet. She thought I had been sleepwalking again and I desperately wanted it to be solely that. I wanted to tell her what I had seen, but the words never came out of my mouth; saying it out loud would make it real and I wanted to believe it hadn't happened.

A week later, my mother switched to working days. She had requested the change when Grandmama passed away a couple of months ago so I wouldn't have to be on my own at night. We had a barbed wire fence put up around the house because Mama wanted to rear chickens. The enclosure would keep them in and wild animals out, but I suspected she was more concerned about me rather than the chickens. It was no coincidence Reverend Jackson stopped by that same week with a couple of the church elders. It was meant to be a quick stop for iced Mauby and coconut cake but turned into an impromptu blessing and my head doused in holy water. I wasn't given an explanation and I didn't need one.

I would never be sure if that night was a dream, a hallucination brought on by Mama's tea, or had I unknowingly answered a forbidden call that beguiled me to a likelihood that was very real. Years later, I moved off the island, choosing to settle in the suburbs away from nature's rawness, enclosed by picket fences and manicured lawns. The lure of the wilderness remained an underlying current that electrified my skin whenever it was close, exuding both wonder and brooding danger; opposing forces hidden in plain sight. Sometimes late at night my horror stirs, echoing from across the years and I recoil at the image of the thing, but then I remember the fireflies and their soft trails of light leading me home. The memory lives only in my head, I've never told anyone about that night. Words have a way of breathing life into things.

If you speak it, you invite it.

The Grandmothers That We Leave Behind

by Christine Lucas

No one talks about Grandma Evlabia anymore. Not Mama, not Papa, not even the neighbors, since an ambulance whisked her away one Sunday morning a month ago. And Bia wants to talk about her so very much. She wants to ask Mama what's going to happen now that Yaya is in the hospital, when the next Loop happens. Who is going to keep them all safe? But Mama doesn't know about the Loop.

Bia knows.

"The ability to sense the Loop often skips a generation," Yaya had told Bia the first time she noticed the Loop, when she was six years old. Yaya had held Bia close to her chest so that her heartbeat could help Bia keep track of seconds, while Time had the hiccups and moved in cycles. For the few minutes it lasted, Yaya recited the ingredients for moustokouloura and then the steps to bake them—*grape molasses, olive oil, cinnamon, cloves, all-purpose flour.* By the time the world whooshed back in order, Bia was drooling in her grandma's arms, craving those cookies, safe from those who dwelled in the Loop.

And now Bia is twelve years old and Yaya's away. Whatever protection spells she knew, Yaya shared them with no one. It's neither in the geranium pot she kept at the windowsill, nor woven into the colorful rugs she brought in this cold land from the old country. If her grumpy, scar-faced cat who pees on everything knows her secrets, he doesn't share them. He's busy evading Bia's parents' attempts to rehome him. Perhaps the spell is in the handwritten notebook with Yaya's recipes? Its pages carry olive oil stains and smell of thyme and oregano, the words written in old-fashioned pencil, smudged at places. Bia cannot read Greek; her mother insisted she should focus on learning their new homeland's language first. There would be time for such useless hobbies once they had settled in—once they'd been *accepted*.

Perhaps there's time before the next Loop. Perhaps Bia is lucky, and it takes years again.

She's not.

It happens again on a Monday morning. Bia picks at her eggs—they're runny, and bland, and the two bacon strips are not enough. "This is not how Yaya made eggs," she grumbles.

"Well, your grandmother isn't here anymore," Mama says. *Neither are Grandma's colostomy bags and the constant stench of feces, mothballs, and liniment.* Mama doesn't speak those words, but they linger loud and clear in the room over their breakfast table. "I won't have this apartment stink of cumin and pastrami." She points at Bia's plate with the tip of her buttering knife. "Eat up. This is how proper people eat their eggs around here."

"But ..." Bia leans over her plate to hide the moisture in her eyes while struggling to keep her voice calm, so as to not sound like a s*poiled, ungrateful brat*. "But, Mama ..."

Mama keeps buttering her slice of bread over and over again, her eyes fixed on some point on their kitchen table. Bia's heart dives for her feet and bounces back up into her throat like a sob. Beside Mama, Papa dips his bag of tea into his steaming cup of water again and again, until water splashes into the saucer beneath and then some, leaving tea stains on the tablecloth. They're both caught in the Loop, doing the same thing over and over again until it ends. Outside, a sparrow repeats the same chirp countless times. Inside, a fly traces the same circle on the kitchen window above the sink. Only Yaya's cat measures everything and everything with his cold, amber stare. He makes a quick snack of the looped fly and bolts to find more looped prey around the house.

Then Bia spots *It*. Like a living, writhing shadow, *It* slithers out from corners, cracks, and crevices, between shelves and from under the stove and the washing machine. It's not easy to notice *It*, unless one knows what to look for: the shadow that goes against the rays of sun, the floating dust that soars against the draft from the open window, the deep, burning hunger that goes against Time. If Bia tilts her head that way, she can almost see a humanoid shape in a loose swirl of dust and crumbs and fragments of dead things. Its arms—or are those tentacles?—stretch and curl around her parents' necks. Bia knows that tomorrow Mama will have more grey hairs, and Papa will have forgotten another little thing from his childhood—perhaps the name of a pet, or the taste of kaimaki ice cream from his summers back home, or Yaya's lullaby that kept him safe from the

Loop in the crib. Then Bia's head snaps up, the knot in her throat a fiery ball of terror.

What if she's next? What if the Loop Dweller steals her memories of Yaya?

Her eyes then return to the drops of butter coagulating around her tasteless eggs. Nothing—no one—will steal Yaya's memory from her. She shuts her eyes and forces herself to remember the taste of Yaya's egg dish. She forces herself to remember her younger self on a low stool next to Yaya, watching as Yaya whisked together everything for her kayanas dish, and she counts in her fingers all the ingredients she can recall: *eggs, tomatoes, cumin, thyme, oregano, basil, paprika, feta* …

By the time Bia gathers the courage to open her eyes again, the Loop has ended and Mama scowls at her again. With trembling fingers, she scoops a bite of runny eggs into her mouth.

They taste like tears.

Bia is fifteen years old now. These days, her parents won't talk about Grandma, unless to list her as a chore.

Mop the floor. Scrub the toilet. Feed Grandma.

Yaya is back now—back in a room that's no longer *hers*, with no potted geraniums or colorful throws and rugs. Or any vibrant color at all. Half of it resembles a hospital, with the stainless steel rails at the sides of the bed, the medical supplies and the mixed smells of disinfectant and urine. The other half is a dump site for everything Mama has no use for anymore, and yet has no heart to throw away: hole-ridden clothes and shoes, an old fan that might work if they replaced the cord, an ironing board with no balance whatsoever, and all of Bia's childhood clothes Mama saved for the younger sibling she'd hoped to conceive and never did. Bia wonders if the Loop Dwellers had anything to do with Mama's persistent fertility issues every time she sits with Yaya, in this room that overflows with little merciless slices of life lost.

Yaya's changed too. She's a shell of her former self; she lies agape, her nightgown hangs several sizes too big on her narrow shoulders, her eyes remain vacant and yet focused at some spot at the opposite wall. This spot sometimes moves, as if something only she can see glides in slow spirals and circles over there. Is Yaya now caught in some greater loop, one that spans in weeks, months, even years? How much of her 'self' have the Loop Dwellers devoured while she was away, so that she doesn't know Bia when she holds Yaya's spotted, bony hand in hers?

When Mama suggests moving Yaya to a 'home' again, Bia responds with a tantrum of epic proportions—if she's going to be labeled an "ungrateful, spoiled brat," she might as well earn her title.

"If you're going to abandon Yaya again, I'm out of here," Bia yells, strategically positioned by the open window so the neighbors can hear.

When Mama shushes her and rushes to shut the window, Bia moves to the balcony door, left cracked open so Papa's smokes won't stink up the living room.

"I'll go stay with Uncle Thodoris and Ayse," Bia yells and moves to the next window, so that neighbors from all sides can get enough gossip fodder. The mere mention of her uncle's Turkish wife is a certain way to rile up her mother, who turns deeply red. Mama never really forgave her brother for marrying one of *those*. "Ayse makes the best imam bayıldı, perhaps even better than Yaya's. I've missed eating real food," Bia yells at the top of her lungs, moving to the next narrow window by the entrance.

It takes Bia a while, and earns her a sore throat and midnight cravings for feta cheese dipped in olive oil and sprinkled with oregano with a side of retsina wine, but Mama finally yields. Yaya stays in that awful room. Bia tries to make it a home again with a basil plant on the windowsill and photographs of the old country across from Yaya's bed, so that Yaya's fixed gaze falls on something wholesome.

Life goes on in a stalemate of bland meals—or just another sort of loop of their own making, weaved out of stubbornness, pride, and countless little unresolved grudges. Yaya's care falls on Bia, who's still trying to read Yaya's handwriting, to learn her recipes and her stories and all those little things that keep the Loop at bay. Then Yaya's health takes a turn for the worse.

The doctor suspects dehydration and possible kidney failure. A nurse comes over to insert a catheter to monitor her urination, and determine if she'll need to be admitted. Bia wants out of there. She doesn't want to be the one to hold Yaya down, while her knees are bent and spread to expose her private parts to a stranger. The nurse is soft-spoken and patient and ever-smiling but still a stranger. Yaya squirms and weeps when her genitals are wiped down with a cleansing solution, and turns her eyes to Bia in a wordless plea.

The Loop whooshes in as the nurse moves to insert the catheter, with the lubricated tip poking at the exposed urethra. And poking again. And again. And Yaya cries, and squirms in Bia's arms, and tries to break free, but the nurse's left hand is firmly on her genitals, the elbow keeping Yaya's right knee from moving. Her left leg is useless anyway, since she came back. Bia weeps and a howl chokes her, a howl at the merciless universe that won't give Yaya a *fucking* break. At the foot of the bed, just behind the nurse, shadows amass—a Loop Dweller. Its upper limbs reach out and churn around the nurse's neck, and coil further down her arm, towards the hand that holds the catheter—towards Yaya.

"No!" Bia cries but her voice carries no power. It leaves her throat muffled, as though she's screamed into a pillow.

The prodding continues, as if fueled by malice, as if the shadowy tendrils drive the oblivious nurse's hand to poke a little harder. Yaya squeals and grapples onto Bia, and Bia can barely breathe, she can barely move. She struggles to wiggle Yaya a little onto the bed, and her hip hits the bedstand and knocks down the bowl of trahana soup she's made for Yaya's supper. It crashes on the floor, the thick gruel sploshes around, and Bia's nostrils fill with the scent of warm winter nights by a fireplace she's never seen. Something clicks in her mind—a piece of a cosmic culinary puzzle cooked in fear and consumed with hope.

"One cup of trahanas," she yells. A coarse, desperate yell, and the shadowy tendrils slow their advance. One of them, the nearest to Yaya's privates, recoils as if measuring Bia's worth. Before the accursed things can move again, Bia yells the rest of the ingredients. "Half a cup of olive oil! Two cups of crumbled feta! Four cups of water! Salt and pepper!"

The Loop whooshes to an end. The dark entity dissolves. Yaya's head falls onto the pillow, drool dripping down the corner of her mouth. Then the nurse blinks, confused, and grumbles something about spoiling this catheter, and reaches for a fresh, sterilized one.

Yaya has stopped struggling, her chest heaving a little faster than usual. Bia wipes Yaya's thin, sweaty hair back, and mumbles empty words of comfort, empty promises that everything will be all right. The procedure is over in minutes this time, and Yaya dozes off afterwards.

Bia rests her head by Yaya's pillow, both relieved and a little envious of Yaya's deep slumber. Something important happened today. She needs to find out what.

Loop in, Loop out, the years pass her by and Bia finds little in Yaya's writings. She finds little *anywhere* she looks—those who could tell her more about the Loop and its denizens are either dead or back in the old country. She has no way to contact them; she lives paycheck to paycheck and cannot afford transportation back home. The old-timers are not familiar with the newest communication technologies, and who will look after Yaya if she leaves even for a short while? All she has is the old notebook and her memories, fragments of songs and stories. She'll make sure that the Loop Dwellers won't take those. They won't, like they took her parents. She's certain it was *them* who caused the accident.

A drunken driver, the police told her. A hit and run. *Sure it was.* Bia was home, in Yaya's room when it happened, showing Yaya cat videos on her tablet—the only way Bia could make Yaya smile these days. Just a whoosh against her face, a blip on the screen that could be a connection error, and chuckling at the edge of her hearing from the shadowy corners of the room. The approaching sirens came shortly after. No one told Yaya; Bia had no heart to do so, and how much would the poor woman understand anyway? Yet Yaya never smiled again after that night.

And now no one talks about Grandma Evlabia, only the nurses and the doctors in the hospital she's been admitted to *again* for yet another respiratory infection. They don't talk about her like Bia *needs* them to. Yaya is so much more than the sum of her withered parts: her airways, her circulation, her bladder, her bed sores and her emaciated body that has long shed the smells of her cooking and the home she's left behind. Sometimes Bia dips Yaya's comb in rosemary infusion, and sometimes she dabs the dry skin of Yaya's face with a washcloth with chamomile tea, and spoon-feeds her small portions of moustalevria that smells like the old country at early Fall. The staff don't mind Bia; they welcome another pair of hands in their ward of old souls.

Grandma Evlabia isn't the only grandma in these rooms. Not by design—Bia asked the ward's head nurse about it. But those three rooms at the far end of the ward seem to be always occupied by old women. There was Babusya Oksana, and Nani Shloka, and Abuelita Maria, and many others. Some with frequent visitors, but most of them alone on their beds for days on end—even in death. Right now, the other old-timer who shares Yaya's room is Babaanne Melek. Like Bia's Yaya, she left her village outside of Ankara to follow her family to the cold north. Sometimes Yildiz, Melek's grand-niece comes and sits with her when Bia is also there, and they all sit and watch TV shows in a language that's not their own in a thick, weary silence. Sometimes Yildiz brings lokum to share with Bia and the staff and those in their nearby rooms. Other times, Bia brings spanakopita squares that can never be as good as Yaya's, but she tries her best. She's never left the hospital hungry. There's always some treat from many different cultures.

On some days, though, everything about the hospital crushes Bia like a giant thumb. She needs air. She needs out, away from the smell of antiseptic, away from the sounds—blips and buzzes and wheels squealing on the linoleum floor—and the ever-lingering anticipation of the inevitable. Does the staff notice her hurried escape? Do they judge her for abandoning Yaya? Bia cannot tell. She keeps her purse clutched onto her chest and her gaze on the floor and bolts.

There's a little coffee shop past the small garden at the hospital's entrance, with tables on the pavement, overshadowed by large-leaved Linden trees. It's a little pocket of spring filled with hope against the bulk of despair that's the hospital across the street. It's also a little more upscale than the places she usually frequents, but she needs real, potent caffeine. So she plops herself into a seat, and orders her coffee black and strong. If the server noticed her white-knuckled grip around the handle of her purse or the sweaty collar of her shirt, he doesn't show; they're probably used to distressed customers.

The coffee is indeed strong, like a shot of adrenaline into her veins that lifts the fog from her mind. She reaches into her purse for Yaya's notebook. There's a recipe she needs to study that she's been postponing for months now: kollyva, the dish traditionally made for funerals and memorial services. There's this knot between her heart and throat that always insists to leave it for tomorrow. If she flips the pages to the list of ingredients—wheat and cinnamon and sugar and nuts—she might attract the evil eye and rush Yaya's passing. But she has to. Yaya has outlived everyone she's ever known, and the inevitable cannot be far away.

Then a gust of wind blows back her hair and linden leaves fall around her like confetti. She reaches to her coffee to shield it with her palm. Bia raises her gaze just so, only to see a man in scrubs two tables over spooning sugar into his cup, until it overflows. At her left, a shameless—and Loop-free—pigeon nibbles on a bagel from the hand of a man in a dark suit. He doesn't notice, only wipes his mouth with a tissue over and over again. Others open and close purses and phones, a kid kicks an empty soda can, until the can rolls away and the boy stands kicking thin air.

Not everyone is caught. Sparrows and pigeons have swarmed the bistro's patio tables to appropriate everything edible. A baby in a stroller wails its lungs out in various notes, and an old guy sitting on a bench keeps feeding the pigeons, scratches his groin and sips from a paper foam cup in no fixed order.

The hospital.

Can the Loop reach that far? She's never seen any Loop that extends through more than a few rooms, but this one feels stronger. Bia's heart takes a dive for her sneakers. She downs the rest of her coffee in one breathless, throat-scorching gulp and runs. She sprints past the pigeon that pecks on a long-gone crumb and onto the pavement, past the bored hospital guard who thumbs on his phone typing the same two letters over and over, past the gardener who mows the same spot on the lawn, and through the ER entrance.

If hell exists, this is what it must be like.

Over there, a tech pricks someone's vein over and over again to draw blood that now drips on the floor and forms a small puddle. Next to him, another patient keeps downing long-downed pills from a now empty paper cup. A pregnant lady on a wheelchair screams at the top of her lungs caught in a never-ending contraction. A kid at the corner barfs over and over again in a waste basket, until greenish slime is all that comes out. At the bottom of the stairs, a janitor mops urine from a broken sample container in a never-ending circle.

Five floor up to Grandma's ward. She cannot trust the elevators. The stairs, then? But first, Bia moves the tech's hand just enough so to leave the mauled arm alone, and presses some gauze onto the bleeding vein. She cannot do much to help the others, so she turns towards the stairs ... and falls face first on the floor that smells of disinfectant and is probably crawling with things Bia would rather not think about. Did someone shove her? She rolls around but there's no one there; only shadows in corners that shouldn't be there. Loop Dwellers—more than one. She's never seen more than one together. Is it the hospital that feeds them and makes them stronger to keep such an extended Loop going? She doesn't know. Yaya needs her, that's all she knows. She pulls herself up, climbs the steps two at a time, and reaches the fifth floor winded and lightheaded.

Mayhem meets her through every open door in the ward, through the nurse's station, even the cooler and the waiting area. Bia shouldn't waste time to help anyone. But it takes only a moment to redirect a hand from doing harm, and there are so many hands that inadvertently try to do harm that she loses count. When she makes it to Yaya's room, Melek appears to be looped, caught in the same little cough over and over again. As for Yaya, her eyes are fixed right ahead, to her other visitors at the foot of her bed.

What little Bia had seen of the Loop Dwellers before had made her picture them like creatures of smoke and shadow, monsters with no physical form, only a thick, hungry fog that devoured moments and memories from everyone they touched. But these three look almost human. They seem a little blurry around the edges, as if not totally in sync with this time and place. All androgynous, in pristine perfectly fitting dark suits, they could pass for well-off bankers or lawyers, if not for their lidless, pitch-black eyes. The middle one reaches out with their long, manicured fingers to touch Yaya's bare foot.

"Leave her alone, you monster!"

Three sets of lidless eyes made of darkness turn to Bia, as if they just noticed her presence. While she still has their surprise in her favor, she lunges at them. The one at the left and nearest to Bia catches her wrist in an unrelenting grip with one hand, and with the other they shove her back against the wall, by Yaya's bed. The impact pushes the air out of her lungs and she collapses on the floor, misty-eyed and panting. Her wrist burns where the creature touched her. But in the few seconds their connection lasted, Bia *saw*. Now she *knows*.

The Loop Dwellers were human once. Always in a hurry, from one place to another, meetings after meetings, deals after deals, games after games. Just one more race, just one more page, just one more drink, never enough hours in a day. Never really savoring a single moment, always seeking the thrill of what the next moment harbored, until they ran out of moments, out of time, out of life, with their hunger still burning. And now they remain caught between moments, until they manage to squeeze through to where they no longer belong. Their presence creates a paradox that freezes Time and creates the Loop that they use to steal moments from their unsuspecting victims.

And, oh, how they love the hospital! Such fertile feeding grounds, enough stolen moments that they've regained substance.

Now that Bia knows, she still has no clue why some people are immune and why her yaya's recipes seem to keep them at bay. But they do. And when the middle one reaches towards Yaya again, Bia tries to stand up. Her knees still tremble, and she falls back on her butt.

"Leave her alone! I won't let you steal Yaya's time!"

All three gawk at her, then something akin of mirth lights up their otherwise blank faces.

"Silly girl," says the middle one, their voice distant as if coming from the depths of a well. "We're not taking your grandmother's time."

Bia blinks. "What?"

A thin, bloodless grin, and a tilt towards still-coughing Melek on the other bed. "*Those* are our Time-cattle. Your grandmother, though …" The grin widens, now too white, too sharp, too wide to be human. "We're *giving* her time."

"What? Why?"

The creature waves around their pale hands. "What can be worse than an eternity in here? A prolonged illness in a useless, aching body, the dying that drags on for days, months, years? She shouldn't have meddled with her betters' affairs."

Bia sits agape, her shoulders slumped, her heart defeated. She sits at a loss for words and for thoughts and for any plan to get rid of the infernal creatures. Her left hand reaches up the squeeze Yaya's limp arm on the bed, as if their touch could somehow lessen her suffering. The fingers of her right hand fiddle with the tassels of her bag she's still wearing cross-body. She reaches into the bag and pulls out Yaya's notebook. A prolonged death, they said. Yaya had a recipe for deaths and funerals. But the words won't leave her lips. How is this different than sentencing her own yaya to death? But then Yaya moans and sobs, and Bia forces the words out.

"Wheat. Sugar. Cinnamon—"

"No. Two cups of flour." A weary, raspy voice.

Bia looks up. The Loop Dwellers seem just as surprised. It can't be Yaya.

And yet it *is* Yaya Evlabia who's found the strength to recite one of her recipes. Did the shot of time from the Loop Dweller boosted Yaya enough to speak? Whatever the reason, Yaya continues in a low, faltering, *determined* voice.

"One cup of sugar. One cup of vegetable oil. One cup of fresh orange juice."

That's not the recipe for kollyva. Bia flips through the pages of the notebook.

"Add the baking powder, cinnamon and cloves."

That's it! Yaya recites the recipe for fanouropita, a Lent dessert dedicated to Aghios Fanourios, a miracle-worker saint of the Greek Orthodox church. Those who need lost things found, bake these pies and bring them to his shrines so he'll reveal what has been lost: health, fortune, loved ones. Even, perhaps, stolen time.

"Whisk them together, until the sugar melts."

Bia adds her own voice to Yaya's. The Loop Dwellers shriek. It's a high-pitched shriek that cuts and pierces through every pore of her body and burns like hot wire along the length of every muscle and nerve. But Bia won't give up. Not as long as she has breath. Not as long as she has Yaya's voice to guide her own.

"In another bowl, pour half a cup of orange juice ..."

Then another voice joins them. Melek, from her own bed, says something in Turkish that Bia cannot understand. The cadence of her words suggests that's another recipe. If Bia holds her breath and focus, she's certain she'll hear more voices—more recipes—from the adjoining rooms in several different languages. Yaya's voice has released the other grandmothers from the Loop, all those who've been left behind, to aid her during her last stand.

The Loop Dwellers gawk at them, shifting their weight from one leg to the other, glancing about, confused and undecided. The more they linger, the more they diminish in substance. Their costumes now hang loose from emaciated forms, their heads grow elongated and malformed, their mouths widen to dark, toothless holes. Once or twice, an arm gets raised only to fall back down again, as if stripped of strength. All around them, the litany of recipes continues.

No, not just recipes. Each list of ingredients with its instructions is molded out of moments: births, deaths, prayers, birthdays and festivals, anniversaries and condolences, comfort for the ailing and the grieving. Whisked together with care, baked with love, consumed with gratitude. They're the backbone of every family, every culture, every civilization that ever flourished. Little acts of selfless service that clash with the Loop Dwellers' selfish, insatiable need.

They're almost gone now, mere shades against the sunbeams of the midday sun through the blinds, a swirl of dust that disintegrates as the Loop whooshes away. Outside, people yell and scream, alarms blare, and doors open and shut. Inside the room, the beeping from Yaya's monitor becomes erratic. Bia clenches her teeth, ignores every ache in her body, and climbs on to the bed. The erratic beeps seem to count Yaya's deeds and days, until they too will stop. Bia pulls her close and holds her in her arms in her last breaths.

One final, glorious moment, that no one will ever be able to steal from them.

The Visitor

by Hiro Finn Hoshino

The doorbell rang and Hana Chouno's hand shook as the strawberry she was eating slipped from her fingers. It bounced dully on her spotless white carpet, leaving splatters of crimson. She sighed as she sat on her sofa and took a sip of her tea; the strawberry was the last of a punnet her sister had sent from her trip to Tochigi.

You must try these strawberries, Hana, they are so good, the enclosed note had read. *I believe in a heaven now that I've tasted them! What was that Beatles song about strawberries again? My husband said I was humming it for the rest of the day. I know you've been having trouble with your mail lately, so let me know when you get these. I'm back in Tokyo now. I have to finish an important work assignment by next Friday (if it goes well, then I'll be eligible for a promotion! You know how rare these chances are. Not bad for ex-secretary Miyu!) but then I'll fly over as soon as I can.*

The fruit was indeed delicious and Hana had intended to email her straight after afternoon tea, mentally drafting her message as she nibbled the last strawberry.

You didn't have to send me the strawberries, Miyu, but I'm glad you did. Thank you for thinking of me these days, I really don't want to be a bother ...

Lost in her thoughts, the doorbell had sounded loud and disconcerting, driving every thought from her mind. Hana Chouno was faced with a decision. She could go answer the door, or she could stay here, finish her tea then perhaps take her time to carefully clean the strawberry stains. She took pride in keeping her apartment immaculate. Afterwards, there was an amusing TV show she planned to watch undisturbed as she prepared dinner. She mulled it over as the doorbell rang again, insistent, demanding, and Hana continued to sit on her sofa, watching the unshapely red splotches on her carpet soak in. She wondered how long it would take to lift the stains and whether she would have to buy a strong bleach. Her slender fingers tightened on the handle of her teacup. The doorbell rang for the third time and Hana stood so quickly she knocked over her tea, the brown liquid sloshing over her coffee table like an oil spill. She walked across the room—away from the front of the apartment—to the glass double doors that led to her balcony, where she would look out every morning over the spectacular views of Sapporo from her lofty penthouse. She did not step out now, however, but stood there for a moment, thinking how nice it would have been to finish her tea out there on her Art Deco dining set, a rare splurge she and her sister had invested in at the local homewares store when she moved in.

It had been so much fun shopping for it, she remembered, as the two of them laughed and sat at various tables and chairs, arguing practicality versus aesthetics. It had promptly arrived at her new apartment and the deliverymen were courteous and efficient. Hana was abashed by their overzealous smiles and she stood awkwardly by the door as they kept a stream of bows, excuse-mes, and thank-yous.

"They bend over backwards if they think you have money," her sister said with a wink, as the deliverymen methodically pieced together the furniture on her balcony.

"Oh hush, Miyu, they'll hear you," Hana said, bringing a finger to her lips. "They're just nice people. And I don't like the thought of people assuming I'm rich."

"Relax. Come on, you should be happier! You're a single woman who just bought her own *penthouse*. That's a win in my books."

Hana gave her a reproving look, but couldn't help an affectionate hint of a grin for her sister. Sixteen years. It had been a long sixteen years before she had saved enough for a deposit, and when she and Miyu sat in the real estate agent's office to sign off on the paperwork, she felt so giddy she even let slide the excruciating, teeth-sucking pause the agent gave when he asked if Hana's husband would be arriving later to sign the papers (Miyu opened her mouth to speak, but Hana prodded her underneath the table). Her father, although begrudgingly, had been the guarantor for the bank loan and everything was set to go, and Hana felt nothing should get in the way between her and her long-awaited home.

"A fine way to celebrate," her sister had announced once the dining set was complete. They lounged on the plush chairs and cracked open cans of beer, their joking and giggling rambunctious as they drank before the setting sun.

The doorbell did not ring again, but the silence ate away at the warmth of her memory. Hana had a disquieting feeling her visitor had sensed her move within the building and was now patiently waiting to be let in. She checked the monitor of the doorbell camera to see who it was, then, with a sharp exhale of breath, pressed the button to unlock the gates to the building. A few minutes passed, then there was a knock at her door. Hana tiptoed to the entranceway. She told herself she was being silly and, with knuckles white as she grasped the handle, creeped open the front door.

He was an ordinary looking man, roughly the same age as her, clean shaven, wearing a baseball cap—pulled over a mess of wavy black hair that cast a shadow over his face—and a rugged jacket over a T-shirt and faded jeans. They stood there, regarding each other, before Hana stepped aside to let him in. The door clicked neatly shut behind him and the sound was odd to Hana's ears, like a rock hitting the bottom of a well. Wordlessly, she returned to the sofa and sat with her legs crossed. The man, keeping his jacket and hat on, paced the living room, carefully examining her furniture and trinkets with great interest.

"How's your sister?" the man asked as he held up a decorative plate to the sunlight.

"She's arriving here this afternoon," Hana said quietly.

The man turned to her. "I thought she was in Tokyo until next week."

Hana pursed her lips. The man wandered into her kitchen and turned on the faucet at the sink, watching the water run for a few seconds before shutting it off. He then opened the fridge, stooping to peer inside. He took an apple from the top shelf and bit into it. He came back to the living room, one hand in his jeans pocket, the other tossing the apple up and down in the air.

"You haven't been to work in over a week," he said, munching the fruit. Hana couldn't bear the sound of his chewing. "What's happened?"

She glared at him. Her fists clenched in her lap. "What do you want?"

"Now, now, let's not get all moody," he said placidly. "I was hoping we'd have a nice talk, that's all."

Hana stood without looking at the man and stalked past him to her balcony doors. She put her hands against the warm glass, willing her trembling arms to be still. It was such a lovely day outside and she saw a pair of brilliant blue monarch butterflies weave amongst the tendrils of her potted ivy that grew densely over the railing and the walls, the soft leaves shimmering as they caught a gentle breeze under the spring sun. With patient nurturing, she had teased the ivy to grow the way she had wanted it to, transforming her balcony into a green oasis. She breathed deeply and turned to face him.

"Fine, what do you want to talk about? How about you tell me your name?"

"Ah," the man said, smiling. "First, let's talk about *you*. How has your day been?"

"I told you my sister is coming this afternoon. She's going to stay for a while."

"I won't be here for long." The man took another noisy bite of the apple.

"If you have nothing to say, you need to leave right now." Hana felt a vein pulse at her temple. "Go. My sister is coming and she expects me to pick her up at the airport."

"If your sister is indeed arriving, I'll take care of her." The man's expression became fixed, his lips thinning to a clay-like smirk. He pocketed the half-eaten apple. "Did you receive my package?"

Hana's eyes darted to the corner of her living room where a brown paper parcel lay unopened. The man went to pick it up and pushed it into her hands.

"You should open it," he said.

Hana stared blankly at the parcel, then edged her unwilling fingers beneath the crinkled wrapping and tore it apart to reveal a pair of repulsive dolls. They were poorly made—with twisted faces and clothes raggedy with rough stitching—but it was their hair that sent awful shivers down Hana's spine. It was black and wavy, almost as if …

"I made them myself," the man said, watching her carefully. He pointed to the male doll. "See, this one is me. And that one"—he looked down at the female doll and his nostrils flared—"Well, that one is you."

Hana threw the dolls to the floor and a searing panic rose as her hands scrabbled for the door to the balcony. The man held out his palms.

"Hey, I don't mean any harm," he said, though something coiled within his black pupils.

"I … you …" Hana choked on her words and hot tears sprung to the back of her eyes. *Why isn't it opening?* she thought, desperately rattling the door handle.

The man took a step forward. "You called the police on me last week, didn't you, Ms. Chouno? Or can I call you Hana? Anyway, luckily for us, my good friend Okamura works at the station. A quick phone call and it was all smoothed over."

Hana shrank against the glass door and the man let out a barking laugh.

"You see how I saved you! I couldn't let you be that *dumb local girl* who sent an innocent man away in handcuffs. Think about what the people would say, dear Hana."

The man suddenly moved and Hana let out a strangled scream, but the man had bent down to pick up the dolls. He placed them on the coffee table side-by-side, gently patting them on their heads, and stood back to admire them. The tea Hana spilled earlier soaked into the hems of the dolls' clothes. She felt a wave of nausea. She clamped both hands about her lips, uncertain of what might issue from her shivering mouth. The man made his way to the front door and turned back with his hands on his hips, surveying the apartment with apparent satisfaction.

"Go back to work, Hana." His voice was barely a whisper. "Go back to work or they'll suspect something's wrong."

He continued to stand there, staring, as if to elicit a response, but Hana glared determinedly back at him. There was something that chilled her to the core in those flat, viper-like eyes; there wasn't a shred of warmth, yet it felt to Hana that those eyes knew more about her than she did herself. A bead of cold sweat trickled down her back. She cleared her throat.

"Leave."

And then he was gone.

Hana's legs gave out and crumpled, and she grasped her knees and cried. She hated how her sobs sounded as they echoed dimly around the apartment. She forced herself under control, reminding herself of what she was to do. She took a moment to collect herself—she gazed absent-mindedly at the strawberry stains, now looking much like splatters of dried blood—then dabbed her eyes with a tissue and blew her nose quietly. She ran to the front door to bolt it and bent under the sofa to pull out a small voice recorder she had planted earlier in the day. She sighed in relief; the red light was still unwaveringly on.

She remembered her conversation with a police officer when she had mustered the courage to head to the local station.

"Mail-tampering? Stalker?" the officer had said, not bothering to hide his exasperation. His prematurely lined face reminded Hana of an old basset hound. "I'm sorry, Ms. Chouno, I understand you are upset, but we get reports like this every week."

"Please, Officer. I get doorbells. Phone calls at midnight. I always feel like someone is following me to work." Hana wrapped her arms about her. "I hear this click as though someone's taking a picture of me and I dare not turn around because it's just so … creepy."

"So, you've seen him through your doorbell camera. Can you explain to me what he looks like?"

"He always has a hat on. And a jacket and jeans."

"That could be anyone, Ms. Chouno. I'm asking what his face looks like."

"I've never seen his face. He never shows his face."

"Has he spoken to you?"

Hana shook her head. She wished the floor would swallow her whole.

"We need hard evidence before we bring people in," the officer said, shaking his head. A flotilla of dandruff settled on his hunched shoulders. "Look, we'll file a report and alert the patrol, but that is all I can do for now. Come back if anything actually happens."

Come back if anything actually happens.

The words had seared into her as though with a branding iron. Hana gritted her teeth and felt cold triumph as she brandished the voice recorder like a weapon. She would have liked to set up a video camera, but her nerves got the better of her (what would he do if he found it?). Surely the police would access the apartment CCTV footage to confirm his presence if she brought the recording to the station. Her finger trembled on the playback button—she felt a flood of terror as she entertained a horrible thought.

What if the man's voice isn't there? What if it's just me talking to myself?

She whipped around to her coffee table—the ghastly dolls were still there, their sunken, unseeing eyes fixed on her.

No. He was here, then he was gone. I made him go.

Hana tore her gaze away and rammed the playback button.

In the muffled recording, she heard herself shifting on the couch, then there was the doorbell. Then the second and third. Hana's heart raced as she heard the knock on her door and the sounds of feet shuffling into the room. There was an unhinging silence, then that low, rasping voice asking how her sister was. She felt an odd mix of relief and dread as she listened; she had what she needed, but the conversation was more terrible than she remembered and the desire to toss the recorder away was immense. She reached for the off button, but a new sound crept through the playback of the recording and made her ears prickle. What was it? Their arguing voices intensified in the background, but there was something else. Breathing? It was breathing. Hana brought the recorder close to her ear and she heard it get steadily louder. *Closer.* She screamed and dropped the recorder. The bitter tang of adrenaline burned the back of her mouth as the breathing steadily amplified and filled the room with horrid, wracking heaves. She tucked herself in a tight ball and rocked back and forth. She thought she might soon faint when the recording abruptly fell silent. Hana peeked between her clammy fingers at the device. The red light was blinking.

"It's still playing," she croaked.

Then she heard it. A sly cackle, barely audible, and the light turned off.

Call Miyu.

A bodiless voice whispered urgently in her ears, and Hana scurried across the room for her phone.

"Oh God, where is it?"

Her floundering arms knocked the contents of her desk to the floor and she spotted it next to the note Miyu had sent with the strawberries. She paused as she picked them up. She desperately wanted to call her sister, but what would she tell her? And what would Miyu say?

"You have a stalker?! And you let him *into* your apartment? Hana, you are insane!" Miyu would be hysterical. "How will you explain this to the police? I am flying over right now."

Yes, Miyu *would* fly to Sapporo on the next flight out. Miyu *would* flush her prospects of a sorely needed promotion down the drain to fly to Sapporo to be with her, to fret with her, to comfort her. Hana felt a fierce rage build inside of her and, with shaky fingers, held up her sister's letter.

I have to finish an important work assignment by next Friday (if it goes well, then I'll be eligible for a promotion! You know how rare these chances are. Not bad for ex-secretary Miyu!) but then I'll fly over as soon as I can.

She paced the spacious living room several times.

"I must have heard my own breathing over the playback, there was no one else after all."

As she passed the dolls on the coffee table (were they grinning?), she remembered the grating words of her visitor.

If your sister is indeed arriving, I'll take care of her.

She flung her phone to the other side of the room.

"You will not harm my sister!" she shrieked at the dolls. Her heart was pummeling at the top of her chest, sounding to her like a runaway train, and she nervously patted the base of her neck. She tried to take a deep breath, but her lungs seemed to have lost their capacity to take in air. Darkness glossed over her vision. She swung a firm hand across her cheek, the resounding slap cracking like a whip, and her sight cleared immediately.

She looked around the apartment; it felt like the walls were closing in on her like a ring of schoolyard bullies, and at the same time, the ceiling was dissolving, melting away so that if Hana would look up, she might see a far-off sky if the walls didn't fall inwards to crush her where she stood. And the dolls were grinning, she was sure of it.

She held Miyu's letter out in front of her, like a crucifix against the undead, and stood frozen in a bizarre standoff with her coffee table. It was then the head of the female doll (*well, that one is you*) twisted in its socket, its neck bending at an impossible angle, and pointed its terrible face to the floor where the strawberry stains were still bright red on the carpet. Hana thought she heard a sharp snap, perhaps from the recesses of her own mind, and she jumped.

"Enough!" She tore her sister's letter to shreds and flung the pieces over her head—they scattered and drifted like crooked snowflakes. "You don't know me very well, do you? You may have neither myself nor my sister."

She seized the dolls around their necks and ran to the double doors of her balcony, which flung open to her touch. She was momentarily stunned as she stepped out, greeted by the caress of the warm spring breeze and the gentle twittering of songbirds. It really was a lovely day. She whisked past the Art Deco chairs to the steel railing covered in ivy at the edge of her balcony, and peered down at the pavement of the courtyard, almost forty floors down. It was blindingly white under the sun. Beyond the apartment gates, people milled past the shop windows of the boutiques and cafes, looking like colorful dots on canvas. With a savage cry of triumph, she lobbed the dolls over the railing. Her chest heaving, she watched them soar through the air, their little faces staring accusingly up at her as they plummeted, and soon they were nothing more than specks hurtling to the stone pavement far below. Hana turned and collapsed against the railing, running a sweaty hand through her hair. The glass doors of the balcony creaked on their hinges, then swung closed with a smart click, as if they had locked themselves. It was a strange sound, and vaguely familiar, like something small and hard hitting the bottom of an empty well.

"I wonder if I can get back into my own apartment," she said.

She fell to her hands and knees and burst into long, uncontrollable laughter. It felt wonderful. Coughing and spluttering, she pushed herself up and leant against the railing, drinking in the spectacular view of the city. She felt a brush against her arm and saw the pair of monarch butterflies fluttering beside her as they danced amongst the green leaves.

"'Strawberry Fields Forever'," Hana said, remembering her sister's letter. "We used to listen to it all the time when we were little, Miyu."

Miyu. The name sounded somewhat distant to her. Hana rubbed her face and nestled her aching head in the dense foliage of her ivy, feeling the butterflies coming to rest on the back of her hand.

"You know, that song has such funny lyrics," she muttered. "Something about going down to Strawberry Fields."

She wearily looked up and the butterflies quavered their wings, looking like jeweled sailboats, beckoning, beckoning to her.

A Lesson in Obsolescence

by Christopher O'Halloran

"Would you?"

George glanced at Raj's newspaper as he slid it across the breakroom table. A silicon doll peered up from the pages. Her eyes held no vitality, no emotion. Dark marbles reflected the photographer's camera in her irises.

"Would I what?"

"You know." Raj bounced his shoulders up and down. "Would you?"

It was a loaded question. George felt the eyes of his coworkers on him. The other men in the lunchroom were the same age as his dad. They wore the orange coveralls mandated for work in the refrigerated warehouse. With shackled legs, they'd look no different than a roadcrew of convicts taking a break.

"How much?" George asked.

Raj, in his mid-forties, rotated the paper to skim the page. He slid it back to George. "Ninety bucks for half an hour."

"Is that the sex doll brothel?" asked Daniel Du, another middle-aged coworker of George's. With a quick knuckle, he pushed his glasses up his nose. He had his own copy of the paper before him.

"Yeah," Raj said. "You see it?"

"Ninety dollars, waste of money," he said. "You can get sex dolls that good for a thousand. Pay for itself in ten uses." He chortled.

Raj turned back to George. "Would you?"

George put his phone down and considered the doll. She wasn't bad looking. Just … vacant.

"We don't bat an eye at fake boobs," he said. "This … this is just fake everything." Laughter. "Sure, I'd do it. Find a coupon or something."

Raj groaned. The bait had been taken.

"Fucking millennials," he said. "Your generation is going to kill off the human race."

"Don't tell us you're too good for robot sex, Raj," said Dareeq with his deep voice.

"Why pay to bang a lifeless doll?" Raj elbowed George. "My wife's usually free!"

He and Daniel laughed. Dareeq smiled in the corner, stroking his salt-and-pepper goatee and sipping his tea.

"Speaking of robots," said Daniel, once the laughter had died down. "I hear the company is looking into an automated picking system."

"Who said that?" Raj asked. He and Daniel were both order pickers. Automation would send them back into the job market, an uncertain and scary prospect in the current economy. Their strong union contract had secured higher wages than most other blue-collar jobs. They made a dollar every two minutes, simply assembling various dairy products on pallets for stores across Western Canada.

It was a good gig.

"Sheldon saw a truck in the parking lot," said Daniel. "*Dynamic Automation* written on the side."

Raj scoffed. "Sheldon's full of shit. Tell the big man to stick to singing and let the adults handle the important stuff." He winked at George.

"He's right," said Dareeq. "They've been talking to the union about it."

"Well," said Raj, "those machines tend to break down if you catch my meaning."

Dareeq shook his head, blowing on his tea. "It's the way of the future. Machines."

The discussion ceased abruptly when Jason Tennant came through the doors. The production supervisor shuffled his feet, shoulders slumped, holding his mug with the company logo on it. From where he sat, George could see the coffee stains embedded in the ceramic—Jason was too busy to give the dishes more than a cursory rinse.

"Hey, George," Jason said as he filled his cup. "Steve's had to go home. Wasn't feeling good, but he said you should be ready to run the blow mold on your own. What do you think?"

George hesitated. Logically, he was sure he knew the basics of running the machine, but the size and complexity of it was overwhelming, even with his trainer present. Could he say no? Would it make a difference, or would they force him?

Sink or swim, kiddo. His dad spoke as clear as if he were standing beside him. He had done backbreaking work his entire life. They passed each other every morning as the sun kissed the horizon; George coming home, his dad getting ready to leave. Both father and son communicated in inarticulate grunts that said all that was needed. His dad was proud of him for finding a good, strong union job and said as much to the whole extended family.

"I can do it." As the youngest employee at Pure Life Dairy, he had his own dues to pay.

"Thanks, George." Jason clapped a cold, clammy hand on the boy's shoulder, then left slurping his coffee noisily.

Raj shivered. "Tennant gives me the creeps. Seems like the kind of guy who would 'dine and dash' at a robot brothel. Quasimodo with a Supercuts hairdo."

"Hey," exclaimed Daniel. "Don't knock Supercuts. They have good deals."

George stood before the control panel to the blow mold machine, mentally going over the checklist of procedures that would spur it into action, forming one-gallon jugs from tiny beads of plastic resin. At the moment, it hummed quietly, the eager machine standing immovable as a tank and twice as big. The temperature was high, primed to efficiency from extruder to cast-iron die tip.

Okay, he thought, breathing deeply.

Die tip heaters, off. He tapped the illuminated square on the touch screen.

Extruder drive, on. George depressed the dull green button. Clear tubes of plastic dropped from eight die tips in a neat row.

Test shots. The tubes pinched off, no longer cascading onto the steel catch tray in long runners, but forming foot-and-a-half-long cylinders.

Here goes nothing. He pressed the start button.

The hard molds clamped around the plastic tubes. Air forced its way inside through pressurized blow pins, inflating the jugs to fill the molds. Eight fingers came up and gripped the jugs as the molds opened. They dropped onto a cooling rack trundling mechanically towards a trimmer that would remove any excess plastic.

Easy. George breathed a sigh of relief and relaxed.

Something nagged at him, however. Something missing.

Take off the first row, he remembered Steve saying. *The first row will have bits of dirt and burnt plastic from the die tip cleaning embedded in the bottom.*

The first row was almost to the trimmer. Almost out of reach.

George jumped forward and began to grab jugs off the cooling rack, throwing them to the concrete floor. As he was gripping the third jug, the cooling rack shuffled forward.

Something pinched his hand.

He swatted a jug away in time to see the heavy steel pipe roll over his fingers.

It flattened them like pizza dough, drawing sticky, crimson blood through tears in his skin. Sparks flew from the cooling rack, though its motor was six feet away.

The pipe chewed up his hand, rolling up his palm. George howled as bones snapped. He tugged, but the cooling rack held firm to its track. Sweating, he reached for the emergency stop, but his free hand was inches too short.

"Help!" he shrieked, his voice cracking.

George was all alone. Nobody was going to help him. If he did nothing, the rack would press him flat like a clove of garlic.

He put a foot on a metal strut to brace himself. Summoning the image of his gruff father, he growled and pulled.

His skin tore apart at the wrist, stretching like melted cheese before separating with a wet rip. Blood gushed forth amidst more sparks, and George's hand separated from his arm.

He screamed in triumphant agony and fell backwards onto the hard concrete. Bloodstained milk jugs moved forward through the trimmer and along chutes that brought them to the fill room. George laughed despite the pain. The lab was going to have their hands full with this one.

George laughed more, noting the hysteria with a distant, second mind. *Hands full.*

When he looked at the stump of his arm, the blood drained from his face. His racing heart shuddered within his chest.

He had expected to see blood and bone.

Cold, blood-slicked steel stuck out from his flesh, as mechanical as the machine that had almost crushed him. Nylon wrapped wires dangled limply instead of veins. The blood had stopped pouring out. The pain was gone.

George looked underneath the cooling rack.

His hand lay there like a dead animal. He shuffled closer and saw steel poking from the torn flesh. His finger bones gleamed like the legs of a metal spider.

Servos whirred within his arm. He leaned his ear towards the ragged stump and heard a faint, electric beeping.

"Daddy ..." The word slipped out of his mouth, the only one his perplexed mind could fall upon.

An electric, ride-along pallet jack stopped ten feet from George. He looked up to see Daniel's shocked face. The Chinese man's glasses dangled on the end of his nose. Absentmindedly, he lifted a hand and pushed them up. He blinked once. Twice. Then continued onward to the cooler.

George didn't know how long he sat on the concrete, dumbfounded. Eventually, he felt cold hands under his armpits.

"There we go," said Jason Tennant, lifting him up and leading George to his office. His breath smelled of stale coffee.

George was placed on a worn office chair within Jason's locked office. He held his stump up in front of him, keeping his eyes glued to the metal pipe jutting out.

Jason rummaged through his desk drawer and pulled out a card. It read *Dynamic Automation*. The production supervisor called the number.

"Hang tight," he said to George, pulling a thin tablet from a drawer crammed with file folders.

George heard the phone ring once before an automated teller answered. Without hesitation, Jason muttered, "Maintenance." The ring came again as the call was transferred. Jason looked sidelong at George. The production supervisor lifted a hand to his head and flattened his lifeless hair.

"What's going on, Mr. Tennant?" George's mouth felt incredibly dry. He had an idea of what was, in fact, going on, but at the moment he found his plethora of questions hard to articulate. Any one of them would sound ridiculous.

Jason ignored him. Into the phone, he said, "Hey Terry. Got another issue. Nope. Uh huh. Hardware this time."

Automation. They had all been worried about machines replacing them. George had assumed his job safe. Somebody would always need to observe the blow mold.

"Mr. Tennant?" His voice shook. "Jason?"

Jason glanced at George, annoyed. "Your men told us they gave him a natural learning curve. What they should have said was they made him borderline incompetent." He tapped a code on the tablet. "Industrial accident. We're lucky nobody saw. Actually, scratch that; *you're* lucky nobody saw."

George started to rise. How much of his body was machine? He still needed to breathe. Panic stiffened his lungs.

"I'm going to get some air, Mr. Tennant."

Jason tapped out a sequence of buttons on the tablet. George sat against his will. A chill spread over him. His skin broke out in goosebumps.

Skin? Was it skin?

"Yeah," Jason said, "I've got him right here … Tomorrow? Why not tonight? I don't give a shit!" He leaned back on his desk, hooking his leg over the corner. George was positioned right in front of his supervisor's splayed crotch. He couldn't look away. He couldn't move at all.

Jason looked George over, listening to the technician's excuses. He leaned forward and peered into George's ear. Seeing something that made him grimace, he grabbed a pen from the disorganized mess of his desk and slid it halfway into the canal.

George's head jerked with the force of Jason's insertion. His supervisor grunted his displeasure and withdrew the pen. It was covered in a dark oil. A string with dusty remnants clinging to it was wrapped around the makeshift dipstick.

"Fine," said Jason, wiping the pen on his thigh, "but I want him serviced in the morning. His skill set will be very important to us." He hung up and sighed, still looking at George.

"Don't worry; we'll wipe this whole incident from your memory. I can see how traumatizing it is."

What the fuck? Wipe his memory? Nothing like this had ever happened to George.

Had it?

The other door to the office opened, and Reggie, the warehouse supervisor, popped his head in.

"Hey, Jay," Reggie said, nonplussed. "We're going to have to bring in some storage trailers if these numbers you gave me are correct. They're a little high, don't you think?"

"PriceSave is having a sale on four liters. I'd put the two percent in trailers. We should have room for everything else."

"How much?" Reggie asked.

"Three bucks, I think."

"Damn, I'll have to tell my wife. Can I get your signature on a few invoices?"

Jason tossed the tablet on the desk and darted out of the office, rapidly clicking the pen in his hand.

As Reggie closed the door behind them, George saw a flash of orange. It was probably wishful thinking, but it looked like the coveralls of one of the order pickers. Had they seen anything?

George couldn't even close his eyes. The conditioned air blew over him from the ceiling vent. It dried his tears, making his eyeballs feel stretched thin.

It was so quiet. The only sound was the humming of Jason's work computer.

Except ... that wasn't it. The humming was coming from inside George. He was aware of it now, making his organs vibrate. It was too much. His heart raced. Blood—or oil, or transmission fluid—coursed through him in a way that tickled his flesh from the inside.

It would drive him mad. It would fry his brain before Tennant could return and wipe his memory. George would beg for it—anything to erase this awareness. Nobody was meant to know this much about themselves.

The unlocked door through which the supervisors had left crept open.

"He's in here," hissed Daniel.

Daniel came into the lunchroom holding the tablet. He walked towards George who sat immobile where Dareeq had placed him.

"Okay, I think I got it." Daniel tapped on the screen. George could breathe deeper. He flexed the fingers on his remaining hand. The digits obeyed. He stood, moving his body at every point of articulation: ankles, knees, shoulders, neck. It all moved the same. He felt no more robotic than he had his entire life.

"Why didn't you tell us you were a cyborg, Georgie?" asked Raj.

"I didn't know ..."

Daniel handed the tablet over to George. "How did you not know?"

"I remember growing up! I remember being a kid. That doesn't happen to robots, does it?" George sat hard. "When I was thirteen, I broke my leg falling off my bike." He looked Dareeq in the eye. "I saw the bone! It wasn't ..." George brandished the steel pipe jutting out from his wrist. "It wasn't this."

"You said Jason was going to wipe your memory?" Dareeq asked.

George nodded.

"If they can delete memories, who's to say they can't create them, too?"

George's mouth fell open. They couldn't do that. He knew the face of his father, his brown mustache flecked with grey, his drooping eyes, his thick hair. He knew the shape of his life in such great detail, from the smell of his mother's cooking to the sounds of his sister's muffled sobs when the boyfriend of the week inevitably dumped her.

Hell, the walk home was only five minutes. George *knew* every bump in the road, every crack in the ground. There was no way they could fabricate all that!

"I need to leave." George stood.

"Hang on," said Dareeq, "let's figure out what's going on."

"I need to get home. My dad will have answers. He'll know what to do." He always did.

Raj put a hand on George's shoulder, but George brushed it away.

"We can help you, Georgie. You're still one of us."

"Aren't you worried about that?" He looked at each of the three. They examined him with wide eyes.

"I know I'm real," George said. "I know I've gotten paid, spent the money. I know I went to Disneyland last year and I know I have a pair of stupid fucking Mickey ears with my name on it. Yet …" He held his stump aloft and pulled out the slack wires. "I can't know any of it. I can't be certain. If I can't, how can you?"

Daniel looked around confused. "I have kids …"

"Do you?"

The men looked at each other, searching for evidence of unnatural composition. Daniel shook his head in blind denial, eyes squeezed shut and mouth pinched into the shape of a balloon knot.

Raj eyed Dareeq.

"What?" Dareeq stood, the dark and peaceful man bristling like a cornered animal.

"Nothing," said Raj. There was none of the usual humor in his voice, only direct speculation that countered his word.

Dareeq took a step forward, but George got between them.

"Wait," he said, playing the mediator.

"He thinks I'm a robot," Dareeq shouted. "Look at me. Do I look like a robot?"

"The kid doesn't," said Raj.

"I sweat for this company. I put in my hours so I can put food on my table." Dareeq slammed his fist against the countertop. The coffee pot fell from its spot on the warmer, clattering against the Formica. "I've got eight fucking kids. If you're trying to tell me they don't exist—"

"You're not the only one with kids," said Raj. He had a daughter. She was in soccer. He was taking her to a tournament in Vancouver that weekend and had told George as much.

"Check the tablet," said Dareeq, finally relenting. "If there's controls for the kid, maybe there's controls for others."

Daniel sat in the corner, examining the tendon on the inside of his elbow. "Guys?" He pinched it, wiggled it back and forth. "Does this feel normal?"

Raj dropped the tablet in Daniel's lap.

"Get us some answers," he said.

Daniel picked up the tablet, but after tapping at the screen, tossed it back on the table.

"Locked out," he said. "Everything else is password protected."

"You know who isn't password protected?" Raj asked.

"Tennant," answered Dareeq.

They left George, united beyond their membership in some workers' union. They didn't need a contract for what they were about to do. Everything about their lives was up in the air. It needed to exist, or someone was going to pay.

George needed his life to exist. He needed his family.

His dad. His dad would have answers.

The first steps towards his home felt right. Business as usual. The sidewalk narrowed until it disappeared, so George crossed the street as he did five days a week.

How lucky he was to live so close to work. Didn't need a car. Didn't even need a bus pass.

Traffic passed, unaware of his predicament. The drone of it was almost enough to drown out his racing thoughts. He held his stump inside his sweater, so as not to draw attention.

George was cold. Why should he be cold? They had thought of everything. Would a couple taps on the tablet warm him?

Dad will know what to do.

Clearbrook Road was ahead. One right turn, and his house would be a few blocks down the road. There he would find the answers he needed.

Maybe his whole family were robots too. Androids, cyborgs. Whatever he was. Would that be so bad? They had lived a normal life thus far, what would stop them from continuing?

George rounded the corner and stopped dead in his tracks.

Nothing was the same.

He had expected residential areas, tall apartment buildings that dotted Clearbrook Road, broken up by the odd convenience store.

Instead, endless warehouses stretched out before him. The street appeared as industrial as it got.

"No …"

His arms fell to his side. A cool breeze played on the ragged flesh at the end of his stump.

The street was a fabrication. His house was not where he remembered it. Did it exist? Did his family exist? He could come to terms with them being machines, but if they weren't real ... If they were implants in his mind ...

His mom, his sister. His dad. That silent patriarch.

Sink or swim, kiddo.

Everything he knew was blown away like wind-tossed leaves. Here one minute, gone the next. The street cleaned of any evidence that a new season had come. He was the blank slate. The raw asphalt, stripped and erased.

His family might be out there, but there was no way of knowing. Chances were, they were inside his head. A backstory. A reason to work.

The only certainty was work. The men—his friends—at Pure Life Dairy. He knew they were real, mechanical or not. He could count on them.

Raj, the joker.

Daniel, the sceptic.

Dareeq, the wise.

He could still keep his family in his mind, tucked away and safe. His friends and coworkers needed him.

He knew the blow mold. His insecurity was only programming. Surely the knowledge of how to run the machine like an expert was in his head? Maybe he could access it on the tablet.

There was a lot of milk to run. PriceSave was having a sale.

Low Contact

by Simo Srinivas

I was low-key in lust with Davey Othonos, which is why I agreed to raise his great-grandmother from the dead. Note that I said "in lust," not love—if you love someone, you're supposed to talk them out of necromantic endeavors, not join in.

Usually, people beg necromancers to raise their relatives from the dead because they want to say goodbye one last time. Or because they want to kill them again. Davey's great-grandmother died before he was born, so I was pretty sure it wasn't either of these things. And it turned out Davey wanted to ask Efthymia Xenakis about a mystery ingredient in a recipe he'd found while he was cleaning out his mother's basement. It was for a savory Greek pastry, and the paper it was written on must have been delicious because rats had chewed most of the ingredient list away.

Come on man! our friend Bilesh said in the group chat. *You already know the secret ingredient is love!*

This is some monkey paw shit, our other friend Lillian said. She sent a gif of a monkey slapping a laptop. *Put that recipe back where you found it.*

I just wanna eat malathropita again, Davey said, wildly misspelling it. *My mom used to make it for me*.

Everyone started typing at once, but no one asked the obvious question, which was, if your mom used to make malathropita for you, why don't you get Kevin to raise *her* from the dead? And the body would be fresh, too: she'd only been in the ground a month.

We knew why. Davey and his mom didn't get along. The last time he saw her alive, she'd thrown a paperweight at his face. An hour later she was gone. Davey had never told us how. I only knew about the paperweight because he'd popped by for a patch-job right after it happened. She'd scratched up his cheeks and knocked his left eye out of his head.

I didn't get along with my mom either, but that's because I dropped out of med school to become a necromancer.

Yeah, that's right. Kevin the Necromancer. It was my username on Reddit, too. KevinTheSorcerer was already taken.

I was self-taught. I used to practice on roadkill and the bodies in the cadaver lab. It was *highly* unethical. You donated your body to science to further the enlightenment of humanity, not to have yourself dragged back into the light screaming and crying. There were at least three of us raising the dead at that lab, by the way, and I know for a fact both of those guys stayed in the program. They made it to residency. Just let that sink in.

My necromantic influencer career never took off. No one raised the dead #ForTheGram or streamed resurrections on Twitch anymore, unless they wanted a SWAT team kicking in their front door. To make ends meet I worked nights at Sunoco.

Davey was between jobs. He showed up at the Sunoco at 3 a.m., bought a piss-water coffee, and whispered that he'd pay me in malathropita.

While he was there someone overdosed in the bathroom, someone tried to rob the gas station, and someone called me a squinty-eyed c-word. I hauled the overdose victim back to life—Narcan, not necromancy—and kept her there until the paramedics showed up. Davey dealt with the robber and the racist by beating them into unconsciousness. Davey's berserking kind of freaked me out, but as the song goes, when I get knocked down, I get up again: nothing was going to put a damper on my fantasy about having my way with Davey against a shelf of Doritos.

"So?" Davey said, chewing the edge of his Styrofoam cup. "Will you?"

Davey was big and blond and did crew in college. We'd known each other since we were twelve. We were sixteen when I realized I wanted to climb him like a tree.

"Davey," I said, "you know I will do anything for you, for free. Where's the old lady buried?"

We had to get Lillian involved. She was an archivist at a certain Ivy League college in New Jersey. It was a coveted position, tenure-track with benefits. One of those one-in-a-million opportunities that got swarmed by a million desperate bodies, but no one who knew Lillian was surprised that she'd clawed her way to the top of the pile.

Lillian and I went to Chinese school together. It was purgatory for kids like me who wanted to spend their Saturday mornings watching cartoons, but for Lillian Chinese school was an all-out battle royale to show everyone in our immigrant community whose kid was the best of the best. She memorized Tang Dynasty poetry, did extra homework, and emceed Lunar New Year events. She got along great with her mom.

So I'm not saying Lillian killed someone to get the archivist gig, but I'm not *not* saying that.

I skipped out on the rest of my shift and Davey drove us into New Jersey in the dead of night. We watched the sunrise from a truck stop on I-78, ate breakfast, napped for a while, and showed up in Lillian's office at noon.

"Diaspora, diaspora," Lillian muttered to herself as she clicked around. She moonlighted at the local historical society and spent her spare time doing genealogical searches for grandmas. Diaspora: she turned it into a song. Diaspora, Efthymia; Efthymia, monkey's paw.

"How old was Efthymia when she died?"

"Twenty-seven, I think," Davey said.

"Shit, dude," I said. *We* were twenty-seven.

I'd been imagining a wizened crone. I started imagining girl Davey in an old-timey dress. Then just Davey in a dress. The thirst was real.

Lillian cleared her throat. She'd pulled up a grainy black-and-white photo of a headstone with a floral-looking cross carved into it. We could just about make out the "X" for Xenakis.

"Congrats, Davey," Lillian said, "your great-grandma's famous."

"Really?"

"Efthymia Xenakis of the Long Branch Xenakis," Lillian said. "Oldest daughter of Spyridon Xenakis, baker. Poisoned by her stepmother, Myra Xenakis, also a baker."

Poisoned via honeycake, Lillian said. A gooey, golden, arsenic-laced pouch of filo and walnuts.

"You're getting all that from Ancestry.com?"

Lillian swiveled so we could see her screen. She was getting it from a 1972 issue of *The Rutgers University Law Review*. "'Hungry Heart': the New Jersey Cadaver Synod of 1918." Like the other Cadaver Synod in Italy, Lillian explained, the one where they'd put the pope's corpse on trial.

"They dug her up?"

"They dug up the stepmother," Lilian said. "Myra died of influenza three days after the poisoning. Efthymia survived the honeycake and wanted justice. She wanted *revenge*. She died a year after the trial, in childbirth."

She was buried in Long Branch, New Jersey. Both of them were. Lillian pulled up the directions on Davey's phone.

"Wanna come with?" Davey offered.

"Yeah," I said, hoping she'd refuse, "the more the merrier."

"God, no," Lillian said, shuddering.

Obviously, you can resurrect people at any time of day, but nighttime necromancy is the standard. Sure, resurrection by moonlight is more #Aesthetic, but it's also more practical. I mean, come on. You dig in the cemetery in the daytime to put people in graves. You dig in the cemetery at night to yank them out. Only one of these things is socially acceptable.

So Davey and I bummed around campus all afternoon, waiting for sundown. It was the kind of fancy place a rower like Davey could have ended up, but he'd wanted to go somewhere farther from home. As for me, I'd applied and been rejected. I used to joke that they'd sent my acceptance letter to the wrong Kevin Chen.

We took a snack break at two. We sat on a bench at the edge of campus dissecting apple crullers from Starbucks.

"Bilesh says we should get on a train and go to Astoria," Davey said.

I opened the group chat. Bilesh was clearly copy-pasting from a list. Top 10 Greek Pies to Try Before You Die, 10 Greek Bakeries in New York City to Put on Your Bucket List, et cetera.

Spanakopita malathropita bougatsa kotopita eat your heart out boys!

"Thanks for not telling me to go to Greektown," Davey said.

I shrugged. "No, I get it, man. It's not the same."

Davey scraped a trail through his icing with his teeth. "Is there anything your mom makes that you'd, you know ..."

"Raise the dead for?"

The dish that levitated to the front of my brain wasn't even culturally significant. It was a bowl of instant noodles. And it wasn't the noodles but the fact that she'd gotten up in the middle of the night to make it for me.

"Nah," I said, "not really."

Davey and I were eating dinner at a Malaysian restaurant when my manager called to demand where the hell I was and what the hell I thought I was doing.

I was on my third cup of Malaysian iced coffee. It was strong and sweet and rubbed the inside of my mouth like a velvet-tongued kiss. I decided that would be TMI.

"I'm taking a mental health break, Suraj," I said. "I was held up at gunpoint."

No guns had been involved in the stickup. But I must have sounded jittery because Suraj backed off and told me to take the week.

"Sweet," Davey said. "Let's go to Ocean City tomorrow. Hey, can I try some of that?"

I passed my cup over and watched him put his lips on the rim.

After dinner, we drove an hour to the cemetery and hopped the fence. It took us another hour to find Efthymia's grave. We found Myra first, actually: Myra Xenakis, born 1882, died 1918; only ten years older than her stepdaughter, she'd been reburied with honors after being exonerated of all crimes. She'd definitely poisoned Efthymia, the law review article had explained, but because Efthymia was alive and Myra was dead, the judge presiding over the cadaver synod had decided to call it even. Those had been his exact words—*Call it even*. He had been some kind of official in the town government. In his spare time, he judged the dead and pies and smuggled moonshine into New York City. What a baller.

The record was silent on how Efthymia had felt about the verdict. I couldn't imagine she'd been happy about it.

"We could do Myra too," I said. "Get her side of the story. I'm kind of curious."

But Davey shook his head. "I'm just here for the secret ingredient, bro."

We'd bought shovels at the Home Depot. We kicked our shiny new blades into the dirt. It had been raining all week, and the soil was heavy and smelled like worms. We looked at each other and started to dig.

Efthymia had been buried long before concrete vaults became standard. Most of her coffin had rotted away. Most of *Efthymia* had rotted away. But there was enough. I picked up a thread with my fingernail and followed it.

At 11 p.m., I raised Efthymia Xenakis from the dead.

It was immediately apparent that we had fucked up. Efthymia rose from her grave screaming in Greek. According to the law review article, she had spent most of her life in Chios, Greece—she didn't speak a word of English.

Davey had been raised by his mother and grandfather, Constantin Othonos, and had learned some Greek along the way, but it wasn't enough. And there was no Greek school in the tiny Pennsylvania town where we'd grown up. Of course, I didn't know what Davey was saying, but I understood the gist. I want you to imagine the scene: my beautiful Davey, six feet tall, yelling, "How are you? My name is David, and you?" at a wailing corpse.

She was looking for her baby. Her hands, mostly ether, partly bone, ran rustily over the pit that had been her pelvis.

"Malathropita," Davey started yelling, over and over. He was probably pronouncing it even worse than he had spelled it. "Malathropita, malathropita. Good morning. Good evening. I am called David, malathropita."

They had buried her in black. Scraps of it were fluttering around her, turning blue-green under the trembling beam of Davey's flashlight app.

The thread was going to break. I didn't want to let her go yet, so I did a stupid thing: I tied a knot around my little finger.

"Please, malathropita," Davey shouted.

I wondered if Efthymia was actually screaming the recipe at him. There was no way to tell. We should have been recording her, I realized. But before I could get my phone out of my pocket, the thread snapped.

Efthymia fell back into her grave, a dime-bag of bones and old cloth. My finger was bleeding. I put it in my mouth and sucked on it and felt Davey watching me.

We didn't bury her. We didn't have time: someone had heard the screaming and called the police. We clambered over the fence, our shovels banging and clattering against the iron like a pair of bell ringers falling off a church tower, and made it across the street to Davey's car just as the first blue lights rolled up to the cemetery gates.

"God damn it," Davey muttered as we drove away, "I'm going to have to ask my mom."

***

Davey's mom was buried back home in Pennsylvania at the bottom of a grassy hill. It was about 4 a.m. when we reached her. The wreath propped up against her headstone was gleaming in the watery light of early morning.

It looked fresh. Davey said it was part of the funeral home package: a new wreath every month for twelve months.

I had been to the funeral and the reception. I had nibbled the grocery store baklava and watched Davey shaking everyone's hand. When he got to me, he'd leaned in and said, "Thanks for coming, Kev. Are you still doing that necrophile shit?"

"*Necromancy*, Jesus," I'd said.

There had been an open-casket viewing before the service. I had gone to that too and looked at her, at this woman who had gouged out Davey's left eye with a well-aimed glass orb from Bed Bath and Beyond. A quick glance at Davey—his eye was where I'd left it, swiveling nicely in its socket.

Eliana Othonos had been embalmed. She looked more or less exactly the way she'd looked a month ago—unnaturally pink, a little bloated, and extremely dead. I couldn't tell, but I knew the side of her head was crunched up like an eggshell. Davey had mentioned it to me while he was griping about how much the mortuary services had cost. Worth every penny, I decided.

No concrete vault here either. Davey had picked a plastic liner that pried off easy. But the wood of Eliana's casket was thick and varnished. It would be a while before the worms could get to her.

"Ready?" I asked Davey.

"I guess," he said.

She hadn't gone too far. Maybe there were things she felt she'd left unfinished. When I tugged on her, she came quickly, almost like she'd been waiting.

But when Davey asked his question, her sightless eyes opened wide.

"Google it," she wheezed. Her dead hands flopped around and beat the sides of her casket, looking for something to throw. "Can't believe you dug me up for this. Dug me up and not even going to say sorry. Can't believe, can't fucking believe, oh, oh, oh you, oh *you*, you lazy know-nothing good-for-nothing *faggot*, you—"

I balled up her spark and skipped it back into oblivion like a round river stone.

We buried her deep. We Googled it and went to Whole Foods. I drove: Davey was crying too hard to see.

Whole Foods opened at seven. Red-eyed, Davey paid a premium for organic fennel, mint, and parsley. He spent about a decade examining the onions, fingering their papery yellow skins, and we had to make a second stop at a Wegmans because he remembered he was out of olive oil.

Then Davey took me home. It was his mother's house, and it was creepy. He'd taken down all of her decorations, but he hadn't replaced them, and the walls were full of nail-holes. Dents, too, and an arc of old blood that disappeared into the matted red carpet in the den. It looked like there'd been a struggle, but Davey said that was just how she had fallen. She'd sliced herself up on a picture frame.

I said I didn't care what had happened. Davey said okay.

As the sun rose, Davey kneaded the dough, and I prepped the greens. We shaped the pies into discs and fried them on medium heat until they were golden brown and fragrant.

"We can talk about the faggot in the room," Davey said. Quietly. I had to lean in to hear him over the sizzling. "If you want."

"Faggots," I said. "Plural."

"Oh," Davey said. "Wait, really? Since when?"

"Birth."

"Okay," Davey said. "I walked into that one."

I wanted to put my thumbs on the corners of his mouth and jolt a smile into him, but it didn't feel safe to smile in that house. Bad vibes. I didn't feel like smiling myself. I couldn't stop thinking about Efthymia Xenakis howling in Greek.

I used to have nightmares like that when I started raising the dead. Not about zombies or anything but about my mom in a nursing home, so demented she'd forgotten every last bit of English. I would be there shriveling up in the corner with a tray of strawberry Jell-O Cups, wishing I'd given Chinese school a Lillian-sized effort. *Hello*, I would say. *Hello, how are you? I am called Kevin. I am your son. Mama. Mama. Mama.*

Davey eased a pie onto a plate, cut it into wedges, and took a bite. According to the internet, the secret ingredient was fish roe, but we hadn't been able to find any. Did it taste like "just like Mom's"?

Davey was tearing up again.

"Ugh," he said thickly. "Burned my tongue."

He stuck it out to show me, swollen at the apex and caked with white pastry gunk across the body, and handed me a wedge.

It wasn't terrible. Very fennel-forward, and slightly gritty: I'm pretty sure some grave dirt got mixed into the filling. You'd think a necromancer would recognize the taste of grave dirt, but like I said, I wasn't exactly the cream of the necromantic cream.

After I finished my wedge, Davey took my hand and looked at the sore red line around the tip of my pinky.

"Thanks for everything, dude," he said. "It means a lot. It means so much. I wish there was something I could do to repay you."

"Actually," I said, "there *is* one thing you could do." And we made out in Davey's mother's kitchen.

Then we sold Eliana's house and rented an apartment and adopted a cat and lived happily ever after until I died of colon cancer and there was no one to bring Davey back from his heart attack the next year because I was dead. Or we sold Eliana's house and rented an apartment and adopted a cat and twelve or thirteen months later while I was restocking cigarettes at the Sunoco and flirting with Davey across the counter, the shade of Efthymia Xenakis erupted through the glass and killed us both.

You can't tell what happened, can you? Our soft tissues have rotted away. But that's all, Necromancer. That's the end of the story. You can put me back down.

The Last Train

by Jen Mierisch

A baby's miserable shriek erupted from an exam room down the hall, stabbing an icicle through Kenna's aching head. Squeezing her eyes shut, Kenna cursed the temp agency for sending her here.

Her workspace was a tiny table in a back office, sandwiched between the copy machine and the file cabinet. Its only advantage was its location, far from the waiting room filled with snot-nosed, germy children.

The jangling of the telephone knifed into her forehead. Opening one eye, Kenna squinted at the wall clock. Ten more minutes until she could escape to CVS for headache medicine.

She picked up the receiver. "Good morning, Downtown Pediatrics ... Yes, I can schedule that for you." Kenna's stomach growled like an irate bear. She wondered if the caller could hear it.

"I don't see any weekend appointments until July ... We can do the 7th at 9 a.m. ... Any change in insurance? ... Okay, Ms. Williams, you're all set."

She clicked to submit the appointment. The clock read 11:55. Please, she silently begged the phone, stay quiet for five more minutes.

The ringing seized her brain and shook it, like a child with a snow globe. Kenna rubbed her temples and answered. "Downtown Pediatrics."

"Hello," said a woman's voice. "My name is Shana Middleton." The voice sounded worn out, raspy, as if its owner had recently been screaming.

"May I help you?"

"I understand you have a colic specialist on staff. Dr. Milar?"

"Sorry, ma'am," said Kenna. "Dr. Milar is no longer with the practice. He retired in April."

The caller was silent for a minute. "Do you have another doctor with this specialty?" she asked. Her voice caught, followed by an unmistakable sniffle.

Kenna shifted in her chair, itchy with embarrassment for this woman, breaking down over the phone. "No, ma'am."

"I'm sorry for getting upset," the woman said. "I haven't slept in … several weeks now. Jacob's two months old. He never stops crying. Can I speak with one of the doctors?"

"Dr. Nasser is out today," said Kenna, checking the schedule. "The other physicians are with patients, and the nurses are in clinic. I can transfer you to voicemail …"

"No!"

Kenna flinched.

"No," said the woman, less harshly this time. "Please don't transfer me. I don't know what else to do. I've called everywhere. I've tried everything. I'm alone, my husband's out of town …" The voice trailed off, replaced by the sound of a baby fussing. "Is there anyone you could refer me to? Doesn't matter how far away. I'm in Devonshire, but I'll drive out of state if necessary …"

Kenna pictured Devonshire, the suburb where she'd worked as a server at bar mitzvahs and quinceañeras to pay her college tuition. She remembered the slim people in gowns and tuxes who had lifted champagne flutes from Kenna's tray with manicured fingers and looked right through her.

"I don't know what to tell you, ma'am," she said.

In the background of the call, the baby started howling. Kenna held the receiver away from her ear.

The caller was crying again. "Please," she whispered. "Please help me. I just… can't handle it anymore. I'm afraid of what I might do."

"Ma'am …"

"Please." She was sobbing now.

"Sorry," Kenna said flatly. "I can't help you."

"Is there anyone …"

"I can't help you."

She replaced the receiver on its cradle more forcefully than she'd intended. The bang struck her pounding head like a mallet on a gong.

"Kenna."

She jumped. Her boss, Debra, stood in the doorway, arms folded.

"Yes?"

"Got a minute?"

"Uh …" Kenna glanced at the wall clock.

"Come see me when you get back from lunch." Debra held Kenna's gaze, then disappeared back to her office.

Swallowing, Kenna grabbed her purse and hustled out the door.

The street noise comforted Kenna as she stepped onto the sidewalk, joining the river of pedestrians. The cars' engines, the chattering strangers, even the buses' squeaking brakes soothed her brain like a bath. She kicked a pigeon off the curb, chuckling at its affronted warble.

Inside the store, Kenna hummed along to the piped-in pop music, selecting an ibuprofen bottle from the shelf. On her way to the checkout, she nearly tripped over a stroller parked in an aisle. Muttering curses, she grabbed a package of Super C. Might as well protect herself against the little plague rats.

As she stepped outside, Kenna glanced at her phone to check the time and muttered curses. Quickly she turned down an alley, a shortcut back to the pediatric office. Condensation from window air-conditioners dripped against the pavement as she dodged litter.

At first, the footsteps were so quiet that she barely noticed them. High heels clicked against concrete, staccato taps reverberating off the brick walls. Kenna ignored them. Hearing a man's footsteps, she might have picked up her pace, or at least taken a look. But there was nothing to fear from a woman, even if the steps were coming closer.

Emerging, finally, onto the sunlit street, Kenna glanced back. Except for a Dumpster and a scuttling rat, the alley was empty.

"And then I had to listen to Debra give me a speech about empathy," Kenna complained into her phone as she strode home from the subway. "What the hell. It's not my fault Dr. Milar retired." Something was pinching her heels. She looked down and sighed. She'd forgotten to swap her pumps for sneakers before leaving work.

"Dude. That sucks," said Tyler. "What did the lady say again? The caller?"

"She said her baby cried a lot. Like, duh. Babies cry a lot." Kenna perched on the edge of a planter and kicked off a shoe. "She clearly hadn't slept in a while. She was crying as much as the baby was."

"Probably colic," said Tyler.

Kenna blinked. "How do you know that?" Tyler boasted expertise in cannabis varieties, Xbox games, and rock-climbing equipment, but not, to her knowledge, babies.

"Sounds like Ashley, right after she had Lucas," Tyler said. "She, like, never slept. Mom went over there every day to watch the baby just so Ash could nap."

"I don't get it," said Kenna, pulling on her sneakers and stuffing the pumps into her bag. "So you lose some sleep. Big deal. I slept like four hours a night during finals."

"Yeah, but not for months on end," he said. "That shit is intense. I've never seen Ash like that. She looked like hell. She cried all the time. I was worried about her for a while there."

"Ugh," Kenna said. "I am *so* never having kids."

Usually, Tyler would have chimed in with something like, "Yeah. Seriously." Today, he said nothing. The silence stretched out.

Kenna felt a rush of irritation. "So what should I have done with her, then? If you're so smart."

"I don't know. Give her to Debra, I guess. She's the boss. Let her deal with it."

"Fine. Tomorrow, you can go in, instead of me, since you know so goddamn much."

"Hey, don't take it like that. I'm just—"

"Mansplaining, maybe?" Kenna stepped off the curb. A taxi blared its horn as it rumbled around the corner, inches from her feet. She quickly hopped backward.

"What?" Tyler said. "How am I mansplaining? I'm just telling you about my sister. I'm just saying colic is a real thing."

"Call me crazy," Kenna blurted, "but I would have thought my own boyfriend would be supportive instead of criticizing me."

"Kenna—"

She ended the call and stuffed the phone into her pocket. A minute went by, then another. She waited for it to ring. Tyler always called back.

The phone stayed silent.

Kenna strode forward, her face a storm cloud, her sneakers slapping the pavement. A minute later, she had cooled off enough to wonder if she'd been too harsh on Tyler. He didn't deserve to bear the brunt of her bad day.

But no. She wasn't in the wrong here, she thought. She'd had a crappy day and he had barely listened; he'd just launched into that story about his sister. Let him be the one to call back.

A few steps later, Kenna's anger cooled and her resolve waned. It wasn't like him to wait this long. Maybe she'd really pissed him off. She pulled out her phone.

"Hey! Shana!"

The unfamiliar voice pierced Kenna's ruminations. She ignored it and kept walking.

"Shana! Hey, girl, what's up?"

The voice was closer now. Kenna turned to see a young, smiling, red-haired woman whose face quickly morphed into a mask of surprise.

"Oh," said the woman. "Sorry! You look just like my cousin's friend. My bad." She turned and jogged back the way she'd come, glancing over her shoulder to chirp, "Sorry to bother you!"

Kenna frowned and shook her head. Another bizarre event in the weirdest day she'd had in a while. She stuffed her phone back into her pocket. She'd deal with Tyler later.

What had the redhead called her? Shana. How funny. The same name as the woman who had called the office about the baby.

The baby was crying, drawing deep breaths and belting out its misery. The sound grew louder until it blotted out everything, like an ambulance passing on the street with its siren searing straight into your brain.

Kenna woke with a gasp, fumbling for her phone, swiping to kill the beeping alarm. Squinting at the sunlight, she shoved aside the bedspread and stumbled toward the bathroom.

In the kitchen, Kenna flopped into a chair with her coffee mug and breakfast Hot Pocket. Across the table, Kenna's roommate Renata set down her cereal spoon and glanced away from the TV news.

"Dang, girl," Renata said. "You look as tired as I feel."

Kenna yawned. "Did someone with kids move into our building?"

"Not that I know of. Why?"

"I couldn't sleep at all last night. Some baby kept crying." Kenna gulped her coffee and cringed as it burned her tongue. "You didn't hear it?"

Renata's earrings swished as she shook her head. "Nope."

"Lucky. It went on all friggin' night long. I think I was asleep for maybe an hour." Kenna glanced at her phone and frowned. Still no call or text from Tyler.

"You've been working at that pediatrician's office too long," said Renata, standing and carrying her bowl to the sink. "Babies on the brain!" She laughed.

"Shut up," said Kenna. "I do not have babies on the brain. Except maybe in my mom's dreams."

"See you tonight for Margarita Fridays!" Renata closed the dishwasher and flounced out of the room.

"Later," Kenna replied, taking a bite of her sandwich. Her eyes drifted to the countertop TV display. On screen was a photo, taken from social media by the look of it, of a smiling white woman with long dark hair.

The newscaster struck a somber tone. "Tragic news this morning from Devonshire. Thirty-one-year-old Shana Middleton was found dead yesterday evening in an apparent suicide, just yards away from her infant son."

The image changed, showing a tiny, pink-faced baby. An oversized sticker on his onesie read "2 months."

"Police responded to a 911 call placed from the Middletons' home," the anchor continued. "Officers found the baby alone in the living room in a portable crib. They discovered the victim's body in a bathroom on an upper floor of the residence."

Kenna dropped her breakfast and stared.

"Middleton was on maternity leave from her job as an executive at Morse Investments. She had no criminal record and no known history of mental illness. The young family had recently relocated following a job transfer. Middleton's husband, reached by phone this morning, requested that the family's privacy be respected during this terrible time."

"No way," whispered Kenna. "No fucking way."

Shana Middleton's blue eyes gazed confidently at the camera. Her brown hair was long and shiny, like a Barbie doll's. She looked like someone who was used to succeeding, someone who needed nobody's help, someone who'd had every reason to think things would always go her way.

Kenna jabbed the power button on the remote, and the screen went dark. She gulped down the coffee and pushed the rest of the Hot Pocket into the garbage disposal. As she gathered her coat and purse, she could hear it still: a baby's woeful wail, bouncing between the tall buildings, all the way up to the sky.

"Kenna," said Debra, "a word."

Sighing, Kenna forwarded the phone to the front desk and trudged into Debra's office, sitting on the plastic guest chair. Down the hall, a toddler bawled.

Debra folded her hands and leaned forward. "That's the third caller you've snapped at this morning."

"Sorry," Kenna muttered, avoiding Debra's brown eyes.

"And Reception asked you for more HIPAA forms two hours ago."

Kenna shifted awkwardly, feeling her heart thump, bracing herself for Debra's announcement that she was fired.

"Is everything okay?"

The gentle tone made Kenna look up in surprise. "Um. I had a rough night last night. Didn't sleep much."

"Aren't you feeling well?"

"Not really." For a second, Kenna contemplated telling Debra about the caller, about the news broadcast that had replayed in her head all morning. Just as quickly, she tossed that idea. She was already in enough trouble.

"You're free to go home if you're not well." The concern in Debra's eyes brought pinprick tears to Kenna's.

"No. I'm good," said Kenna, thinking about the short paycheck that would result from an afternoon off. Her student loans weren't going to pay themselves. "I'll try to do better."

"Are you sure? Everybody has rough days, Kenna, but being rude to customers is not acceptable."

"I understand."

"All right," said Debra. "We'll give it one last shot."

Kenna stared at her folded hands.

"Go on back now."

Kenna rose and scurried back to her table.

The afternoon dragged. Kenna felt like a piece of taffy, stretched thin and liable to break. She chugged office coffee from a paper cup. Phone calls slowed. The copy machine clacked and whirred as she ran off more HIPAA forms. As she stood waiting, lulled by the drone of the machinery, the newscaster's words returned unbidden. Shana Middleton. Body found in a bathroom. She wondered how they'd determined it was a suicide.

She would not Google the news story. She would not. If Debra caught her on her phone, that would be the end of it.

At the front desk, Kenna deposited the still-warm papers into their trays. Hefting the stack of patient files from the day's appointments, she walked to the file room.

The shelves spanned the room's height, floor to ceiling. In the back, near the Fs, Kenna set the file folders onto a stool and peeked between the shelves. Sliding her phone from her pocket, she opened the web browser.

The dead woman's husband had been away on business, she read. Neither she nor her husband had family in the area. Neighbors said they'd heard the baby crying sometimes and were shocked that something like this could happen to such a nice young couple.

According to investigators, the cause of death was electrocution. The new mother had swaddled her son, called 911, stepped into the tub she'd filled, switched on a hair dryer, and dropped it in.

Kenna ran down the hall to the restroom. Breathing hard, she splashed cold water on her face and looked into the mirror. Her eyes, blue like the dead woman's, looked sunken in shadow.

A woman had done a horrible thing, and Kenna was possibly the last person who had spoken to her while she was alive.

Kenna forced herself to walk back to the file room. She concentrated on tucking away the folders in alphabetical order, telling herself not to picture an upstairs bathtub in an elegant house, willing herself not to imagine what that Barbie-doll face had looked like ... afterward.

She felt her eyes prickling with unexpected tears for the second time that day. A sudden surge of anger streamed through her veins. "It is not my fault," she muttered, swiping away the hot salt water. What kind of mom would just kill herself, and leave her baby all alone, just because she was tired?

When 5:00 finally came, Kenna burst through the door like a tiger from a cage. The air was thick, threatening rain, but she gulped in greedy breaths as she started walking. Overhead power lines buzzed with static in the moist air.

Near the subway entrance, the gray man paced in his usual place, sneakers shuffling along the pavement. His hand-lettered sign bore a single word: REPENT. He fixed his milky eyes on Kenna, extended an arm, and pointed at her face. She hurried past him and down the subterranean steps.

"Kenna!" said Renata in greeting, as Kenna hung her damp coat in the closet. "You're coming out with us, right? You look like you could use a drink."

Before Kenna could reply, the door buzzer sounded, and Renata jumped up from the couch to answer it. Seconds later, their friends Henry, Paul, and Marie strolled in through the apartment door.

Kenna's bleary eyes watched her friends, laughing and bantering back and forth. They were so relaxed, so carefree. Every cell in her body ached with strain and exhaustion, and she longed for some way to feel normal again. La Ciudad Mexican Restaurant made their margaritas strong. One or two of those should take the edge off.

Something tickled at the back of her mind, something she'd read, about how you got drunk faster when you were tired. Screw that, she decided. Her alcohol tolerance was pretty good. She could handle a drink or two.

They assembled around La Ciudad's corner table and ordered every appetizer on the menu. Kenna reached for the salt-rimmed glass and felt the green liquid flow down her throat like sweet fire. Mariachi music blasted from the speakers. Several more friends showed up and joined them. Kenna was grateful for the big group, so loud they wouldn't notice if she was quiet.

Across the room, a waitress with long dark hair turned her head and looked directly at Kenna. She had Shana Middleton's face.

Kenna gasped, blinked, and looked again. The waitress was just the Friday regular, stuffing signed receipts into her apron as she hoisted a tray full of empty glasses.

Absurdly, Kenna thought about proposing a toast to Shana, to remember her life. The concept was so ridiculous and terrible that she started giggling hysterically, unstoppably. "No more for Kenna!" hollered Marie. Their laughter roared in Kenna's ears.

Later, they all careened down the sidewalk, on the way to some bar where some friend's band was playing. Kenna's mind wobbled, a boat adrift on an alcoholic sea. It was raining again, but Marie was singing as she threw an arm around Kenna's shoulder and another around Renata's. A taxi splashed past, its horn a shrill whine trailing off into the darkness. Its blonde passenger, gazing out the back window, resembled Tyler's sister Ashley. Kenna pictured Ash, who'd always been so sweet to her at Tyler's family get-togethers, holding a screaming baby in the pitch-black middle of the night, her pretty face crumpled in misery.

Inside the smoky bar, Kenna's stomach roiled, tequila threatening to erupt. Clutching her abdomen, she put out a hand to lean against the bar.

"You okay?" asked Renata. "You don't look so good."

"I don't feel so good. I'm gonna head home."

"Want me to come with you?"

Kenna looked up. Renata stood next to Henry. His head was turned away, talking to their friends, but his hand rested on Renata's shoulder. That was new.

"Nah," she said. Henry's fingers stroked Renata's arm, his body swaying, his voice too-much-liquor loud. Renata, in contrast, seemed her clear-eyed self, her hair long and dark, like Shana's.

"Hey, listen," Kenna told her, "get yourself home after this, okay?"

"I'm planning on it," said Renata.

"Be safe. Take an Uber."

"Sure."

"By yourself."

Renata laughed. "Okay, Mom. See you back home."

"See you there." Kenna smiled weakly as another wave of nausea gripped her innards.

The Uber app refused to load, displaying an error message about an unavailable server. Wiping raindrops off the phone, Kenna tried hailing a taxi, but they all sped past, filled with passengers. She turned back toward the subway. If she hurried, she could still make the last train.

Kenna gripped the rail as she lurched down the damp stairs to the platform. She skidded a little, then flopped down onto a bench, slapping the sides of her face as if sobriety could be applied by force.

She took out her phone, thinking about the passenger who looked like Ashley, thinking about Tyler, who still hadn't called. She loaded her call history. Her finger hovered over his name. She should call him, she felt. But what would she say?

Shana had chosen motherhood, thought Kenna. She had brought her fate onto herself. But so had Ashley. And sometimes people made choices whose consequences spiraled out of control.

Kenna looked down the length of the platform, a flat plane in a tube-shaped cave. She was alone. And yet it seemed that Shana Middleton was there too. Kenna imagined Shana sitting on the bench next to her, wearing a business suit and heels, the two of them facing forward like commuters waiting for the same train.

As suddenly as a smoke alarm, a baby's angry wail flooded the station, echoing off the soggy walls. Kenna leaped to her feet, trembling, and looked around. The dim platform was empty. The stairs leading to the street were vacant, littered with soggy shreds of garbage.

Get a grip, she told herself, her breath coming in ragged gasps. There is no baby here, Kenna. No baby.

The baby's cry was growing louder, as if someone were pushing a stroller toward Kenna. Heart slamming against her chest, she stumbled backward, tripping over the bench. Her arms flailed, and her phone went flying, bouncing against the floor and skittering toward the track. She dived for the phone, landing on the damp cement and sliding, too fast. She swiveled, trying frantically to stop, but her legs sailed over the edge.

Somehow her arms locked against the yellow-painted rim of the platform. And then her elbows were the only thing stopping her from dropping into the shadows that concealed the third rail. In terror, she kicked at the slippery tunnel wall.

A flicker of movement appeared at the stairs. Kenna squinted at what looked like a homeless woman, with long, ragged hair and stained clothes, walking slowly toward her.

"Help me!" Kenna screamed. "Please! I'm slipping. I can't hold on!" Her arms trembled alarmingly.

The baby was still crying. The shrieks bounced off the tunnel walls, multiplying themselves, swallowing up the narrow space, all the way to the tiny light in the distance, the headlamp of the approaching train.

The woman studied Kenna with her head cocked to one side. She seemed to have something bulky underneath her coat. She shook her head sadly.

Kenna's arms began to shake violently with the effort of holding on. Her abdominal muscles clenched as her feet fumbled fruitlessly for a hold. The train sounded like rushing wind, growing louder as its light grew bigger. Her elbow slipped.

"Please! Is there something I could grab onto? Anything?"

The woman was just a few feet away now. She looked into Kenna's eyes and leaned down, causing Kenna's heart to leap with hope. Then Kenna saw what was bundled in the woman's coat. It was one of those wearable baby carriers. It was empty, its fabric sagging against the woman's chest.

"I can't help you," the woman said. "I can't help you."

Her voice sounded exactly like it had on the phone.

The light approached inexorably, like dawn. Kenna screamed, as loud as the baby now, as deafening as the screech of the train's brakes as it barreled into the station and her arms gave way and she fell.

Mad Lullaby

by Ray Pantle

Fate isn't written in Link's DNA—or in the straps fastened to his ankles and wrists. He doesn't belong in this place, bound to a wheelchair. That psychiatrist seated across from him—the one with the Smart Focals attached to his head—doesn't know Link. He doesn't realize how normal Link is, not like Gwen does. He must get out of here and get back to her, his salvation, his Star.

But he can't break free. The restraints are buckled so tightly that his arms have gone numb, and the slightest struggling against his bonds sends pain shooting through his bruised eye.

And using that other trick to escape, the secret he's been carrying for years? No, there are less desperate ways.

Dr. Hans flips on the EgoMate next to him and speaks to the machine. "Freud," he says to his virtual assistant, "begin note: It is June 5, 2019, 2:30 a.m. Patient is Lincoln Redfield, age 19. He is exhibiting no signs of his illness at present. I will continue my observation as we get deeper into the night and report any changes to his mental state. End note."

Dr. Hans turns to the back wall. "Freud, get the Intake Team on screen."

The EgoMate's lens projects an image onto the back wall. In it, a line of whitecoats waits for their boss's command.

Link's jaw tenses at the sight of the Intake Team. They're the ones who had strapped him down and jabbed a needle into his thigh. The ones who hovered around him, flipping between typing notes on their electronic pads, bantering about the Ohio State game, and studying him as if he were a dead insect pinned down for display. Not a single one had bothered to hold his hand, offer him water, or promise everything would be okay.

"I've read his file." Dr. Hans taps his Smart Focals. "It says here you sedated him."

"Correct," a lanky resident speaks on screen. "He assaulted the police officers who brought him in."

"In self-defense," Link says. "Look at my face. They're the ones who busted into my dorm room. *They* attacked *me*."

"To protect the public," the lanky resident says.

"Enough," Dr. Hans says to the resident. "What the hell were you thinking? Link has TSD. Sedating him is contraindicated with his illness."

The resident opens and closes his mouth like a beached fish. "I'm sorry, I didn't know. I thought TSD is like schizophrenia, except it hits in the evening."

"No, no, no, they're nothing alike. Twilight Syncopatic Disorder. The main symptom's right there in the name. How could you possibly miss that?"

The resident mutters an apology and lowers his gaze. Dr. Hans tears off his Smart Focals, scrubs a hand down his face, and takes a deep breath. "This can't happen again, okay? TSD is rare, yes, but very serious. Those inflicted fall unconscious at night. Their brains aren't like ours. They can't function without this period of rest called sleep, not without treatment. That's why we brought Link here, to get him stabilized so he stays awake. But thanks to your sedatives, he's now *more* likely to sleep. I'll be lucky to get a full history on him."

Dr. Hans taps the EgoMate, and the screen blanks out. "Unbelievable," he mutters, shaking his head while moving to the back window to peer into the night.

Link views the outdoor courtyard from his wheelchair. Its greenery and picnic benches might have made him forget he's trapped in a locked ward, if not for the barbed wire fence bordering the area. No patients or staff roam at this hour. Instead, the courtyard teems with an army of workers donned in Hazmat suits. They carry out their assignment under garish pole lights, aiming their guns at the foliage and spraying it with a thick chemical mist.

"Locusts," Dr. Hans says, his lip curling in distaste. "A real problem as of late. Patients end up stuck indoors, restless ... harder to control."

Even in his current state, Lincoln recalls what he learned about the locusts in biology class, how the creatures had been largely absent from the United States until last year, when locust sightings began cropping up throughout the Midwest. But what interested Link most was their curious behavior during droughts when the otherwise solitary creatures would band together and forge a swarm.

Dr. Hans returns to his desk. "I'm sorry about what happened with my team. Let's start over, okay? Have an honest chat."

The doctor works his mouth into a smile, but the attempt does nothing to calm Link's nerves. "I need out of here," he says. "I'm seeing my girlfriend in an hour. If I don't show up, she'll worry about me."

"Your girlfriend." He speaks to the EgoMate. "Freud, go to the subfolder titled Gwendolyn Marvel."

Click, whirl, groan. A beam shoots from the lens, transmitting Gwen's high school picture onto the wall, the same one Link carries with him. She's frozen in classic Gwen mode: mouth upturned, gaze upturned, everything glimmering, aimed skyward.

Dr. Hans reads from the lines of text claiming space on screen. "Born August 3, 2000. Double majoring in deep space exploration and interplanetary botany, with a minor in math."

Gwen's image on screen jolts alarm through Link. Her likeness shouldn't be here, tied to this awful place, yet his heart swells with gratefulness as memories of her burst forth. He remembers the two of them lying in an intimacy pod under a canopy of stars while Gwen points to Orion through the glass ceiling. (She's hell-bent on joining NASA; he's hell-bent on being there to wrap his arms around her bulky spacesuit to say his goodbyes). That had been a night of unbelievables: of learning the rhythm of her body, of hearing her heartbeat with his ear to her chest. He had briefly forgotten the invisible mark branding him a freak and had seen himself through Gwen's eyes—as someone with a future as golden and bright as hers.

"She's not aware you're sick," Dr. Hans says. "Same with your pals at school. Clever of you to ask for a separate dorm, for when the symptoms take hold. But you can stop playing games with me. I know everything, Link. I know how ill you really are. And I know about the crimes committed to cover it up."

Dread roils through Link. After all those years of worrying himself sick, of taking great lengths to hide the truth, his worst fear has finally manifest.

"I checked the Mental Illness Registry. Your name's not on the list. Someone must have swabbed another boy's mouth and sent his DNA in with your name. Someone lied to the government for you."

On screen, Gwen's photo is replaced by a scaled-down version of Link's childhood home. Inside one room, a digital boy resembling Link sits in the RealGames dock he used to own, shooting at the virtual villains of his favorite superheroes, while his digital mother across the hall dresses for work.

"You kept it secret at first," Dr. Hans says. "Easy enough with your mom having two jobs, and the babysitters drifting in and out barely noticing you're around. And why bother telling her? Your father's leaving has been hard enough on her. Why add to the stress? Then one night, when she should be at work, you have an attack."

As the doctor talks, the digital version of Link on screen frowns, and the hand holding the electronic gun drops to his side. Dazed, with his eyes on the floor, his mouth opens into a yawn. This reenactment pitches Link into the past, to the first time night had tempted him.

That summer had been so sticky-damp it had been impossible to relax. But, one evening, things improved. A breeze stirred outside. The air rustled the curtain, swaying it back and forth, beckoning Link to follow the rhythm, to close his eyes, let himself give in.

His muscles melted like warm butter. Curling into a ball on the floor, he let his eyelids slip down, then shut.

His mother's scream jerked him awake. Spit had crusted down his cheek. His mother stood over him, a dropped laundry basket at her feet, the hand clamped over her mouth failing to mask her shock.

"She thought hiding it would protect you," Dr. Hans says. "For years, refusing to get you help. Thankfully, she eventually came around."

The doctor's words pulse through Link like fever chills. "What do you mean ... *she came around?*"

"Winter break rattled her. You'd been sleeping more often, in longer stretches. Imagine how alarming that was for her, especially after what happened with that sleeper in Dayton. Finally, she understood the risk and gave us a call."

"You're lying," Link says. "She wouldn't do that."

"Don't be upset. You're lucky she turned to us when she did. The sooner treatment begins, the less impaired you'll be."

"I'm not impaired. I've got a scholarship to a top school. My track team's number one. Everything's fine."

"Freud, go to the subfolder titled Link's Transcripts."

Click, whirl, groan. The EgoMate throws another image on screen. Fanned in a row are the As and Bs he'd received first semester, alongside the more recent Cs and Ds.

"You've slipped," Dr. Hans says. "And with only sixteen credits, not the standard twenty-one. How can you possibly keep up? We're talking forty hours of sleep each week. Forty hours with no attention to school or sports. Medication can improve the symptoms, but it isn't a cure. You'll still suffer bouts of sleep multiple times a week."

"Fine. I'll drop a class or two. Quit track for a while."

"Link, you're not listening. This illness is serious, with real handicaps. Imagine a world, an altered reality if you will, where everyone has your sickness, where everyone sleeps. Technology would be far less advanced given the wasted hours where people did nothing but sleep. Students would have to spend more years in school, meaning more loan debt to pay off."

"Yeah, and it would be normal to them," Link says.

"But it isn't. Not to us."

Dr. Hans sighs. He removes his Smart Focals and rubs the bridge of his nose. "I know this is hard to accept. Go ahead and hate me for being so frank, but it'll save you a lot of heartache in the end. People like you … they never lead normal lives. Most end up living at home, fully depending on their folks, doing menial jobs. Think about Gwen. You can't expect someone so ambitious, someone who surely wants a family someday, to give that up."

The room seesaws. Dr. Hans's words garble, as if coming from deep inside a well.

"Enough," Link says. "Shut that damn screen off."

"We haven't covered everything."

"I don't care." Link's gaze darts to the far wall, fixing on the towering bookshelf.

"Please stay focused. You've had a sedative, and I still want to discuss more of your history and treatment plan—"

"What the hell is that?"

"What is what, Link?" Dr. Hans says, his maw a tight knot. "Are you falling asleep, *right now*?"

"That." With one restrained hand, Link points across the room. A single insect has gargoyled itself atop the bookshelf.

Dr. Hans eases around his desk, creeps across the room, and cranes his neck to study the creature. It appears no different from a grasshopper, with its lime-spotted body pod, its swab of head, and membrane honey wings.

"A locust," Dr. Hans says. "Must have escaped the spray."

Its head at a tilt, the locust regards its observer with twin coal eyes. There's a long pause while the two stalemate, the doctor lip-pinched and oddly amused, the insect tense and on guard. The locust crouches down as if preparing to leap from the bookshelf, away from the doctor's reach.

Without warning, the doctor's hand shoots out and captures the creature by its hind leg. He flings it to the floor and stomps down, breaking its body with a sickening crunch.

"What the hell," Link yells. "You didn't have to kill it."

"It'll defecate on my floor," Dr. Hans says. "Who knows what it's carrying."

The doctor pulls a tissue from his desk and wipes up the locust bits before tossing the remains into the trash. Then he sits and steeples his hands under his mouth.

"Link. I'm trying to help you. But the more you won't cooperate, the longer you'll be locked up. You want to go home, right? So, work with me here. Tell me about the things you haven't mentioned, the other ... disturbances. Most people like you hallucinate while asleep. Ever have that happen? Ever ..." The doctor's mouth twists, and he spits out the word. "Dream?"

Link remains silent. He raises his leg as far as the restraints permit, until his shoe touches the desk, as if lengthening his limb could stretch the moment and allow more time to decide how honest he should be.

"I see things," Links says at last. "I hear things, too."

"Yes, that's part of the dreams. What patients describe, the hideous monsters, people chasing them, I could only imagine how hellish that is."

"Most of my dreams aren't like that," Link says. "I dream about fishing with my dad. Once I dreamed about Chuck, the dog I had as a kid."

"And the other ones? The ones where you *do* things? Violent things."

"What? No, it's nothing like that. I do have surreal ones, though, like where I have gifts. Strength enough to lift a house. Hearing so sharp I catch water dripping from the neighbor's sink. The ability to control animals. Sometimes, I can even fly."

Dr. Hans types notes on his pad. "There's nothing else you do with these powers? Maybe to a teacher who gave you a bad grade, or the faster guy on the field?"

"No. Why?"

"I'm not denying that dreams can be comforting. It's obvious you use them to deal with problems in your life. Flying particularly, that's classic escape. But sometimes, dreams turn deadly. One woman dreamed of hacking up her newborn son. How deeply disturbed she must have been."

"You mean, she *actually* killed him?"

"No, but sleepwalking is common with TSD. She could have wandered into the kitchen for a knife. And that's not the only concern. Remember the accident in Dayton? The man with TSD who fell asleep while driving? His doctor had warned him to take his meds, but he wouldn't listen. He survived with only broken ribs. The family he rammed head-on wasn't so lucky."

"But I've never fallen asleep at the wheel."

"Not yet. We live in a sue-happy culture. You can't afford the risk."

"But you can't lock someone up for what they *might* do, or because they see and hear things others don't. I've never harmed anyone. I'm not dangerous."

"You lack insight. It's common with the mentally ill." He types in his chart. "Ten milligrams of Prestia, one of our newer meds. Once therapeutic levels are reached, it will cut down the number of hours you sleep. But the good news is, the dreams should stop right away."

"No," Link says, shaking his head. "No drugs."

"Once stabilized on meds, you'll be discharged. Isn't that what you want?"

"Yes, but I want to dream too. I like that part of it."

"I'm sorry, but I'm afraid you don't have a choice, not with the new law in place." Dr. Hans takes a breath and folds his hands on the desk. "After the tragedy in Dayton, Congress had to act. Now, once a psychiatrist orders treatment, the patient can no longer withhold consent."

Again the doctor delays, as if waiting for the words to sink in. "Once a week you'll appear at the clinic for your shot. If you don't, you'll be put in restraints and hauled in by police. You don't want that. It's best to cooperate."

Link's vision warps. An image from an old documentary on the European witch hunts fights its way into his mind. A woman accused is stretched out on the rack, her agony so fierce that a confession of guilt howls from her lips. The guard takes her broken body off the rack, but instead of setting her free, he drags her screaming to the pyre where he binds her to a stake, and within seconds the kindling catches fire and a blazing inferno engulfs every inch of flesh.

Because choice was a lie.

Because either way the soul of the outcast would be destroyed.

The adrenaline that had been rushing through Link now flows out like blood from a wound. Heaviness settles into his bones. The room blurs under a sheen of tears.

Dr. Hans rises, comes to the wheelchair, and pats Link's arm. "It's a lot to digest. Let's chat more in the morning, after your first dose of meds."

Link watches the doctor press the intercom and call orderlies to come for him. Within minutes he'll be escorted back to his room and the door will click shut. There, he'll stare at the ceiling for hours ruminating about school next fall, the students bustling through the quad, his friends making weekend party plans, everything he'll miss while holed up in his old basement, smeared on the couch binge-watching shows. Because that's how it must be after he's released: his future job manning the register at the corner store, with his mother's friends who ask how school is, his old classmates who pretend not to recognize him.

He propels forward in time, to Gwen's big day. She stands tall in her NASA suit and poses by the spacecraft gearing up to launch; her husband graces her with a kiss, a well-respected scientist in his own right, a man perfectly matched for her, one deserving of her love in a way Link is not and never will be. He might pass as normal in some other world, one full of sleepers like him who set a slower pace, but here, there will always be an unbridgeable gulf between what functional society demands of him and what his brain has condemned him to be. So, he'll always be incurably sick. Defective. And with no escape.

Except in his dreams.

Link closes his eyes. He imagines a breeze stirring outside. The air rustles the grass, swaying it back and forth, beckoning Link to follow the rhythm, to close his eyes, let himself give in, before he's forever robbed of the thrilling phantasma of dreams.

The room shivers back into place, but it's a murkier, more surreal version of itself. A shadow has draped over Dr. Hans's face, and something has melted his grin away.

Dream-Link reaches out with his mind, beyond the hospital grounds, and sends out a wordless call for help. Moments later, he hears the tiniest of sounds. A steady echo coming from someplace beyond the room. It resembles the beating of wings against air, but to Link it sounds musical, like a sweet lullaby.

Dream-Dr. Hans cocks his head as the fluttering gains strength. Its source no longer emanates from some undefined point but from above, inside the ceiling. The air-conditioning ducts rattle with a thunder of pings that stop in the vent directly over their heads.

Link grins. His aerial troops are here, ready for his command.

Now.

Tiles explode. A cloud of locusts burst through the grate. Dream-Dr. Hans stands frozen, jaw slack, eyes bulged, as they descend.

The swarm mushrooms throughout the entire room. Mighty wings thrash and buzz, their metered pulses growing faster, fueled by rage. Dr. Hans strangles out a cry. He loses his footing and crashes into the desk, his electronic notepad clattering to the floor. The blitzkrieg encircles the doctor's head. Locusts tangle in his hair, beat their wings against his ears, pry open his mouth with their legs while the footsteps of orderlies thunder down the hall toward the screams.

Despair falls from Link, like skin that's been shed, excitement blazing through every inch of him. His atoms rearrange, morph, enhance. Two lumps grow under the flesh of his back. They expand in size, too painful and large to contain, until wings tear through skin and spread above the wheelchair. His restrained arms shrink in width, taking the shape of needle-thin insect limbs that slip free of the straps.

As the first orderly barges into the room, Dream-Link stops for one last look at Dr. Hans. He's crumbled and sobbing on the ground, looking fractured and strange through Link's compound eyes. Link's legs rub against his wings, producing a gleeful buzzing, and he turns to the window, takes one giant leap, and crashes through the glass.

The locusts circle Link as he breaks into flight. Together, they ride air, lifting toward clouds, claiming sky. Earth fades, Earth is gone, but Link moves beyond the miseries of his past, toward galaxies of unimaginable sights. He scours the universe and its vast pool of space until he locates the spacecraft carrying Gwen. He dives down and takes her into his spindly arms, pressing her close to his thorax; she nestles and touches his hard chitin shell, caresses his wings. Together, they blast off to a new planet they claim as their own, where they can trace new constellations in the nighttime sky, and he can name each one after her.

This will be his home. A safe place for those like him, where they can sleep and weave wondrous tales without living in fear. A place where other sleepers can come and worship him as a god, and he can lead them to dream.

Someone Who's Not Me

by Micah Castle

At the kitchen table, I nurse a cooling cup of coffee. Dirt-caked hands pressed into vinyl. Sunrise peeks through the window over the sink, washing the room in soft orange-yellow. Take a sip, another. Warmth blooms in my chest, burrows into my hands and feet. Someone knocks at the front door. Sighing, I glance at the clock over the hall.

"Not even seven," I mumble, rising, abandoning my mug.

"It's his teeth," Mrs. Canelo says, her hands, knuckles dry and cracked, on her little boy's shoulders. "Says it hurts, even when swallowing."

I hunker, hands on knees. Face level, the tan-skinned boy recoils but his mother's grip tightens.

"*No se mueva,*" she whispers.

"Don't worry," I say, adjusting the glasses sliding down my nose. "Can you open up your mouth? Good, good; a little more, wide. Say 'Ahhh'."

Blood seeps between two yellowed teeth near the back right. The one farthest away nearly all cavity. "All right, close your mouth. Thanks." Straighten, hold back a groan.

"I think I can help," I say to Mrs. Canelo. "But I'm not a dentist. I don't know much about teeth."

"That's fine," she says. "You're still a doctor, no?"

"Kind of but not really," I say.

She shakes her head. "Doesn't matter. I've heard you help people; cure them. Much cheaper than the hospital."

"All right, if you're okay with it." I lean out the door, pointing over the porch's side. "There's a sidewalk over there. Just follow it around back. I'll meet you there."

"Okay, Doctor. Thank you."

Wish she wouldn't call me that but I say, "You're welcome," anyway.

She still holds her son by his shoulders, standing idly a few feet away from the greenhouse. Like she's afraid of it, or maybe he is. I would be too at that age. The giant opaque plastic walls strapped to curved metal rods, the smell of soil and manure, and other earthy aromas he can't place. A strange middle-aged man, not a dentist, who'll pry into his mouth like he's searching for something in a cabinet.

Terrifying.

"Just wait there," I say to them, passing by to the greenhouse. I unzip the arched door, slide in, seal it. Humidity immediately seeps through my clothes. Though I just left before dawn, everything's noticeably grown. Vines uncurl from soil heaped behind potted innards, climbing the support rods. Tiny white buds sprout from their underbelly, dangling like bells. Soon they'll ripen and help others.

Crouch in front of the pile of unused parts in the corner, rifle through wood and loam and broken bits. Typically they grow in wholes: hearts, lungs, eyes, fingers … But not teeth or nails or little things. The soil doesn't offer those for reasons beyond me.

"Ah." Hold up a small sliver of wood, still deep brown with etchings. "This could work." I reach for the nearby toolbox, pull it over and open it. Grab a carving knife. It won't be identical to the others, but it'll do.

"Now, just to let you know what's going to happen," I tell Mrs. Canelo outside. The sun's halfway in the sky. "I'm going to give your son a shot of a numbing agent on the inside of his cheek. Then after about ten minutes, I'll give another." She nods after each sentence, eyes attentive. I like people like her. Listeners. "After he won't feel any pain, then I'll remove the bad tooth with sterilized pliers." I lift the pair I'll use, sunlight glinting off stainless steel. Crude but they work. "Once removed, I'll place this"—I raise the wooden tooth—"into the empty spot. Then he'll be good as new."

"No pain?" she asks.

"No pain." I try to smile but it feels awkward, so I don't.

"When can we start?"

"Let me grab the medicine from inside, then we can begin."

She smiles, tears starting in her eyes. "Thank you, Doctor."

Pliers in boiling water, two syringes with donated Novocain on the table, and the book opened before me. Even after this long, I don't remember the exact tune. Each human piece has a different harmony. Flip until I find a small section with a faded, ink illustration of bared teeth.

I lift the tooth in cupped hands to my mouth, hum to it like whispering into a lover's ear. The melody is soft, light: whimsical. I start swaying in rhythm without noticing and finish the short song. I stare into my hands. Tiny emerald beads dimly glow within the wood's etchings.

Water streams over the pot, hissing on the stovetop. "Shoot!"

"Are you ready?" I ask the mother, who's holding down her son lying on the ground. Empty syringes on the laid-out towel. The pliers' handles dig into my washed hands, its teeth pinching the ruined tooth.

She nods.

Before the kid can say anything, I rip the tooth out and blood immediately pools into his mouth. "Turn his head," I say. She does and it trickles out onto the grass. I set the pliers down, pick up the wood tooth. "Now sit him up and lean his head back, quick." She does, and I gently set the tooth into his gums. Prod and push it until the emerald beads drain from the wood into him, vanishing as it reaches his gums. A moment, two, then the blood's gone, as though vacuumed by something under his tongue and the wood forms into a replica of his other teeth, though brown.

"Swallow, please."

He does and it's as though nothing has happened. "Can you run your tongue over where the tooth was?" He does. "Feel anything different?"

He shakes his head, smiles. "*Nada*," he says with a numb mouth.

I stand, lower back wailing, and wipe the sweat from my forehead. "Wonderful." Face his mother. "Your son's fine now, Mrs. Canelo."

She wraps her arms around her boy and cries. 'It's only a tooth,' I want to say, but don't.

"Is that all?" she asks, handing me a twenty-dollar bill.

I pocket it. "Yup, that's it."

"Are you sure? I can pay more." Her hand in her wallet, pinching another twenty.

"Positive, that's my normal rate." I lie. Don't have a rate, just charge whatever I think fits the work.

She puts her wallet back into her purse. "Thank you, Doctor. Really, thank you."

"No prob—" Before I finish, she reaches up and hugs me. "Uh …" I pat her back, look at the wall until she releases me.

After adjusting her blouse, she takes her son by his hand. "Have a good day, Doctor."

"You too," I say, closing the door.

The exhaustion of being awake before sunrise and the unexpected tooth removal weighs on me like lead. If I was doing this in my twenties, I'd be fine—energized from the procedure, running on an adrenaline high, excited for the next patient—but now, I sink into a kitchen chair, run my bloody hand through my thinning hair. "If only the earth could fix aging," I say for what feels like the thousandth time.

Randomly, I wonder how my son's doing. Michael would be in his twenties himself now. Does he have a wife? An accidental kid, like his father at that age? Maybe a boyfriend. I grin. "Be more like me than he knows." But then a subtle dread seeps into my gut.

No, I hope he's not like me, his life not a repeat of my own. The pain, hurt; the divorce, the loss of a family, the shame and guilt of what I only discovered …

Things are different now, but then … even workplaces vilified attractions. Kathy was hurt—I did that—but she took more than necessary, tearing away my career, my livelihood. No longer a planetologist, no longer welcome at the university, no longer anything but a person with nowhere to go.

"Okay," I say as though speaking to someone else. "No more of that, Nick." Shake my head, wipe my eyes. "Get out of your head." It's a little after twelve. "The next appointment's at three, so get up; get a shower, some food and, if possible, a nap."

Another mug of coffee sits by the one from this morning. Drowsiness still lingers as I stare into the steaming cup. "Should probably eat before they show up." But my legs still feel sleepy. Take a sip. Still too hot. Rub my eyes, blink away the grogginess, recall information about the upcoming appointment.

Timothy-something. Early twenties. Said something stupid to his girlfriend mid-oral, and she bit down, *hard.*

I wince just thinking about it.

She must've had sharp teeth for him to visit me. Must be without insurance, too. Take another drink. Cool enough. Caffeine slowly trickles into my veins.

I haven't seen it—yet—but I don't imagine a full replacement will be needed. A scab, maybe, or a coating should do …

"Wonder if he's still with her?"

The sky's awash in cotton candy pink, the clouds pumpkin orange. Timothy-something showed up an hour late, and now it's nearing six o'clock. Out back, I crouch before his unzipped jeans, the porch light throwing my shadow over his lower body.

"You still with her?" I ask, using a gloved hand to raise his member, the other holding a lit penlight. Peer at the underside of the scrotum.

"What?"

"The girlfriend—you two still together?" Gently lower it. The swelling isn't too bad, but bruises cover it like an overly ripe banana. Deep red teeth indents ring the flesh near the tip. Definitely not going to lose it.

"I—uh—yeah, we are."

I click off the light, straighten. "Why?" I don't care if it's awkward. He was late, after all.

"I love her."

I snap off the gloves, toss them in the bag on the grass. "How long have you been together?"

He takes a moment, then: "Fifty-six days."

I almost laugh but that'd be rude. "Uh huh." I sigh. "Well, here's the good news: it doesn't need replaced, but the bad news, if it happens again, it will." His blue eyes widen. Sometimes it's fun to lie. "So I'd think a lot about staying with this girl, if it's worth risking your manhood."

"So … for now, what can you do?"

"I'll coat it, let it marinate for twenty-four hours—no baths or showers or sex, no foreign liquids but your own should touch it. After that, it'll be good as new."

He adjusts his weight, his hands still holding his unzipped pants, his shriveled penis lying flat against them. "Will it hurt?"

"As long as you listen, it won't."

He nods. "Then let's do it."

"All right, be right back."

The cover on the twenty-gallon bucket in the greenhouse is peeled off. Sweet ripe odor erupts into my nostrils, cloying at the back of my throat. I cough, cover my mouth. Like smelling a hundred rotten oranges, burns like a mouthful of cinnamon. With two fingers, I scoop out some of the brown-green cream, quickly seal the bucket and leave the greenhouse. Breathe in the cool evening air deeply. Thankfully this stuff doesn't need to be hummed to. Just works on its own.

In my haste, I forgot to use gloves to remove the cream, so now I gingerly paste it over Timothy's member with bare fingers.

"Oh, it's cold."

I ignore him, covering down to his testicles, over the head, ensuring a circle of flesh is open for the urethra. Then I'm done and wipe my hands in the grass. Wait ... A peppering of dim green appears, dancing within the mixture, then dwindles as it sinks into him.

"Damn," he hisses. "It just got really warm all of the sudden."

"That's normal," I say, standing. "You can zip up now."

He does, then wipes his hands on his striped polo shirt. "So how much is this going to cost?"

"How much do you have?"

He's taken aback, but pulls out a battered wallet from his back pocket. Peels it open, counts bills. "A hundred and twenty. You don't take cards, right?"

"Right." The sky's darkened, night heavy over the neighborhood. Crickets chirp and fireflies appear and disappear over the grass. For a second, I picture us from the sky, two guys in a fenced in backyard in the dark after one has lathered the other's dick, his two fingers still oily. Sounds like a scene from a bad TV show. "So, I'll just take the one-twenty."

"Really, dude?"

I nod. "Really."

He hands me the bills like they're the last he'll ever have. "Thanks, though. A day, right? Then I should be good?"

"Yup," I say, pocketing the money, and realize I used my cream hand. Darn it. "Remember, no foreign liquids for twenty-four hours. Period. Got it?"

"Yeah," he says, and we fall into an awkward silence. "Well, I guess I'll see you later."

"Hope not, but have a good one."

He wishes me the same, and leaves around the house.

It's that in-between at night where I could go to sleep but it's too early to, as though there's an unspoken rule against being in bed before nine. After washing my hands several times, and the bills left on the counter to dry, I dump out the two cold mugs and let them sit in the sink.

Plod into the living room down the hall, switch on the lamp and drop into the threadbare recliner. Grab the TV remote.

Click.

News.

Infomercial.

Soap opera.

Another infomercial.

News.

Commercial, commercial, commercial.

Click.

Set down the remote. Sigh. I don't know why I bother turning it on—the eight free channels are always the same, no matter what time I check.

I settle into the cushions, close my eyes. An image forms of our old living room. Dull colored rope rug in the middle, a thrifted couch, the same chair I sit in now, and an old, giant tube TV we inherited from my parents. But we had cable and that's all that really mattered to Michael.

I smile, my body sinking to the brink of sleep.

No matter how late I stayed at the university on Fridays, I made sure to set an alarm for six the following day and wake up before him. Get the TV warmed up with Saturday morning cartoons, while I brewed coffee and made instant pancakes and scrambled eggs. We didn't have orange juice, but we had a few oranges, so a half of one apiece.

When he stumbled out from the hall in his faded pajamas, his thick brown hair askew, rubbing one eye while yawning, I'd greet him on the floor in front of the TV, a plate of food at the ready. He'd smile a smile that could melt ice, run and embrace me with his small arms. Then we'd eat as we watched his shows.

I gasp, open my teary eyes. Sit up.

"Gotta stop doing that." Elbows on knees, heels of hands in sockets. Groaning. "But what else am I supposed to do? Can't be bothered to read anymore. TV's a wash. No interest in new hobbies, constantly too tired to exercise, and too old to date." I debate with myself even though I already know the answer, the same cycle over and over again.

The greenhouse.

But I'm beyond exhausted, even for that. So screw the rules. I raise and trudge upstairs. Wash in the bathroom sink, undress to boxers, and go into the bedroom. Weave around the stacks of books, step over the ones bordering the mattress on the floor. Fall into the comforter and quilt, cocoon myself. Sleep comes quickly.

Knead the warm soil underneath the growing vines, their bells now blooming, white pedals streaked green. The purple hanging LED lights along the ceiling's middle give them a reflective sheen. Soon the bells will be ripe to pluck and plant. After the soil, I use a shovel to cycle the heap of dirt with leftover pieces until there's no more clumps. The pots are watered, nothing new has grown, though some buds with emerald saplings have broken the surface.

A muffled knock at the zipped door. Halt, stare, hold my breath. There's no appointments, I know for a fact. Never any before sunrise. And no one comes back here, ever. Why would they?

Another knock.

I go to the door, dirty fists to my side. "Who's there?"

"Wow—you still sound the same after all this time, Nick." A familiar, deep voice says. "Or are you going by Dr. Dawn now?"

It feels like a slap in the face to hear my maiden surname. I was one of the few men who preferred to take their wife's last name. No one knows it but … "Step back." I hear that he does, and I unzip the door and quickly sidestep out. Seal it and turn. Hold back a moan.

"Good morning, sunshine," says Benjamin Cherry, Head Faculty Advisor of CBU. The heavyset man who fired me years ago. Still wearing the same outfit: olive sweater vest with a khaki shirt underneath, and dark tan pants over worn loafers. His short hair has thinned but there's enough to cover his protruding forehead. His hands are in his pockets.

"Ben," I let out. "What're you doing here?" And how did you find me? And what the *hell* are you doing here?

"Heard through the grapevine you were a doctor now." He rocks on his heels. "And I'm in need of one."

"Why don't you go to a hospital?" I look at my feet. "CBU had good health coverage, if I remember right."

"Not there anymore," he says. "Got canned a few years after you were."

"Wow," I say. "Sorry that happened." Why do I apologize?

He nods. "No worries. They gave me enough severance to float on before I got hired by another school doing the same work."

I want to ask why he was fired—was it his bigotry under the guise of poor performance? Caught in a scandal? Sleep with students? Stealing money from the treasury? But I want him to go away more than appease my curiosity, so I say: "Well that's good. Doesn't this place have insurance, too?"

"Yeah, but not good enough to cover what I need done."

"And what's that?"

He takes his hand out, pokes his chest. "Need a new ticker."

"A whole new one, or just fixed?"

He kicks dirt, slides his hand back into his pants. "Well the doc I visited a few years ago said if I kept eating the way I like, I'll need surgery. As you can see, I haven't listened."

"Can't you ... I don't know, eat better and exercise?"

"Too late for that now." He shakes his head. "But, getting back on track, Nick. Instead of getting it cleaned, I'd rather start anew. Like you did, right? And I heard you were able to replace organs."

I grit my teeth behind closed lips. I didn't *start anew*; I was thrown to the wolves and fought my way out, because of you, Ben. It was only luck I found these damn books in the first place, only really dumb luck I was able to understand them, find somewhere with land that would listen to the weird songs and bend to the melodies. Our situations are not the damn same. You're a stubborn fat man who couldn't put down a burger; I'm a gay man who was outed by a lying ex-wife who stole everything and a faculty who believed her.

All this roars in my head, but, "It's not cheap," comes out.

He chuckles. "Always a funny one, a comic. It has to be a helluva lot cheaper than the hospital, right?"

"Right."

"So how much we talking here?"

"It's based on the work and process, but somewhere in the range of six grand. Could be more or less, but probably more."

"I can manage that." He puts out his hand. I take it, skin revolting, and shake. "So," he says, "when can you start?"

Two days, I said. Two days of only low-fat foods and water. Nothing else. No strenuous activity either. I wanted him only eating Jell-O and watching TV. He agreed and left.

Sitting in the kitchen awash in burning morning glory, fresh coffee held in dirty hands, I stare into nothingness. Still can't believe he found me after so many years ... I wonder if the other faculty know of my work and I worry that helping Ben will only result in more of those who snickered and leered and didn't raise a voice to help me keep my job will show up on my porch soon ...

Does Kathy know too?

Michael?

My breath hitches, chest shutters. My nose tingles with numbness, fingers cold despite the warm porcelain mug. I have no idea how I'd react if either of them were at my door. Twenty years changes people; I'm no longer the father he once knew, the husband she didn't accept ...

"Why'd I even agree to help Ben?" I curse. "Him of all people?"

Money.

Always comes down to money, one way or another. Something I hardly valued when I was receiving it regularly, now something I need to get meagerly by and do what I know. Without it, I'd be left applying to entry level jobs at supermarkets and groceries, retail stores and other places an almost fifty-year-old man shouldn't be doing.

"But I shouldn't be doing this either," I say, so what do I know?

Then, the ultimate question appears from the roving sea of thoughts: When Ben's under, will I save him? Will I be able to? The man who cast me into homelessness under my hands, will I still want to save him when his death is only a misspoken melody away? His life in my total control ... I could leave him under forever, lost in the gauzy limbo of the roots; could do a lot of things to him, unconscious ...

"No."

I'm not a killer, no matter how much rage boils in my gut. And what would happen if I abused the soil and melodies? They're sentient in some way, so God only knows if they could turn on me or stop listening altogether ...

Sip the coffee, exhale as the heat warms my chest. It's almost eight, and I have an appointment at eleven.

"May as well get ready." I go to the sink to wash away the dirt and Ben's handshake.

We stand out back. Zayne's hands shoved in tight, faded jeans, his wrinkled long sleeve covering pale skin. He still hasn't told me exactly what his problem is. "So do you have any pills I could take?"

"For what? Pain?"

He shakes his head, his brown hair falling from behind his ear. "More like for numbing. Like, so I can't *feel* anything."

I shift my weight, feel suddenly uncomfortable. "I don't give anything out without a reason. My work can be ... addictive."

He stands on tiptoes, peering over my shoulder. "Is it in there? The stuff?"

I step into his line of sight. "No one's allowed in there." This is annoying. "And if you don't have any ailments, then I'm going to have to ask you to leave. I'm not a pharmacy."

He removes his hand and places it flat on my chest. I recoil at first but stop. An unfamiliar current radiates through my shirt. A yearning I haven't felt in years. Is he ...? I meet his gaze. Seemingly he reads my mind and nods. "It's not for an ailment, per se," he says, "but in my line of work, it's good to have something to numb the world, you know?"

Tongue stuck to the roof of my dry mouth. I lick my lips. "Ah—what kind of work are you in?" His hand remains on my chest, fingers splayed. It's been so long since I've been touched, and I can't stop my groin swelling. I keep my clammy hands at my sides.

"You'll find out"—he grins, revealing perfect teeth—"if you agree to help."

"I can't—" His hand lowers, pressing against my sternum. "I can't," I repeat. "Just give it out, I mean. There, there has to be a reason."

"Can boredom be a reason?" His hand lowers, stopping above the navel. "Or just wanting to be away from my own body for an hour or so, when clients are there? Or, I don't know, just not wanting to feel anything at all, a break from everything?"

"Sounds like you need therapy more than what I have," I blurt.

His hand at my waist, two fingers hooking slacks. "I've met enough therapists to know that they're more fucked than I am." His second hand joins the other. "So, Doctor, do we have a trade? Your services for mine?"

I should shake my head. I should remove his hands. I should tell him I'm too old for him. Too inexperienced. I should tell him to leave and so many more things but my head goes up and down.

Hands under shirts, undoing pants, kicking boxers away as cold skin meets warm flesh. Books heeled aside, tumbling. Comforter and quilt chucked over shoulder, the back of his head shoved into the pillow. Throbbing pleasure. Churning stomach. Aching temples.

It's more than my lips on his body, his on mine, my stroking hands, his tight grip. I want to be within him on some plane of existence, our insatiable bodies intertwining as though we're two pieces seamlessly melding together. I want our physicality to be one; him and I into us.

Sweat covers us, heat fills the room. Then he's on his belly, his face in the blankets, his hips arched, his muffled words: "*Please*," sends my consciousness wavering as my desires are fulfilled; with the help of the lube he had in his back pocket and a careful thrust, we are finally one.

Awaking, the quiet's palpable. No wind or cars or birds outside, nothing running in the house. Blink the haziness away as I stare at the popcorn ceiling. Zayne's like a dream I can hardly remember, only flashes of imagery of skin and remembrances of lustful heat and utter pleasure reaching a shuttering precipice I haven't reached in what feels like ages … Realize he's not in bed.

"Zayne?" I call, sitting up. "Zayne?"

Books still knocked over, only my clothes covering some, blankets in a ball below the warped window frame. The door's open. I jump out of bed and grab my clothes from the floor.

"Zayne, you here?"

A stop at the bathroom. The medicine cabinet's open and bottles are toppled over, others spilled open in the yellowed sink. Cabinet underneath is also open: towels, soap, and toilet rolls strewn about.

In the kitchen, the same. Every drawer and cabinet wide open. I don't know what he was looking for here. Silverware, chipped mugs, coffee tins, and boxed food helter-skelter. Open the fridge, things touched there too. "Jesus…" Then it dawns on me: "*No*."

Door agape, revealing what I've kept secret for so long. Inside it's cold, the heat from the lamps escaped. I quickly zip it shut, crank the thermostat up. They must be kept warm. Although it's subtle, I know Zayne has rummaged through things. Oily fingerprints on the pots, divots in the soil heap, the lid on the cream bucket halfway off, blossoming bells ever-so-slightly bent. I grab a shovel, turn the soil, check the pots, delicately adjust the bells. Create homeostasis again, cursing.

Why the hell did I do that?

Why did I let my emotions get the better of me?

He was an escort, a prostitute—I knew that without him saying it, but I still let him pull me in.

"It's not all his fault; you wanted it too," I remind myself, kneading soil. I don't even know what he expected to find in the greenhouse. No one understands this. To anyone it's just dirt and plants, not pills or anesthesia or medical cream or anything similar to modern medicine. And even if they *did* know what the ground could do, they couldn't hum it to life, lilt it to their will.

Everything gradually returns to normal. The heat's back, so I decrease the temperature.

"Okay," breathing heavy, wiping sweat from my brow. "Okay." Run my palms on the back of my jeans—

"Wait."

Check the pockets, find them empty.

He stole my wallet ... All the money I've earned the past few weeks. I hadn't stored it yet in the lockbox. Tears form. The familiar cold of betrayal washes over me. Living pay to pay for months, the little jobs only covering a bill or two, groceries and coffee; big jobs hardly come by ...

Was it worth it? Rings in my mind. Was it worth it to feel loved again?

"No," I whisper, dropping to my knees.

It never is.

"Nick?" Ben says into the phone. "How'd you get my number?"

"The phone book," I say, standing in the kitchen. The phone's awkward in my hand, it's been a while since I've called someone. Evening fuchsia seeps in through the window. "Have you been following the plan?"

"Yes, been doing nothing but watching TV and eating gelatin."

Close my eyes, do mind math. Forty-eight hours is just a precaution, but the procedure can be done under twenty hours, if I'm very, very aware. I need the money, rent and late utilities due soon, so I will be. "Do you want to start now?"

I hear his chair creak. "Like the surgery?"

"Yeah, we can start in an hour."

"Absolutely—let's get the ball going. I'll be over soon."

"Great, see you then."

The Horror That Represents You

Shirtless, Ben lies on a metal table in the basement. The overheads make his pale flesh blindingly white. Gray hair peppers his shallow chest, trails over his bulging gut. A paper gown donated by a nurse sometime ago covers his bottom half. A space heater blasts in the corner.

"You okay?" I ask, sliding a false IV connected to an empty bag into his arm. He hisses as I tape it down.

"Not the Ritz," he says, chuckling.

Roll over the anesthesia tank with a mouthpiece. "Now," I say, leaning over him. "I want you to breathe in deep when I put this on. Count backwards from ten. Once under, you'll feel no pain whatsoever, probably not any once you're awake either."

"What if any problems occur?"

"If for whatever reason I can't complete the replacement, I'll wake you up and you'll only be charged for what work I did."

"Wow." He grins. "That's nice of you. The hospitals don't even do that."

"Yup." I put the piece to his mouth. "Deep breaths, count back from ten."

"Ten," voice muffled.

I slightly turn the tank knob.

"Nine. Eight. Seven…"

His eyes close and I quickly twist the knob back, removing the mouthpiece. I'm not an anesthesiologist either; only got the stuff because I had a patient who knew a guy who knew a guy, but it's apparent a little goes a long way.

I remove the IV, roll everything away, and slide open the giant metal door in the far wall. Everything in the basement is for show. Makes patients comfortable with familiar routines and scenery. The real work begins when they're under the greenhouse.

Ben rolled into the cavern, flabby arms splayed over the sides. I take dangling roots and wrap them around his wrists, take smaller ones and hook them in his mouth and nostrils. A larger one with a puckered, ridged end, like a squid's sucker, is placed to his forehead.

I hum soft, fluting melodies into each and peridot beads awaken and stream into him. The puckered end flattens over his skin, and dim illuminance cascades downwards, disappearing within him.

Now that he's truly unconscious, I grab the mason jar in the corner. Unscrew the lid and shake out about ten wooden pieces. Toss the jar back into the dirt. Each piece is different—a sliver here, a knobby one there—but each is perfect for the work.

Setting them in a pile in between his breasts, I cover them with both hands, leaving an opening on top, and hum strongly, deeply, like a Gregorian chant that vibrates my throat and chest. When I finish, the wood chips are gone, leaving behind tiny scars.

I bring the stool over from by the door, sit, and watch. I have no idea what happens once they're inside. I've only done organ replacements a handful of times. I imagine the wood melts into a form that can pass through muscle and bone, slipping between veins, and find the heart. Coats it in a green-speckled brown substance, a form neither liquid nor solid, an in-between the wood and melody create. Oozes into the muscle, working from the inside out. Molding new ventricles and arteries and veins, replacing the old with the even older. Once done and Ben's heart fills with the new, it ... consumes it.

I've never seen it but that must be what happens, for the old heart never leaves the body. It doesn't pass in stool or vomit; the patient doesn't sweat blood nor does their skin get a meaty, red sheen. It's absorbed as it grows and soon it's gone, leaving the better, wooden one.

After an hour, it's time to wake him. I hum the melody backwards to the roots and slowly uncurl them from his wrists, remove them from nose and mouth, gently pull it from his forehead. His arms flop and dangle, mouth still agape, eyes closed. I put my ear to his chest, strain to hear ...

Nothing.

"What?"

I crane my neck, clean my ear with a finger, put it back to his skin. Close eyes, palm the other ear ...

I only hear the blood pounding in my head.

Instantly, I'm sweating. I cover the scars with my hands and hum deeply, profusely, pushing every ounce of hot air out from my lungs and into the wood. My throat becomes raw, mouth dry. Lick my lips, continue. I'm tempted to stop and do CPR but I know it doesn't work, air's useless with the wood. Hum deeper, stronger, louder; make the melody faster but his heart remains unmoving and I begin screaming into my hands, the cavern, myself, the world because this is my fault!

I push off the table, digging nails into palms, yelling, crying.

This is my fault.

I throw the stool, smash the mason jar and stomp on the wood; tear the roots from soil and stretch them apart, leaving them like severed limbs on the floor.

This is my fault.

Heel them into the dirt, grind them into dust and punch the wall again and again until knuckles bleed and I kick until my toes sing.

This is my fault.

The screaming must've stopped because I don't hear it anymore but I'm still brimming with rage and betrayal, bursting with hate and guilt and shame and I try to scream but my esophagus's sandpaper and only a faint whisper whistles out from bloody lips.

I did this. I killed him. I let the soil be tainted.

My knees collapse under me and I smack my head against the wall and collapse to the floor. I can still cry, still sob, still pull my legs to my chest and wrap my arms around my knees and wail into dirty jeans.

Again, I've betrayed the ones I love.

I'm the problem once more, or always have been.

"No," I say like a child to his tirading father. "No, it was a *mistake.*"

Is it still a mistake knowing everything prior? The ground soiled by another; the timing in the red, not even close to forty-eight hours. It can't be. I did this. I did everything I wasn't supposed to let happen.

Squeeze my eyes tight, attempt to force myself unconscious to provide some sort of fucking relief from this agony but it doesn't come. A numbing, high-strung emptiness does instead, flooding over me. There's no escape. No pushing it aside, starting anew. Before I was cast out, but now there's nowhere to go, nowhere to hide. Ben can't fire me now and Kathy can't divorce me again and Michael can't know his father any less than he does already.

Like a broken record, *this is my fault* repeats in my head.

Like waking from a nightmare, I realize I'm in the kitchen, at the table, holding a mug of coffee. Couldn't have been a dream, for I'm caked in dirt and ash. The cup trembles violently in my grasp, so I let it go like it burns me. I try to recall how I got here but can't, all I can remember is Ben, downstairs, dead on the table.

Wipe away fresh tears, mumble: "What am I going to do?"

Because it's more than Ben, it's the soil, too. The wood, the vines, the flowers: my life's work ruined. I know it can't be used. It doesn't listen anymore, or has turned against me for a time. Maybe in the future, the sin will erode and the dirt can be purified and the melodies will be heeded, but for right now … "I have to stop."

No more patients, no more appointments, no more income.

"But the body," I say huskily.

The grim answer's obvious: give him to the earth. Maybe it'll forgive me with the offering.

I scald my tongue gulping my drink but feeling anything is welcome, because not only have I killed an innocent person, I'm also now hiding his body. A murderer and a fugitive. A low I never imagined I could reach, but here we are …

Standing, I finish the coffee, searing my throat.

No more waiting.

Rot reeks in the cavern below the greenhouse. Yellow-green sludge oozes from broken pustules between his breasts, chips of wood poking out. Brown lines run parallel to engorged blue veins under ghostly flesh. I have to cover my mouth as I push the table aside, keep it covered while I manage with one hand to shovel, digging away ground enough to fit him.

Body odor and decay intertwines and I taste rancidity like a fuzzy layer on my tongue. It rakes my mouth, my nose. I feel on my skin, my hair. Even my insides feel as though they're reeling. But I don't leave, I don't complain; I did this, I deserve it.

The grave looks wide enough. I toss the shovel aside, and push the table to the hole's edge. On the opposite side, tipping it little by little until Ben slides off and drops below the earth. Set the table down and walk around Ben's final resting place.

He fits almost perfectly, a bent arm reaching out. I toe it back in, then bury him. When it's filled, I pad it, smoothing it out, and stand over it. The cavern now a catacomb.

"I'm sorry," I say, because what else am I supposed to say? "You didn't deserve this …"

And I leave it at that.

No patients, no money. Can't get unemployment if I'm not on the books somewhere, and I'm not disabled … So before the landlord comes and the bill collectors call, I pack what books I can, a trash bag full of clothes, and whatever else I think I might want to keep.

Inside the greenhouse, my worries are confirmed. The soil's fetid, turning sooty gray, becoming dense dust. Vines are black-purple, wounds replace bells, trickling bruised sludge. Frayed white petals and buds lie on the ground and disintegrate when touched, caking skin. Opening the bucket is like opening a sewage tank and I quickly seal it again before the odor reaches my stomach. I scan the pots, dirt all dry and hard, saplings dark green viscous fluid; except for one, the sapling still lively enough to give a pinprick of hope. I take it with me.

Without a car, I carry everything to the bus stop at the corner, pot wrapped in my arm. Catch it when it comes, and drop what last change I have into the metal box. Drag my belongings to the back where I sink into a hard-cushioned seat.

Gabled houses blur past under a slate overcast. I have no idea where I'm going or what I'll do when I get there, but I need to get away before people come asking questions about the late bills, rent; searching for Ben or me; the sick wanting to be cured.

Maybe somewhere in the country, I'll go. A cabin bordering wilderness, where I can wait and hum into the potted soil, praying day-by-day that it'll grow. Someplace where no one will find me. Go by a different name when I have to go into town for supplies. Dye my hair, shave; lose weight, lie about my age.

Be someone else, someone new, entirely—what I have truly ever wanted since losing my family.

Just Lucky

by Patricia Miller

"Mr. Angelico, two weeks. That's all I'm asking." Robert Penniman was pleading now, near tears.

"I'm sorry, Penniman, but it's in the hands of a private collector." Samuel Angelico wasn't the slightest bit sorry. He did wonder how Penniman had made it past security, but no matter. If the young artist wanted to have it out in public, Samuel was happy to accommodate him.

"Then give me *their* contact information. Let me speak with them. You said yourself it was the best work I've ever done. The show will be nothing without it."

"A *private collector*. Had they wished to be identified, I would have said so." He held up a hand. "And before you ask, no, I will not call them on your behalf."

"Mr. Angelico, please, I'm begging here. I've worked all my life for this. You have no idea how much this show means to me."

"And yet, I am unmoved." Samuel knew exactly how much it meant and didn't care. As much as he loved art, he loathed artists even more, a fact clearly evident to Penniman and several guests curious enough about the heated exchange to hover nearby. He loved winning in front of an audience, particularly when the other side lost *so* much and *so* badly. He would never understand how anyone could create such brilliance with an ego brittle enough to fracture after a minor setback.

And Robert Penniman *was* fractured—weeks of letters, phone calls, emails, and finally in-person groveling had amounted to nothing. Everyone who was anyone in the art world had just witnessed his humiliation at the hands of Samuel Angelico. His show would still go forward, but the reviews would be full of speculation about what might have been, missed opportunities, and unrealized potential.

Samuel allowed himself a brief but satisfied grin. The painting in question was hanging on a stark white wall behind a pair of secure doors leading to his private home collection, not fifty feet from where he had been confronted by its creator. It truly *was* the best thing Penniman had ever done or ever *would* do. Samuel did have a way of drying up whatever muse an artist followed, and if they never again reached the pinnacle of their profession because their best was in private hands, it was less than nothing to him.

Nor was Samuel bothered by Robert Penniman's opinions on his parentage, education, or business acumen, words that trailed behind the artist as he was escorted from the party by security. Samuel knew his own deliberately cultivated reputation, knew he was wanted by some, envied by more, and hated by most, usually in that order of one's acquaintance with him.

He looked around his crowded great room. People mingled, danced to a live jazz ensemble, gazed in awe through the broad expanse of windows at the turbulent sea below. Samuel wandered from one group to another, stirred up conversations, encouraged them to stroll among the pedestals, niches, and artwork on display. Everything they saw was for sale—at a price.

Samuel's current lover echoed Penniman's sentiments the next afternoon, after yet another postponed rendezvous. Emma had previously found him compelling despite the gossip about past lovers' breakdowns and psychiatric care. He had wooed her, concentrated his considerable energy on her, showered her with gifts and the undivided attention of a man besotted. She soon discovered that attention vanished once she said yes. Like the long string of beautiful men and women who preceded her, who wanted him and hated him in turn, she had reached her limit.

"This is unacceptable, Samuel. I heard the rumors, but I dismissed them. After all, *some* people are fragile. *Some* people are ill-equipped to handle your kind of intensity. I thought they were jealous of your success and envious that I had you. But I don't have you! I don't have a life, and I don't have a future here. You can't treat people this way!"

"I treat people as I find them, Emma. I was quite up front with you about my schedule. Things happen." He *had* wanted her, but now Samuel only wanted to leave.

She bored him. So many people did. He cut schoolmates, casual friends, mentors, his parents, and sister out of his life because they'd grown tedious with nothing else to offer but shared experiences or DNA. And now here was poor Emma, who'd been so charming, grown as boring as the rest.

"You have no feelings. None. I don't know how you can go through life without having a genuine emotion once in a while."

"Just lucky, I guess." He didn't even notice her front door slamming shut behind him.

As with Penniman's begging, her tears didn't move him. Few things could. Great art though—at least the acquisition of great art—moved him like nothing else. He'd made a small fortune in Silicon Valley and saw it grow because he was lucky enough to be on the right side of the real estate bubble and smart investments.

Samuel was usually the first of the crowd to discover hidden gems among hundreds of restaurants, musicians, and authors. His real gift though was uncovering the next great artist. He could sniff out talent before the paint was dry, and by the time anyone else recognized their genius, he'd already cornered the market on their finest work. The echo of Emma's slamming door barely faded before he turned his attention to the next genius on his list.

Lilith Chambley was an artist up the coast. Samuel had run into her some months before at an architectural salvage yard and they'd struck up a conversation while he was collecting a few marble pedestals the yard's operator had located for him. Lilith, meanwhile, was waiting for her car to be loaded with boxes of decorative fittings, Victorian gingerbread, scrap metal, and several lengths of scarred molding. That she was an artist was immediately apparent. That she had no interest in sharing her work with him was also apparent.

"I don't sell anything local. I like to keep my work at a distance," she said. "Besides, I like the travel involved with the craft fair circuit."

She had no social media, no website, no email, not even a business card. It was pure luck he'd found her, but luck was his stock-in-trade after all, and she finally showed him pictures of her work. Lilith's fabrications were as odd as they were riveting and had depth and complexity he'd never seen before.

"I can understand that completely. You don't want the people you see every day to get that close to it, particularly when your work is really a reflection of your soul." Samuel laid on the sincerity with a deft hand.

Lilith was wary, reluctant even to take his card. She did agree to call him for coffee next time she was in town. After four months of irregular conversations over scones and strong black coffee, she finally allowed him to visit her studio.

It was a long two hours inland from the coast. Seeing the modest cottage, surrounded by patchy woods and pastures, he doubted the neighborhood even knew her studio existed.

"I keep myself to myself," she replied when he pointed out how isolated things were. "I find the quiet restful."

The studio was a barn at the back of the property. An older RV was parked next to it—for her road trips, she said. The barn's large sliding door had a standard-sized entrance framed inside it, but she slid the larger door open anyway.

"I need the ventilation." Lilith flicked her hand across some switches, turning on the large LED shop lights which ran in several rows along the high ceiling.

"I *am* impressed. What a remarkable space." Samuel didn't need to fake his amazement. He wasn't expecting to find a well-organized barn considering she worked with other people's castoffs. The mismatched shelves and racks lining the walls were stocked with the oddest collection of textiles, scrap metal and glass, old toys, appliances, computer components.

Several completed pieces were suspended from the ceiling with old coax cable. Woodworking tools shared space with sewing machines, a metal lathe, 3D printer, and welding station. A long table held a work in progress—a pretty large one if the frame was any indication. He wanted it, before he even knew what it was.

So, the wooing of Lilith Chambley began in earnest over the course of a summer, not with gifts of fine chocolate or wine but with phrases like 'no catalog,' 'no publicity photos,' 'private collections,' 'overseas markets,' and those words strung together were more effective than roses ever could be. Progress was slow, requiring almost more patience than he had, but he wasn't willing to give up—not this late in the game.

She did not invite him to the studio often, nor would she accept an invitation to his home for a party. She didn't like modern architecture, said it was soulless. His own home was one of those soulless moderns, perched high on a cliff. It was unique, the last residential design by an architect who now focused solely on corporate offices and towers. Artists were not the only people who lost their muses after dealing with Samuel.

He didn't care much about the house per se, only what it contained, well hidden behind those security doors. His private gallery had been designed to his specific needs and featured long gently curved walls for paintings and 3D objects, niches for smaller sculptures, soaring ceilings with cross beams perfect for hanging mobiles and art glass which caught the sun.

Huge banks of UV-treated windows stretched up the walls and over the ceiling, flooding the space with natural sunlight during the day. Unobtrusive overhead fixtures held back the evening darkness. Hidden inside the white walls were air filters, climate controls, and security systems to rival the Louvre. The house was perfect for him, and even if Lilith considered it soulless, Samuel didn't think it needed one.

But Lilith resisted still. "It isn't a question of exposure—I don't *want* my name out there."

"I won't *put* it out there." Samuel gestured to the piece she had named *Time's Eventide*. The piece which had caught his eye on the first studio was now complete, resting against the back wall. "This is for my personal collection. No one else will ever see it."

"And I can't just sell you *Time's Eventide*. It's part of a triptych. What would I do with the other two?"

"I'll buy all three. You've said you wanted to go overseas to the Far East, Morocco, and Africa. What I'll pay you for these would easily cover an extended stay and leave you with more than enough to meet your expenses when you return."

Lilith let out a long exhale. Her resolve began to waiver, her back to bend ever so slightly. After four months of careful, painstaking courtship, she finally said yes to the sale of all three works. He handed over a check, and she helped him load the first two pieces into the back of his Land Rover. *Eventide* was much larger in scale, almost massive, and would require special handling—he'd arrange for a truck to get it to the house.

"I can deliver it and make certain it doesn't need repairs once it arrives," she said.

Samuel didn't know if she was genuinely concerned for its wellbeing, or if she was having second thoughts about parting with it. It made no difference. Samuel didn't need her help, didn't need *her* any longer, and preferred to make his own arrangements.

He was laughing by the time he reached the end of her driveway. He now had three pieces instead of the one he'd hoped for, and the sale of the other two would easily defray the cost of the third. He wasn't interested in a set, didn't care that it was being sold as one, and had already identified two clients who would snap them up at ten times the price he'd paid.

The companion pieces were relatively small, each needing no more than four-foot square of wall space. The first piece, *Time's Dawn,* integrated shards of glass, mirrors and what appeared to be the tumbled bits of a junk drawer into a brightly painted and glazed whirlwind of wire, homespun yarn, scrap copper sheeting, and a disassembled CRT screen. They swirled together in colors sailors would be wary of—brilliant yellows, oranges, and scarlets. The second, the ridiculously titled *Time's Journey*, featured earth-toned scraps from shipping pallets, old maps in blues and greens, guidebooks, stones, and glass fishing weights.

In the week between purchase and delivery of *Eventide*, Samuel sold and delivered the smaller works. The client originally earmarked for *Time's Journey* turned it down, saying they found it disturbing. No matter. He quickly located another client eager to grab it at all costs.

With that task out of the way, he focused on identifying the proper placement of Lilith's masterwork. Trailed by filtered sun, he walked along the curved walls of his inner sanctum to the perfect spot where *Eventide* could lean against the smooth plaster. That section had been left empty, held vacant for just such a monumental piece. Possibly the work might need to be moved after he lived with it for a while, but once positioned, it was rare for any part of his collection to be unsuited for its place among its brethren.

Eventide arrived on a Thursday, crated and tarped against the coastal weather, resting in a canvas cradle to prevent any jostling along the road. Lilith made a good job of the crate, sturdy yet easily opened with a clever arrangement of temporary wheels, handles and strapping. Shifting the contents to its proper position went smoothly. Samuel removed the disassembled crate, stopped by the kitchen for a brandy, and returned to admire his new acquisition.

Those moments, spent communing with art that existed for his pleasure alone, were the only times Samuel felt anything akin to human emotion. He loved knowing only he would ever see the contents of this space. And the new creation before him elicited a visceral response which left him near breathless.

He tried to write a description to fit it—everything in his collection had an entry in his mental catalog—but how to describe something so imposing, so glorious? On paper, it was simply an assemblage of carved wood, framed by miscellaneous pieces of molding studded with glass, braided metal, and polished stones. Twisted strands of brightly colored beaded silk, shaded from pale violet to deepest amaranthine, draped across and around the Victorian fretwork, masking the edges of a rusted sheet of tin. Enameled metal was layered over crimson-tinted glass, hand dyed fabric swirled with midnight blues, and parchment decorated with gold symbols. Hinges, bolts, hasps, dials, knobs, and other hardware were mounted at odd angles. Some were polished, others painted, scuffed, rusted, glazed, studded with tiny crystals.

Samuel positioned himself in front of it, silent and still. The sun overhead bounced off it at irregular angles and cast odd arcs of light and shadow throughout the space. He considered himself lucky to have obtained it so easily. Here was a work that he could study for the rest of his life and never see all it had to offer. He gave one last thought to Lilith, for he knew she would never again capture the magic contained in the bits of wood and glass before him.

Two weeks after he accepted delivery of *Time's Eventide*, Mr. Calloway phoned, wanting to return *Time's Dawn*. He and his wife found it unsettling.

"It doesn't go with the rest of my collection." The stress in Calloway's voice was evident, even to Samuel.

"I don't take returns, Calloway."

"I know. Would you consider a trade?" Samuel did not accept 'buyer's remorse' as a general rule, but Calloway was a frequent client and willing to swap it for a painting that wasn't nearly as valuable. The transaction was settled to the satisfaction of both parties. Samuel decided to display *Dawn* at his next event.

Samuel's great room was cleverly laid out with a wraparound second floor promenade overlooking the room below. The larger space had alcoves and conversation areas divided by panels which swiveled and slid in various configurations. He moved a panel here, re-positioned a statue there, and hung *Dawn* at the end of a long wall where it caught reflections off a nearby antique mirror. He increased its price by five percent.

Dawn attracted a lot of attention, but no buyers. It took two such events before Samuel noticed people avoided that part of the room altogether. He gave it some thought, turned a different set of panels, created a more intimate space and watched closely. The same response. People would step inside, then just as quickly step back out again.

This was a puzzle—Samuel never had anything generate that kind of reaction before, and it was particularly concerning when he received a phone call from Ms. Pasco seeking to return *Time's Journey*.

"I'm sorry, Samuel, but something doesn't track with this thing." Val Pasco liked being thought of as cutting edge, more modern than mod.

"That is unfortunate, Val. I can't just refund your money, of course. Artists must be paid. Would you consider choosing another piece more to your liking?"

Samuel prided himself on his eye for art. *Journey* was spectacular by any standard, but he accepted its return with the same arrangement he'd made with Mr. Calloway. He did something he'd never done before—he hung both pieces side by side and marked them *Not For Sale*. It was an old trick but identifying objects as unobtainable would often drive people to obtain them at any costs.

They didn't sell. He was honestly insulted after all the fuss and bother of pandering to clients too blind to recognize genius laid out before them. Both pieces were removed to his study by Saturday. Perhaps he needed to rethink his strategy.

Samuel resumed much of his normal routine the following Monday, mingling with the same crowd, dining at the same restaurants, going to the same gallery openings. Other clients and other art flowed in and out of his hands. Sales were brisk as summer faded into fall, and the year was shaping up to be his most profitable.

Samuel spent many long evenings in his private gallery, contemplating *Time's Eventide*. He usually renamed all his pieces, but this work proved as elusive to name as it was to describe. He decided to hang *Dawn* and *Journey* on either side.

Once that was done, he recognized the mistake he'd been making. These were not individual pieces, but truly were a single work just as Lilith described: a triptych now made whole. Time and light flowed between them, caused mirrored reflections to weave through and around the trio. No wonder he couldn't sell the individual pieces, for no single one of them was complete without the other two.

He was tempted, just for a moment, to revisit Lilith and purchase more of her brilliance. It was such a startling variation in his usual habits that he talked himself out of it immediately. She would never be able to capture lightning in a bottle a second time. He was therefore surprised to find himself on the road up the coast on Thursday, when he had been scheduled to meet a client for lunch at a restaurant an hour's drive in the other direction. He called to say he'd be unable to attend, then negotiated the twisting country roads to the outskirts of the small town where she'd made her home.

The front door was locked against intruders, curtains and shades drawn tightly in their frames. He walked around the back of the cottage to the studio. The large door was held fast. He could see through the windows of the small door cut into it, but the darkness beyond told him nothing. Samuel retrieved a flashlight from his car and cast a beam through one of the bottom panes. He could make out shelves full of scraps and bins filled with the same tucked under the long workbench. The top of the bench was empty—all her tools, all the work in progress was gone. There were no signs of a hasty departure. No signs of her RV either, so she was probably traveling along the fall craft fair circuit. He made a mental note to check in before the holidays and returned home.

On Friday, Samuel called off a dinner engagement with a prospective lover who could no longer hold his attention. A week after that, he bailed out on a show opening, then a play. In the evenings before he retired, and in the morning before he went about his business for the day, Samuel would stand in front of the triptych, lost again in *Time*. It filled his waking thoughts; became an obsession he could not shake.

This was new for Samuel. He loved to win an object others coveted. He loved making other people lose. He rarely loved the object itself. But *Time*—no one else knew. He couldn't revel in his victory without some kind of acknowledgment, and yet the thought of displaying the masterpiece for all to see was unbearable to him. That left just one person in the world who would understand—Lilith, the reluctant artist, the cause of his disquiet.

He made another unscheduled trip to her studio. There was no sign she'd been back since his previous visit. He asked at the local diner and as he suspected, none of them realized the person living there had even *been* an artist. The only way they'd known the house was occupied was the occasional appearance of woodsmoke from the chimney. No one could put a date on the last time they'd noticed any.

He hired a private detective to find her and waited impatiently for any news. The detective had more in common with an accountant than Sherlock Holmes, but he'd come highly recommended. Samuel had few details to provide. He didn't even have a phone number—she'd called him, and her number showed up on his phone as unavailable.

"Mr. Angelico? It's James Fraser."

"Fraser, where is she?" Samuel could not hide his impatience.

"I have no idea. As far as I can tell, she doesn't exist, has never existed."

"What the hell does that mean?"

"I mean there is no record of anyone named Lilith Chambley in that age range in this state or anywhere else. No driver's license, no voting record, no utility bills, no banking information. The check you wrote her was cashed at your bank—"

"I know. They called me the day she took it in." Samuel didn't think it odd she wanted cash. He used cash for a significant percentage of his transactions. Some artists didn't want a paper trail, and many of his clients found such documentation—inconvenient.

"But she didn't deposit the money anywhere either, Mr. Angelico."

"She must have presented an ID."

"A passport, but my sources tell me there isn't one issued to anyone with that name matching her approximate age or description."

"People don't just vanish, Fraser. What if she left the country?"

"No record on any outbound international flights. I did find her RV—it was a rental under the same name with the same passport used as ID."

"Surely they would have required a driver's license and a credit card."

"No, it's one of those vacation rental things. She paid cash up front along with a significant cash deposit which she did not get back, by the way. The owners found it parked in their driveway with the keys on the seat and a note to keep the money. The rental dates match the times you said you'd been at her studio."

But—but the rental property ..."

"Cash again. The cottage and land are in probate, and the executor was happy to have someone at the place for a couple months."

"The delivery company—what did they say?"

"Nothing. They don't exist either. As a scam, this one was brilliantly executed. I'm sorry, Mr. Angelico, but you're out of luck." The detective was calm, probably used to delivering this kind of news.

Had Samuel actually been fooled by her? He reviewed every interaction with Lilith Chambley. He had watched her work, saw her hand in the pieces in his gallery. No. He could not accept that it had all been a scam. He was not wrong. He was *never* wrong.

And in the meanwhile, there was *Time*, consuming all of his.

He was determined to stay away from it and convinced himself he was successful. At first. Slowly though, it colored his dreams, and they were filled with lights and shade. Individual components would appear on innocuous objects, as handles on cabinets, or decorations on porch swings. Soon, he began to see echoes of it throughout his waking hours in every shape and shadow.

He canceled an appointment with a client coming in from Europe, because it occurred to him that he'd never seen *Time* under the noonday sun. He discovered the sheet of tin serving as *Eventide's* background was not flat, but cleverly scored in thin, wavy strips no more than a quarter-inch wide. The reflections from those variations lit objects from within. He reached through the twisted silk and touched it gently, ran a finger across the striated surface. A burred edge caught and pierced his finger. He pulled his hand away as quickly as he dared, afraid to displace or stain the fine threads. The puncture was deep, welling up with blood. He staunched the wound with his handkerchief without moving away. It was worth it, bleeding for this kind of perfection.

He needed a distraction from *Time*, from Lilith. Perhaps a party, held for no other reason than to occupy his time and redirect his thoughts. He planned it with the precision of a military campaign, catered by a restaurant that didn't provide such services in the normal way of things. Samuel had deep pockets though, and with enough money, one could buy almost anything, including Michelin Star catering.

Clients old and new mixed with the social elite, feasted on world-class cuisine, drank the finest wines, circulated among Samuel's cleverly arranged panels and artwork. It was the same crowd, the same scene, the same tedious way to spend an evening. He almost wished for an irate artist to show up. Even the music sounded wrong, discordant, tuneless, although the guests didn't seem to mind.

Samuel did. Samuel made his excuses and checked with the band and sound engineer. They didn't hear the harmonic fighting against the melody, didn't hear the arhythmic beat under their own. There was an undercurrent of something amongst the attendees though, a not-quite pause in the conversation when he moved between clusters of people, a cadence to his name that let him know the talk was about him.

It was not enough to worry him on any conscious level—Samuel didn't *do* worried. He focused his keen hearing, and soon heard the names Pasco and Calloway. There was no longer any doubt about the topic of conversation.

That night, his dreams gained a musical accompaniment. He didn't know the song, didn't recognize the composer's style, but the same melody became the soundtrack to everything. Sometimes it was played as soft jazz, other times rock, symphonic, or new age. There were voices singing. The lyrics were indistinguishable from the music in the foreground. He couldn't hold onto any of it long enough to remember the tune while he was awake.

The music began to linger, but not in any way he could hear. It was more the aftermath of an echo of a note which filtered into his day, as a drum vibrates long after the sound has passed beyond hearing. It was discordant, with descants that should have been jarring to the ear but weren't.

Samuel called a few of his contacts, ostensibly to let them know he was considering a road trip that winter, but in reality, to discover if they'd seen his errant genius. Several of them followed the craft fair circuit as well—no one had even heard of her. No one matched her description. No one recognized the style of art she created. He worried if she continued her work, perhaps under another name, she just might surpass herself, and he couldn't bear for someone else to benefit from that. In his mind, she owed him.

The obsession ruled his life. With what he paid her for *Time*, she'd have the means to travel incognito. He went over *Time's Journey* with a fine-tooth comb. The maps, the books outlined a trip through a few supposedly mystical locations in Europe and the Far East. He canceled his remaining engagements and booked tickets. He told his clients and social circle he was going on a long-postponed buying trip overseas. He needed to meet with artists in person, he said. He didn't know how long he'd be gone. Everyone nodded. It never occurred to anyone to throw him a bon voyage party.

Samuel stopped his mail, notified the security company. He spent his last night at home alone, finishing the decanter of brandy while contemplating the sunset from an armchair in his study. It was only a lifetime of self-control which kept him upstairs when every fiber of his being wished to be downstairs. But however reluctant he was to leave *Time* behind, he had to find Lilith Chambley. He was still undecided if, once he found her, he should return *Time* to her or beg for more of her work. He fell asleep before he reached a decision.

What finally woke him was impossible to say. It might have been the moonlight streaming in through the floor to ceiling windows. It might have been hunger for he had not eaten dinner. The music didn't wake him—it was too faint to hear without conscious effort. But perhaps it wasn't his conscious self that woke first.

Samuel rose from the armchair, used the washroom, splashed cold water on his face. He was awake, but the music remained, just on the edge of perception. It was the same melody, the same voices from his dreams in a disquieting susurration. He tried to focus, to determine its point of origin. He had no stereo in his study, preferring to work in perfect silence. No sound system in his bedroom, the kitchen, the bath. He walked through the great room. The music persisted, but it did not spring from there. He knew the source of the music—*he knew*—but pride made him reluctant to confirm it.

At last, he keyed open the gallery, shrouded in shadows. The lights were dimmed, but bright moonlight spilled through and around the contents. Samuel secured the door behind him, took his time resetting the alarm, adjusting the lights, checking the environmental controls. He strolled slowly, deliberately through his collection, taking care to study each piece. His other masterpieces had been neglected of late.

The music *was* coming from *Time*, from all three pieces. He was certain he would find some cleverly disguised electronics, batteries, timers. She had strung him along, wasted four—no, eight months—of his life. She had deceived him, mocked him. She was cunning with her shyness, her reticence, all the while using cheap tricks to make the art more than it was.

He walked straight up to *Dawn*, pulled it off the wall, searched it from top to bottom. He heard no music, found no electronics, laid it on the terrazzo floor. *Journey* received the same examination. Nothing again, even though he had not been gentle lifting maps and rifling the stiffened pages of the books it contained. He dropped it on top of *Dawn*, shoved both away with his foot, heard metal and glass fall to the floor.

Eventide was next. He peered around the back. It revealed only that same single sheet of tin—scored and rusty—which had left him bleeding months before. There were no exposed wires, no obvious source of light or sound. He listened carefully on each side; pressed an ear to the fluted woodwork that made up the frame. It might have vibrated, might have quivered against his flesh, but no voices came from there. Samuel crouched down at floor level to check the base. Nothing.

Finally, he stood in front of it, eyes closed, breath held, straining his senses to localize the music's source. It came from nowhere, seemed to be everywhere. A choir singing, chanting, murmuring barely in range. He leaned in closer, closer still.

He braced his hands lightly against the frame. A draft ruffling his hair, a flicker of silk brushing his face, a whiff of incense, spicy and acrid, filling his senses. The voices began to resolve slowly, slowly, one word at a time.

He heard his name.

"Open the door, Samuel, open the door …"

He struggled to open his eyes, didn't, couldn't see a door. There were knobs and hinges studding *Eventide*, but none of them were functional.

Something caught in his vision though, perhaps a whisper-thin tracing of dark gray against the black, just where the frame met the tin on the left-hand side. Ever so gently, he reached out with a single hand, teased the gauze-like silk away from the edge, pushed at the border of dark and darker. A slight give, more music, more chanting, a clock chiming. The voices changed in timbre, increased in volume.

"Open the door, Samuel, open the door …"

Silk fluttered with every word exhaled into his brain. He brushed at them—the silk and the words—batted them away, but the more intelligible the voices became, the more violently they whipped around him, until the beaded fibers and whispered phrases entangled his arms, his torso, his legs, his brain. He thrashed against them, his curses echoing through the moonlit hall. He grabbed at the frame to pull himself free, only to flay his palms on the glass and rusted metal studded along its surface.

The thin tracing of gray grew wider and wider still. The scored tin rippled, bent, melted away into a void of shadows. *Eventide* opened, warped, turned inward. The relentless silk jerked, dragged Samuel inside. He tried to scream but couldn't catch his breath. Couldn't tell which way was up or down. Couldn't sense if he was standing under his own power or hanging by a thread. Couldn't lift a finger against the unbearable pressure weighing down his limbs. Couldn't stop spinning weightless in an unfathomable abyss.

The silken strands bound him in place, burning through his flesh. A door slammed shut behind him, his body swayed with the shockwave reverberating in the cold darkness. The music, the chanting stopped. Only silence remained. It was its own weight against the pervasive black.

And then, a single voice—a nightmare—pierced through the eternal darkness: quiet, implacable. "You have something of mine, and I must insist on its return."

Samuel Angelico had always been a lucky man. Someone once said he had the luck of the devil. Sometimes, the Devil wants it back.

Monster Spray, Monster's Prey

by Sheila Massie

I know you are there under the bed.

I am three years old, and I tell my mother about you, and how you tap your fingers along the mattress, inviting me down into your darkness. I imagine your talons, long and sharp and deliberately honed to an edge. My mother brings a glass bottle the color of the summer night sky. She says it is Monster Spray. She mists it under the bed and in the air around me, telling me it will protect me from you. It smells like her perfume. I can feel you there, swimming circles underneath me, swirling and diving and resurfacing. I hear you sigh. You are patient and will wait for me.

I am seven years old, and you touch me for the first time. It is nothing more than a caress like silk rippling over clean, warm, freshly bathed skin. I am convinced it is a chance meeting, only a mistake. I breathe in the scent of Monster Spray. There are rules for monsters under the bed.

I am ten years old, and you are breaking rules. I do not let my feet or my fingers dangle over the edge of the bed, and yet your claws scrape along the bone of my shin, leaving scars like brick-red crayon marks on clean, fresh paper. You tangle my hair in your fists and tug experimentally. I jerk back, scalp stinging, hearing the strands snapping and breaking off into your palm. I let out a choked scream, sharp and breathless. You lay a finger over your lips and shush me. But it does not matter. My mother no longer believes me, and the Monster Spray lays in her drawer stale and useless.

I am fifteen years old and reckless and helpless both, and I have decided to let you take me. I edge my feet over the lip of the bed. A cool breeze caresses them, the night air stirring. Your fingers are soft and smooth. You touch me hesitantly at first, wondering if I will jerk my legs back to the safety of the bed. I do not. My heart is racing. I want to tell you to let go. But I do not. I am curious and invincible. Your fingers curl around one of my ankles. Then the other. I can feel the strength in you. Your hands are cool and damp, like stones drawn from the river.

Your fingers flex and grip. My bones feel soft under your palms. I hear a sound like sandpaper sliding over rock. And I do not know if you are trying to speak to me or if it is just your body sliding over the discarded toys I have abandoned under the bed. You begin to pull me towards the edge of the bed. It feels like chains of iron, cold now in the room. The blankets slide over my head as you draw me out from the end of the bed, rippling like a stream in its channel. The air under the covers is close and warm and smells of baby powder and sweat and being human. My hips buckle at the edge of the bed, my legs turn downward, but my feet do not touch the floor. You let go for a moment, and I wonder why. Then I feel your body wrap around my legs—the flick of hair, or a tongue, at the backs of my knees. Your hands clamp onto my waist, no hesitation now—iron will meeting iron arms and shoulders and back. My fingers claw at the sheets in a sudden panic, too late.

I am eighteen years old. Strands of me fall away, long ribbons of flayed skin, skeins of hair, and I pluck these from the murk and weave them together. There are stones scraping across my flesh, scrubbing it, and raking it raw and bloodied. Delicate teeth chew at my toes. My gut is raw with hunger and with swallowing the stench of your breath. My lips and my fingertips have become numb. There is light. There is darkness. Once, I hear my mother calling, but I cannot smell her perfume.

I am twenty-five years old, and I have decided to return. I am unmade. Remade. Something other than what I was. Your rules do not apply to me anymore. I understand you now, and I have a strength in me.

I scrabble at the edges of my bed, clutching fistfuls of blankets, feeling them collapse with my weight. I slip, I fall, I claw again and again, hauling my ravaged body away from your tangled embrace. You rage at me, sinking mandibles into scars and tasting my blood as it drips. You beat your fists against my torso. You pluck at scabs and tear away dead skin. I am a starfish clinging to rocks. I unwind a limb and reach upward and hold on, again and again, until I crawl back into my bed and rest my head on my pillow.

I am limp in my exhaustion. I breathe deeply, gulping air. There is a scent weaving itself through the currents. Not Monster Spray. The scent is both new and familiar and it is mine. Your tongue lingers over my skin like receding tides. My toes and fingers hang over the edges of the bed as though dabbling in sea waves. Your fingers flow over mine like bubbles of sea foam, gentle, with longing, but I can deny you entrance into my world now, and I will not return to yours.

Wire Laurel

by Stephanie Parent

Daphne had only been in the tattooist's chair an hour when the scars along her forearms began to squirm.

Phineas, whose intricate designs and vibrant colors were whispered about as Melrose Avenue's hidden treasure, had been inking in the mountain laurel he'd stenciled on Daphne's arm.

Laurel reminded Daphne of her childhood, she had told Phin, of summers spent hiking in the Shenandoah Mountains. She wanted pink and purple blossoms, enveloped in green leaves, to hide all remnants of the lines that striped her flesh beneath.

During their consultation, the scars on Daphne's arms had seemed so faint. Like a rope burn Phin could soothe away with his stubby fingers, the clumsy-looking hands no one could believe created such precise art. He'd said sure, he could conceal those subtle scars beneath bright ink.

But now, as the tattoo pen buzzed and Daphne's moody blue eyes swept across the walls where Phin had hung pictures of his work, the lines on her arms darkened, thickened, swiveled across her skin.

Phin's hand shook.

Phin's hand never shook. Not when that grizzled vet told tales of his days in Iraq while Phin outlined the commemorative insignia for the Army friend who'd never made it home. Not when that blonde twenty-two-year-old swayed her ass as Phin drew details of butterfly wings, and she chattered about some Playboy Mansion party.

But now, Phin's hand shook, and he just managed to drop the pen moments before he would have etched a permanent flaw across Daphne's skin.

"Sorry," Daphne said in the same quiet, steady voice she'd spoken with so far, "I should have warned you."

"It's all right. Just startled me—"

Phin cleared his throat and retrieved the pen from the floor, inspecting it for damage and disinfecting it again. The scars settled, sliding into place beneath Daphne's skin, as he returned to his work.

The walls of this room where Phin made art on flesh were lined with photographs—photos of tattoos. Ink portraits of faces that must have belonged to family members, lovers, the occasional celebrity; flowers of all sorts, from primroses to lotuses emerging from the mud; mermaids and butterflies, the usual suspects; but Phin's renditions had a melancholy to them, an emotion rising up from the skin. Or perhaps that was just Daphne, projecting. Mostly, she saw the body parts, stripped of their owners, facilitating the close-ups of their tattoos: the laddered incline of a ribcage; the arch of a back; the rounding of a buttock or bulging muscle of a calf. Something about those disembodied pieces, caged in their polished frames, set Daphne off. The sight awakened her scars, and sent pinpricks farther inside her than Phin's needles could ever penetrate, till she wished she could crawl right out of herself.

This was what she had feared. This was why she'd waited so long to get these tattoos. It wasn't just a question of money, like she'd told Phin, although that was an issue too. A thirty-year-old who supplemented her freelance writing and editing with the occasional meeting with men in hotels—it wasn't as glamorous, or lucrative, a life as it might seem.

But the more pressing question was:
What if the tattoos didn't work?

"You're wondering where the scars came from." Daphne spoke after fifteen minutes of silent gazing at the walls, during which her flesh had remained calm.

Phin almost jerked for the second time, but held the instinct down. "I'm a professional," he said. "I only wonder when the client wants me to."

Daphne snorted. The most human sound he'd heard from her so far. "After my arms," she reminded him, "we have my ankles and my neck." She cricked her head with the final word. "That's a lot of professionalism to ask from a man."

Phin drew back and crossed his own arms, irritated despite himself. "I may be a man," he said, "but I would never—"

"I didn't mean it like that." Daphne tucked her chin. "It's a lot to ask from anyone. And I think maybe ..."

She looked up again, looked right into him with eyes like the ocean before a storm. "Maybe you need to know. In order for this to work."

Phin broke contact first, glancing down at the bounty of stenciled petals to trace and, over several sessions, color in. "We have time," he said, and returned the pen to her flesh. He steadied her arm with his other hand, the surface smooth as marble. It was hard to imagine those scars rising and shifting like they had.

Another minute passed, only the pen's buzz filling the room, before Daphne spoke.

"I wanted to be seen," she said. "I had moved to Los Angeles for school, a writing program, but that was an excuse. I was twenty-five years old, and no one had ever truly looked at me. I'd spent my childhood in the mountains, picking flowers and reading books, disappearing among the trees. So I moved to this city, with the palm fronds and neon, the concrete and wide-open beaches—backdrop to a thousand movie sets, a million photo shoots, an uncountable number of dreams."

After how quiet Daphne had been so far, this outpouring of words deserved a response. "You wanted to be an actress, or …"

She snorted again. "I was too shy for that. I couldn't speak, or move, in a way that would demand an audience's attention. And modeling—well, I'm short. Not particularly photogenic …"

Daphne had eyes that drew you in like a dream, but after his own decades spent in a city that chewed up and spat out a million dreamers, Phin couldn't disagree with her. Her nose was a little too big, her eyebrows too uneven, for an industry that required scalpels to chisel imperfections away.

"I was shy," Daphne went on, "in some ways. But in others, I wasn't shy at all. A normal modeling agency would laugh me out the door. But there were all kinds of …" She wiggled the fingers of her free hand, searching for the word, making the scars on that arm writhe. "*Opportunities*," she went on, "for someone who wanted to be seen. It was just a question of what you were willing to do."

The Craigslist ad was for a nude bondage model. The artist wanted to tie a girl up and then sketch her. It was, in some ways, less dangerous than other things Daphne had done. There would be no photographs, nothing that could end up online. No slipping her bikini top off on a beach and preparing to cover up quick if onlookers intruded, or worse, the police showed up.

But it was also the kind of ad no sane person would have answered.

Or, more precisely, after meeting the man who posted the ad no sane person would have come back.

They met in a coffee shop in South Pasadena, an hour's subway ride from Daphne's Hollywood apartment. Behzad was barely an inch taller than Daphne, with a shiny, round bald head and small, beady round eyes and a big round belly from which his stocky limbs protruded. He reminded Daphne vaguely of one of the brothel clients in the movie *Belle de Jour*, the man who'd carried a mysterious buzzing box.

Daphne sat across from Behzad with her unmarked forearms stretched before her, her hands circling a coffee mug. She listened and nodded as he described his desire to sketch a bound woman in a room he had rented for the purpose, in this charming neighborhood where band fliers hung on the coffeehouse corkboard and every barista was a filmmaker or singer-songwriter. In his business suit, with his brusque, no-nonsense manner, Behzad seemed out of place. The last thing from an artist. A strange energy emanated from his short limbs, something coiled, snakelike, his bald pate emerging unexpectedly like the hooded head of a cobra.

Daphne had already decided this was a bad idea, that she wouldn't come back and model for him, but for now it was easier to nod and smile and pretend she would. Daphne did this a lot—nodding and smiling because it was easier, and telling herself she was waiting for the right moment to disengage. Sometimes that moment came, and sometimes it slipped away from her. Or, she let it slip away.

"Have you been in bondage before?" Behzad asked, his voice slithering like a snake under the coffeehouse chatter and hissing espresso machines.

"Yes," Daphne lied. She was still waiting to be tied up someday, by some tall, strong man, the way she'd always imagined it, but not by *this* man. Maybe she should leave—

Behzad's eyes on her body fixed her into place, her hands tight around the coffee cup, forearm muscles rigid till the veins stood out in blue ropes. She couldn't get another word out, lie or truth; she could only nod as Behzad told her how he would make art out of her.

Up until the very day they'd agreed on, Daphne told herself she wouldn't do it, that she'd sleep through her alarm and block Behzad's number from her phone. But she found herself riding the subway, barreling through burrowed tunnels and then, as the train neared Pasadena, emerging into buttery sun. Tapping on her laptop, editing other writers' books, her freelance job. She didn't *need* the two hundred dollars Behzad had offered her for an hour's work, but she wanted it.

And she wanted something else.

The room was set up like an intimate artist's workspace, or like a boudoir. An easel in one corner, sketchpad set upon it, pencils on the easel shelf. A plump-cushioned sofa, a door that was always closed because Behzad hadn't rented the entire apartment, just this room. A ritual, needing few words.

Behzad waiting for Daphne to arrive, again in his superfluous suit, though he quickly shrugged the jacket off. Daphne taking off her shoes, dress, underwear. Behzad placing his short, round fingers on her shoulders, turning her so her back faced him, guiding her wrists to touch and securing them with rope from an overstuffed bag in the corner. Another rope for her ankles. Behzad arranging her on the couch, on her stomach. Behzad scribbling for a few minutes—seconds?—flipping the sketchbook page, drawing again. Adjusting her. More doodling. Making her stand, turning the page, scribbling, scrawling.

What was that, thirty seconds per sketch?

The scratch of pencil on paper paused, and Daphne prepared to be moved again. Instead, Behzad's voice slunk out:

"Have you ever had a spreader bar used on you?"

Was it harder to lie when you were naked?

Daphne shook her head no.

The spreader bar was a metal pole, shiny as a snakeskin. Behzad leaned Daphne's hands against the closed door so she could open her legs wide, so he could secure the rope around each of her ankles to either end of the bar. She was glad for the door, then, because she couldn't have stood upright with her legs stretched so far.

Behzad slid slick hands up the insides of her thighs, stopping just below the spot where her legs met. He walked away and returned holding something long and thin and wiry extending from a handle. Daphne's head was not bound; she could have twisted her neck and looked fully; but she only glanced from the corners of her eyes.

Behzad struck the back of Daphne's thighs with the wiry tail that cut into her flesh. Once, twice, ten or a hundred times. Her heart raced with an emotion she couldn't name, and she bit her lip, determined not to cry. She remembered a movie she'd seen, where the heroine was kidnapped by a villain who got off on whipping women till they cried and cried and eventually died. When the hero rescued the heroine, he said, *You were such a good girl. You didn't scream, and it saved your life.*

Eventually Behzad stopped; he dropped the weapon and traced pudgy fingers over her thighs. "You have one of the highest pain tolerances I've ever seen." Wonder cranked the volume of his voice high. In Daphne's head, the words transformed. *You're such a good girl,* Behzad said inside her mind.

Behzad untied her and Daphne put her clothes back on, glad her dress descended almost to her knees. As he walked her out, she realized, after those first minutes, he hadn't touched pencil or paper at all.

On the way home, while the subway car entered the hooded tunnel and descended underground, Daphne gazed into the darkness and decided that Behzad didn't really want to draw her. But then a part of her had known that all along. Just like Daphne didn't want some pocket money in exchange for an hour naked before a strange man.

What Daphne wanted was to be seen, really, truly seen. She would not have chosen this man, with his king-cobra head and snake-bead eyes, to be the one to see her. But you couldn't always choose what you wanted, what you desired. You couldn't choose a whole hell of a lot in this world.

After two sessions spent shading blossoms and leaves on flesh, the problem had become clear:

Daphne's scars were rebelling.

Each session, the scars rose further till they were barbed wire wrapping her wrists, choking the petals made of ink. Phin did his best to work around them, but it became more difficult every time. After the third session, when Daphne gave Phin permission to touch her without gloves, he palpated the metallic ridges intertwining with her veins. She shuddered and bit her lip.

"Does it hurt?"

Daphne hadn't reacted to the tattooing process itself, but now a mere touch seemed too much for her to bear.

"Yes." She clenched her fists so the scars rippled like living things. "It hurts inside my bones. Cold and sharp."

"Should we stop?" Phin asked. "If this is making it worse, maybe you need to see someone else. A doctor—"

Daphne snorted, the indelicate snort Phin was starting to like. "You think a doctor, a scientist, knows what to do with something like this?"

Phin studied Daphne's forearm, the way the wire scars broke through the flowers, highlighting their fragility, showing how easily they might tear. Phin couldn't deny it was fascinating, knowing he'd played some part in creating it.

He couldn't look away.

"If anyone can help me," Daphne went on, "it's an artist." She grabbed Phin's wrist, thicker and stubbier than hers, and one of her wires sliced against his radial artery. A spot he knew by heart; a common request for tattoos.

Phin pulled away—he was not a masochist, did not like to be tattooed himself—but one moment of contact was enough for the wire to invade his blood like bitter ice. Was this how Daphne felt, all the time?

"You're my last chance," Daphne said. She looked away from him, toward the many monuments to Phin's artwork on the walls. "I think we need to move on—finish it all."

Phin swallowed and thought of the familiar buzzing of the tattoo pen, of warm blood flowing, of change and hope. "Your ankles next?" he asked. "More laurel?"

"Yes," Daphne said. "I want the leaves to wrap all the way around, an unbroken garland, like a knotted rope."

The most insane part was not that, after modeling for Behzad, Daphne rode the subway home with blood dripping from her thighs. The most insane part was not how quickly the marks on her legs disappeared; how something so painful, so transformative, could leave no lasting proof of itself behind.

The most insane part was that Daphne went back, and made no mention of the fact that Behzad touching and whipping her legs was completely outside of the arrangement they had agreed upon.

Daphne went back, and after her forearms and ankles were bound; after a few minutes of Behzad's frenzied sketching, when Daphne peered at the papers and saw only some vaguely girl-shaped lines; after she was leaning on the door with her legs spread and a metal whip striking her thighs, Daphne thought:

He said he wanted to make art of me. And isn't this a sort of art?

Daphne would never have looked directly at Behzad; she would never have looked anywhere but down at the floor, in that artist's boudoir with the closed door. But Behzad grabbed her chin, his fleshy wrist against her throat, and turned her face toward his.

"So impressive," he said. "You haven't made a single sound." He swallowed, his Adam's apple a mouse sliding down a snake's esophagus. "Such a good girl."

After those words, Daphne couldn't consider closing her eyes. She couldn't even blink. Behzad looked right into her with his eyes like little beads, like seeds, planting something inside her. Then he turned her head back to the wall, and slid his hand along her neck and bare back, and lower. The fingers that had held pencil to draw her, whip to mark her; those fingers now pierced her, in every place they could.

She should tell him to stop, Daphne thought, but her throat had been pierced too, wires crisscrossing her voice box so that words were only shredded bloody things inside her.

On the subway ride home, Daphne saw the first metallic lines threading across her arms, echoing Behzad's ropes. She would have expected scars where he'd whipped her, or invaded her, but—

The rope was what she'd wanted in the first place. It was why she'd answered the ad, why she came back, the first step that led to all the others. She'd wanted someone to witness that bound-up part of her.

And now her desire would forever mark her.

⁂

"He was a sorcerer," Daphne said, when Phin had finished the last red laurel over her ankle bone. It should have been pink—he'd switched to lighter ink throughout the sessions, as Daphne told her story, but the flowers on her flesh had only darkened. The scars darkened, too, jutting like rusted wires.

"He had the power to stop you from speaking," Daphne went on. "He was a stealer of voices."

Phin drew the tattoo pen away from Daphne's skin, and Daphne gasped, and the scars writhed. "Are you all right?" Phin looked away, at the photographs of safer art contained by their frames on the wall. "Stupid question."

"When the pain on the outside stops," Daphne said, "the pain on the inside wakes up."

"I could keep poking you with the pen if you want." Phin tried to smile, tried to joke.

He was relieved to see Daphne smile back, half-hiding the grimace underneath; but he still had the feeling he was skirting the edges of something he couldn't comprehend.

"That might make things more bearable for a while." Daphne lifted her leg. Metallic protrusions split the red petals and her own skin open till Phin couldn't tell blossom from blood. "But it wouldn't hide this. I'll have to start wearing long pants, all the time."

Phin considered, once again, stopping before the final tattoo. What if the pain got so bad Daphne couldn't walk, or speak? But another possibility had occurred to him, so he held his tongue:

What if the tattoos weren't about hiding the scars, but about pulling them gradually, painfully, grotesquely *out*?

It was an artistic challenge Phin barely wanted to contemplate, but the time to make a different choice had passed. Like Daphne five years ago, Phin had agreed to something without understanding the stakes.

Daphne must have seen the confusion in Phin's eyes, as she went on: "I wish I had an explanation that would make sense." She lifted an arm where blossoms and metal melded. "Not for what Behzad did, these strange powers he had—there's no explanation for something like that—but for what I did, why I kept coming back. Why I was the way I was; why I would give up so much just to be seen."

Phin took one glove off, reached out and asked a question with his eyes. When Daphne nodded, he placed a fingertip on a metal ridge, as if pricking himself with a thorn. The pain shot through his veins like some dark drug, but he forced himself not to pull away. He kept contact even as the agony spiked and tattooed his insides. It reminded him how much he preferred to be creator, artist, the one wielding the needle; the rare tattooist with no ink of his own.

"You didn't ask for this," he finally said.

"No," Daphne agreed. "The pain is getting worse. I can't sleep. I can't think. I can't hide this from clients; soon I won't be able to work." She breathed in, short and harsh. "It's not like the pain of a tattoo or a whip. There's no meaning to it. It's not art. It just hurts."

Her limbs shook and the scars rose and sharpened, and Phin couldn't stand it—he pulled away. The crawling invasion of his insides ceased at once, but for Daphne, there was no escape.

He had to ask again. "Your neck. You're sure you want to …"

She lifted her throat where concertina wire shone under the skin, a choker about to emerge. "Yes," she said. "I want a nightingale singing, with an open mouth."

Even after Daphne realized Behzad was a sorcerer, even after she realized the marks on her arms and ankles wouldn't fade like the whip lines on her thighs, she went back to model for him another time. She couldn't say why; whether it was because of his knowing eyes, the ones that saw how much pain she could take, how long she'd dreamt of being bound. Or whether it was that metal he'd planted, drawing her back to him like filings to a magnet.

Whatever the reason, there she was, naked and splayed against the door. Wrists tied above her head, Behzad's fat fingers wrapped around the whip's handle as he reared back to strike. And maybe it was the metal under her skin; maybe it was the many sketches Behzad had collected, images of a girl wrapped in ropes, a girl who couldn't speak or move, a girl who was only an outline. Whatever it was, Behzad seemed determined to whip her till she screamed, to draw out whatever sound was left inside her and steal it for himself.

Daphne bit her tongue, tasting metal and blood.

Behzad struck and struck, the whip a snake's lashing tongue. He grunted and gasped till Daphne could no longer tell if he was impressed or impatient. The blows ceased but her skin still throbbed, singing a stinging melody that sounded like *good girl, good girl*. Daphne prepared for Behzad's fingers to invade her again, but what thrust its way in was something else—

Something long and rigid and cold. A metal handle that did not belong inside her. Inside anyone. A foreign substance that made her want to crawl out of herself.

This was not art, and Daphne opened her mouth to demand that Behzad stop but metal bit her throat. It coiled, spiraled, circled her vocal cords and kept her from crying out.

When it was over, wire protruded from beneath the skin of Daphne's neck, pulsating like an echo, so faint that from the outside it might have been a mirage. Behzad had made art of her, but around the metal she was still a human girl, flesh and blood and a heart that beat her own rhythm, and she would not come back to him again.

Daphne's nightingale tattoo was the most demanding artwork Phin had ever attempted. On her arms and ankles, the metal had retreated long enough for him to imprint her skin with blossoms; but on her neck, where her pulse fluttered like wings, the scars fought him off. Phin held every muscle rigid as he drew the nightingale's outstretched wings, its open beak, while Daphne's skin shuddered more than the tattoo pen and her wires poked his glove. It took all the effort he possessed to keep the pen from straying, to hold the needle in place and create the image he and Daphne desired.

By the time he'd finished, his own body felt stiff as metal, heavy with an exhaustion he couldn't shake off. And Daphne had turned so quiet, her skin pale and bloodless, so close to collapsing that Phin feared she'd never get up.

"I'll get you some juice." He headed for the mini fridge without much hope it would help. "Get your blood sugar up."

But she spoke in a rasp:

"Finish it."

Phin swallowed. "We should wait for the lines to settle—"

The scars on Daphne's arms and legs emerged, drawing beads of blood. She croaked: "*Now.*"

So Phin colored the nightingale, with a blue patch of feathers below its beak the exact shade of Daphne's eyes. A bluethroat. Wires thickened around Daphne's throat, her own skin turning the faintest shade of blue. Her pulse retreated, her lips parting with no sound.

"You're suffocating, Daphne." Phin's words constricted, as if his larynx had alchemized. "I've got to stop."

She shook her head, and red blood dripped around the metal and down her blue skin, and Phin understood—*Don't stop.*

He was close; he had only the yellow of the nightingale's open beak to fill in now. Every prick of the needle impaled his own skin, his veins, his bones. As though each drop of ink were another step in an inevitable transformation, another ingredient in a magic spell.

And then, even as the needle pierced the flesh above her throat, Daphne's words came one by one:

"Was Behzad really a—a sorcerer? Did he have some second sight, some supernatural power to paralyze me? Some snake's venom, or—"

She paused, her silence like a scream.

"Did he just look at me, really look at me, and know I was a girl who would never tell him no?"

The words triggered something, the click of a key in a lock, and as Phin deposited the last of the ink, the nightingale blurred, shifted, flapped its wings and opened its mouth with a wail that skewered his thoughts. He was fainting, falling, the entire room disintegrating, shedding its skin, the tattoo images in their frames juddering on the wall. He plummeted to the floor and the pen rolled away from him and in his warping vision the metal slithered from Daphne's flesh like a thousand snakes, breaking her open, baring blood and muscle and bone. No human body could survive that, and Phin reached out to reassemble her.

But he was like metal; he could not move.

Phin awoke to the sugary-sharp scent of orange juice beneath his nose. He opened his eyes and saw a pale hand wrapped around a cup, attached to a wrist and forearm covered with pink and purple petals, green leaves—and no metal at all. "It worked," Daphne said, her voice lighter, a hint of birdsong dancing between the words. "The scars are gone."

⚲

Daphne lied. Yes, the physical evidence had vanished; the metal had risen and writhed right out of her skin, splitting her like a scream, a pain that left no trace of itself. The worst kind of pain—the pain you could not see; the pain that was not art. But it lingered beneath her flesh, something she would never cast off: a prickling remnant of those wires, perhaps just the memory of them, a phantom limb. A second skin.

Daphne couldn't say she was surprised. As powerful as Phin's tattoo pen had been, as powerful as it had been to speak her story aloud, no art could conquer reality. They didn't live in that kind of world.

When Phin had collected himself and, with Daphne's support, stood up, Daphne followed him out to the front of his tattoo parlor. She hadn't paid much attention before, but now she noticed, in this little waiting room, the pictures on the wall.

These photos did not seem particularly artistic—they were candid, casual portraits. People in T-shirts; goth girls in all black, their male counterparts with chains hanging from their belts; a pretty woman in a sundress, a serious-looking man in a button-down. A few had tattoos poking beyond their sleeves, crawling up their necks, but not all. Daphne looked closer, and realized the same palm tree appeared in each photo: the miniature one that grew right outside Phin's tattoo parlor, waving to passersby with its fronds.

"The pictures of tattoos in your studio," Daphne said, remembering the peonies along a ribcage, the Celtic design on an upper arm. "Are they—"

"They belong to these people," Phin confirmed, tracing a finger along one portrait. "Those images were my art, inside the studio walls. But once they walk out those front doors—it's not mine anymore."

"You didn't want to take *my* picture, though?" Daphne crossed her arms with exaggerated affront. She wasn't upset—couldn't be upset, with the sensation of freedom like wings taking flight across her flesh. A sharper echo thrummed beneath the surface, but Daphne could live with that. And maybe this new freedom was why she wanted to tease Phin a little. See him clench his clumsy-looking hands, out of his element, without a tattoo pen to wrap his fist around.

"It didn't seem right, considering your story—but if you want me to—"

"I know." Daphne put a hand on his, a tattooed laurel against his wrist. He flinched, then softened.

Maybe he felt it too—the remnants, the things that could not be undone. The new creation taking its meaning from what had come before.

"No photos right now," Daphne said. "Maybe I'll be back. Thank you for listening, Phin."

She opened the door and, like a picture walking out of its frame, she was gone.

Adrift in the Salish Sea

by Bebe Bayliss

"Jack, you look miserable, have a refill," Rosie said as she lifted a glass under the tap.

"Come on, you know I just have that kind of face." He tried a smile as she slid the beer across the bar to him.

"Dude, that's not an improvement." But she laughed as she said it.

"Ouch." He sat up straight. "A good friend will always stab you in the front."

"Oscar Wilde?"

"Of course."

She chuckled as she dried a glass. "I'd bet money you're the only delivery guy in Canada that quotes Oscar Wilde."

"Well, British Columbia, anyway." He drained the glass and left twenty dollars on the bar. "Thanks, Rosie. I'm headed back south tomorrow, so I'll see you in a few weeks."

As he drove the company truck to the motel, he decided he liked Rosie and would probably let her keep her legs. He had a strict selection process for The Project and, anyway, he preferred to work with men.

He'd started The Project accidentally a few years ago when, a little drunk and going too fast on a shortcut to the highway, he hit a hitchhiker. Unsure what to do, he ran over the guy again to be certain he was dead, then stuffed the body in the back of the truck and went home. He put the hitchhiker in the big freezer in his basement while he figured out the next move.

It was fate that the very same evening, he watched a show about currents and tides in the Salish Sea and it gave him an idea. He'd conduct experiments on the drift of bodies in local waters. When he was a kid, he'd wanted to be a scientist, but his mother had said that his father had been a no-good loser so there was no way Jack was smart enough for that. It was a handy argument, and she'd used it when he wanted to be an astronaut, chef, cowboy, and artist. Jack never met his father, so he had to take her word.

By the time Jack found himself with a hitchhiker in the freezer, his mother was dead, and he'd inherited the family farm—twenty acres of mediocre land and an isolated farmhouse—and he was free to formulate plans without interference. He determined that not only was getting an entire body into the water without being spotted problematic, heads and hands made a body easy to identify. He preferred anonymous subjects. Using scientific methods of deduction, he decided to use only legs and feet, detaching them from the body at the knee, but leaving the shoes on so he could identify them when they washed up onshore. His own knees hurt from constantly climbing in and out of the truck as he made deliveries, so he figured they were a weak point.

The hitchhiker was young and scrawny—an excellent test subject as Jack experimented with limb removal. The rest of the body he buried in the meadow, set far back from the road, well behind the house. He hoped the hitchhiker would approve, and it felt good to finally have the family farmland put to use.

Jack delivered dairy products to restaurants and grocery stores. His territory included miles of coast where the boreal forest reached to the water, punctuated by rocky bluffs, small strips of beach, and tiny, hidden coves. He knew all the little marinas and resorts that brimmed with tourists from May to September, then emptied out for the off-season. They were hard to reach in the winter, but early spring and late fall were perfect times to stop by and toss in a leg or two as he made deliveries.

He recognized that, lacking formal scientific training, there were bound to be gaps in his method, and this was evident right away. He had no way to track the hitchhiker's legs and, for weeks after he started the experiment, he was at a loss about how to gather data. Then someone found a foot in a sneaker on the beach, and the news report included a picture. He had the "eureka" moment that heralds so many scientific discoveries. His mother would have been impressed.

News Alert: A man's right foot, clad in a sneaker, was discovered on a beach on the Gulf Islands this morning. The foot was enclosed in a sock and disarticulated at the ankle.

Dis•ar•tic•u•late (dis-ar-*tik*-yu-late) *verb.* Separation of a body part at a joint.

Jack looked up the word to confirm the precise scientific language being used to describe his experiment, and it made him feel even closer to the scientific community. He wondered where the rest of the leg had gone. He needed to conduct more experiments.

Hitchhikers seeking the solitude of the surrounding wilderness were perfect test subjects. He was always ready to give them a lift, and spent the first few miles of the ride evaluating them. Clothing, their way of speaking, who they talked about, all were carefully observed to make sure they were a worthy candidate for The Project. If they didn't pass muster, they were let off at the next junction to find another ride.

Jack knew that lab animals were trained with food, so he offered hitchhikers that made the first cut a single-serve lemon chiffon yogurt. If they declined, they were dropped off at the next intersection. Those who ate the yogurt were dead within minutes, thanks to the homemade cyanide Jack injected into the yogurt. He had never considered fermented milk to be a healthy food, and this reaction to lemon chiffon supported his opinion. His insistence that his mother buy him a chemistry set for his tenth birthday had laid the ground for his current success, and he liked to think that she'd have been proud of how well his cyanide worked.

His refrigerated truck kept the subjects in top condition until he could get home and separate them at the knees, and the first hitchhiker soon had company in the meadow.

He had favorite release points for the legs. The best places were small coves with easy water access, private but not remote, so he didn't have to drive too far off his delivery routes. Gas was expensive and his experiments were self-funded. The best site was about a mile from Rosie's, and he enjoyed his visits to her place.

News Alert: Three feet have been found on local beaches since May. A fourth foot was found on a beach in Washington state. Police said all feet were found inside running shoes. The coroner stated that all feet had become separated at the ankle due to natural decay while in the water. Police do not suspect foul play.

Jack felt the foot discovered in Washington state a very interesting data point and was pleased that neither Canadian nor Washington police thought random feet found on beaches was suspicious.

Months and months went by and, as feet continued to wash up, The Project occupied much of his thinking time. On the long drives between deliveries he daydreamed about the interviews he'd give when he finally revealed the results. He'd paraphrase Oscar Wilde: "To lose one foot may be regarded as a misfortune; to lose a dozen looks like carelessness."

News Alert: A right foot, clad in an athletic shoe, was discovered on the shore near Vancouver last week.

The image in the report clearly showed three stripes on the shoe and Jack was puzzled by this, as he refused to support Adidas, the brand favored by his mother. Any other athletic shoe company would do, although he preferred Nike, and had considered approaching them for a research grant once his preliminary findings were public. According to his observations, many hitchhikers also favored Nike, so he could be selective when choosing experiment subjects.

He thought of the Adidas-clad foot as a statistical anomaly, until it occurred to him that he might have competition. If so, he wondered if they would compare data points and let him include the information in his official Project scientific paper.

He was up to fifteen hitchhikers, and there were still a number of legs unaccounted for. Although he'd been careful in his collection of subjects and release of test legs, the process was becoming tedious, and he was concerned he might make a careless mistake. Perhaps it was time to end the experiment and write his conclusions before he lost interest completely. He'd stop this September, at the end of the season. The back meadow was getting full anyway.

He considered what he'd do next. The Project had consumed so much of his energy that he hadn't really practiced enough self-care. He realized he was tired of all the driving and that he'd like to find a job closer to home.

"Hiya, Rosie."

"Hello, Jack," she said as she slid a beer across the bar. "You look more miserable than usual, and I mean that as a friend." She looked concerned.

Jack took a swig of his beer and sighed. "Rosie, I'm tired of driving, and I think I'll quit and find a different job at the end of the season. I don't spend much time at home, and it's lonely being out on the road all the time. It would be nice to be in one place, maybe even have a dog waiting for me when I got home."

She'd been wiping down the bar as he talked but stopped for a moment before she spoke. "You'll be missed. I feel like we've become friends, and I guess I'll need to get my fix of Oscar Wilde quotes while I can."

"Well, can a friend take you to dinner tomorrow night? Just to share some quotes," he added, to make sure it didn't seem like a date.

"I'm pretty busy here, but it would be nice to have dinner somewhere else. Otherwise, it's just another solitary evening with me and the cats back at the cabin. How about the new restaurant at the north marina? I hear the chef is a magician with seafood."

"I hate people who are not serious about meals. It is so shallow of them," he quoted.

She laughed. "Oscar Wilde again?" He nodded. "Well then, dinner tomorrow night it is."

The restaurant was a bit of a drive, but the logging road shortcut got them there in no time, and it was pleasant to sit at a table next to the big window overlooking the marina.

"In a few weeks the weather will be warm enough to sit outside," Rosie said as she sipped her wine. "You'll miss this."

"I will, but the driving is just too much. I feel like there should be more to life than delivering cheese and milk."

"Well, I hope you'll reconsider. In fact, I insist on it." She set her wine down and leaned over the table to face him directly, her voice low but clear. "I know what you've been up to. I've heard about the missing hitchhikers, and I've seen your truck over and over at odd times at the little cove near my place." She sipped her wine and continued. "I grew up here, fishing and hiking, and I know these waters and currents, how they flow and how they hide secrets. I don't know what your game is, but I know you're responsible for the mysterious feet. Well, most of them."

She leaned back, a smile on her face that Jack couldn't read. His mind raced. She knew. He decided right there that tonight, Rosie would not return home, that he'd finally add a woman to the collection in the meadow. He was so close to completing The Project and would not let her interrupt his plans. His hand tightened on his beer glass, knuckles white.

"Oh dear, you look surprised. Loosen up and finish your beer, I can see your death grip on that glass from here." She motioned to the waiter for another round. "I can also see that you're angry, and that must be clouding your mind. You seem to have missed a key point in what I just said."

He looked up, confused. What had he missed?

"Jack, I said that I knew that you were responsible for most, but not all, of the feet. Can you think how I'm certain of that?" She smiled again.

He felt a thrill of realization. "Rosie … you're the competition?"

She laughed. "That's what you call me? But no, it's not like that. You've inspired me. When my dad died, I inherited the restaurant and I had to keep it running. I can't sell, it would be like losing the family farm, and I'm not a quitter. But I was so bored and lonely. I really needed a hobby, and I was at a loss about what to do until I saw you pick up a hitchhiker summer before last. I can't say when I pieced it all together, but the missing hitchhikers, your job as a delivery man, your repeated trips at high tide to the little cove, the feet that washed up ... it all had to add up to something. It was exciting to me. Imagine getting away with that? There are still things I don't understand, though. What do you do with the rest of the bodies?"

Having decided that this was Rosie's last meal, he saw no sense in lying to her, especially since she was a fan of his work. "I separate them at the knees, then bury the bodies in the meadow on my property down south. I'm up to fifteen test subjects." He was rather proud of that number and in only a few years.

"It's a clever system, for sure. And you're so lucky that your constant movement not only presents you with a wider hunting range for subjects but that you have a place to work. It's been hard for me to reach my goals, tied to the restaurant like I am. I've only taken three subjects, single men passing through town who were happy to join me for a drink back at my place when the bar closed. I've had to send them off from the cove as full bodies, but I feel that I have real potential. Honestly, your work has deeply touched me."

Jack was startled. Full bodies sent off, but only feet found? Rosie was doing revolutionary, even dangerous, work. He looked at her with a newfound respect and wondered if he should reconsider the decision that she'd have to join her test subjects in the water. Maybe he'd made a snap judgment and, besides, a disciple in his work was something he'd never allowed himself to even think about. Still, whatever he did about Rosie, he had to decide right now.

Rosie looked thoughtful. "I have an idea that I might be in some danger, now that you've told me your methods. In case this ever came up, I've put a sealed letter in the hands of my lawyer, to be opened in case of my death or disappearance. It outlines what I know of your activities and will be shared with the police if I don't check in with him according to our schedule. He likes to know I'm safe, being a single woman and all."

Jack concentrated hard on what she was saying, realizing that the decision had been made for him.

"I need a mentor," Rosie went on earnestly, "someone to learn from, and I've found him. Here is what I propose. You'll keep your job, and make your deliveries, and sometimes I'll join you. You'll like some company on your drives, won't you? And hitchhikers are even more likely to get in a vehicle with a woman, so I can expand my range. You can live with me at the cabin, and it will be nice to have a dog. I'm sure the cats will get used to it. We can use your meadow for my bodies, and we can share notes on our work. Really, I'm very excited about the possibilities. After all, as Oscar Wilde says, 'an idea that is not dangerous is unworthy of being called an idea at all.' Don't you agree?"

Jack stayed silent as the waiter delivered their meals. The scallops did indeed look good. He savored them as he rolled his options around in his head. She had him cornered, but her angle was a good one and, anyway, it was all in the name of science. And there was a chance that this could become something more than just a professional arrangement. He allowed himself to hope.

"Rosie, you've convinced me. You're clever, and you've taken the trouble to learn some Oscar Wilde, which means a great deal to me. I look forward to working together." He was genuinely touched at her efforts, and her enthusiasm as a research partner was contagious. He really did look forward to continuing work on The Project. "My scallops are excellent, by the way. How is your salmon?"

"Done perfectly. I can't wait to come back. We can sit outside on the deck, and I can wear the funny T-shirt I found in the backpack of one of my test subjects. It looks great with the skirt I got to wear with it. The skirt's pretty short, but you won't mind, will you?

Jack smiled at her as the waiter removed the plates. "I won't mind. After all ... I am a leg man."

LAGNIAPPE

During a staff meeting one gloriously stormy night, the idea of having a "Lagniappe" near the end of some of the works published by Brigids Gate Press was discussed. The staff unanimously voted in favor of the idea.

Lagniappe (pronounced LAN-yap) is an old New Orleans tradition where merchants give a little something extra along with every purchase. It's a way of expressing thanks and appreciation to customers.

The Lagniappe section might contain a short story, a small handful of poems, or a non-fiction piece. In this book, it is an exemption to the anthology's guideline of no fractured fairy tales.

***

The lagniappe for this anthology is a beautiful and powerful poem titled "The Nature of Me" by Linda D. Addison. It's a fitting end to this anthology, and we hope you enjoy it as much as we did.

The Nature of Me

by Linda D. Addison

I am dreams you can't remember,
nightmares you can't forget,
decisions made, then denied,
love rebuffed, pain embraced.

We are each other's lost childhood,
breath held while joy withheld,
abandoned heart space filled
with shadows hidden behind smiles.

I consume broken space between
here and there, the gaze shared
when you weren't looking, the aroma
of innocence inhaled, then choked.

Waiting for others to cross my path,
to cling within my breathing space,
each breath in rhythm with promised
love will be replaced by soul's poetry.

I am the poem …

About the Authors

Vivian Kasley hails from the land of the strange and unusual, Florida! She's a writer of short stories and poetry. Her words haunt places such as Cemetery Gates Media, Brigids Gate Press, Vastarien, Ghost Orchid Press, Death's Head Press, October Nights Press, The Denver Horror Collective, and poetry in Black Spot Books inaugural women in horror poetry showcase: *Under Her Skin* and *Under Her Eye*. She definitely has more in the works, including her first collection coming in 2025. When not writing or subbing at the local middle school, she spends time reading in bubble baths, walking through graveyards, snuggling her rescue animals, going on adventures with her partner, and searching for seashells and other treasure along the beach.

Vivian can be found at:
https://www.facebook.com/bizarrebabewhowrites/
amazon.com/author/viviankasley
https://twitter.com/VKasley

Sridhar "Sri" Shankar writes fiction inspired by his experiences in India, and as a physician, both in India and the United States. He consults with the forensic department of the University of Tennessee. He has a self-published book of short stories, *Shades of Life*, and a novelette, *The Kite*, and his work has appeared in *Conclave* magazine and the anthologies, *Lies along the Mississippi* and *Blues City Clues*. He lives with his wife and children in Memphis, Tennessee.

A born drifter with plenty of dark stories, childbirth is the closest thing to eldritch **Koji A. Dae** has experienced. Now she finds herself strangely settled in Bulgaria with two kids, a cat, and a whole lot of responsibility. She writes about things mothers see from the corner of their hearts and all varieties of human relationships—with each other, with technology, and with the greater universe. Her first novella, *Mazi,* is currently available.

Megan M. Davies-Ostrom is a disabled Canadian author whose short stories have appeared in venues such as *Fantasy Magazine*, *DreamForge Magazine*, *Cosmic Horror Monthly*, and anthologies such as *Dark Waters* and *Bodies Full of Burning*. Megan lives in Ontario with her husband, daughter, and two (strange) cats. When not writing or carrying out the duties of her civil-servant alter-ego, she enjoys hiking, reading, and playing board games. Megan is represented by Becky LeJeune of Bond Literary Agency.

Nicole M. Wolverton is a writer of (mostly) horror and thrillers for adults and young adults. She is the author of *A Misfortune of Lake Monsters* (2024, CamCat Books) and *The Trajectory of Dreams* (2013, Bitingduck Press). She is Pushcart-nominated for her short fiction, with nearly 50 of short stories, essays, and creative nonfiction published. She also served as curator/Editor of *Bodies Full of Burning* (2021, Sliced Up Press), an anthology of short fiction that investigates horror through the lens of menopause. She lives in the Philadelphia area and has a master's degree in horror and storytelling.

Nicole can be found at: nicolewolverton.com

Scott J. Moses is the author of *Our Own Unique Affliction* (DarkLit Press). An Active member of the Horror Writers Association, his work has appeared in *Cosmic Horror Monthly,* The NoSleep Podcast, Planet Scumm, and elsewhere. He also edited *What One Wouldn't Do*: *An Anthology on the Lengths One Might Go To.* He is Japanese American and lives in Maryland. He is represented by Alec Frankel of IAG for TV/Film.

Scott can be found at:
Twitter: @scottj_moses
scottjmoses.com

Anya Leigh Josephs was raised in North Carolina and is now a therapist working in New York City. When not working or writing, Anya can be found seeing a lot of plays, reading doorstopper fantasy novels, or worshipping their cat, Sycorax. Anya's short fiction can be found in the Deadlands, *Fantasy Magazine,* and forthcoming in the *Magazine of Fantasy and Science Fiction,* among many others. Anya's debut novel, *Queen of All,* is an inclusive adventure fantasy for young adults available now, with the rest of the trilogy coming soon.

KC Grifant is an award-winning writer based in Southern California who creates internationally published horror, fantasy, science fiction, and weird west stories. Many of her short stories have appeared in podcasts, magazines, games, and Stoker-nominated anthologies. Her weird western novel, *Melinda West: Monster Gunslinger* (Brigids Gate Press, 2023), described as a blend of Bonnie & Clyde meet The Witcher and Supernatural, ranked #1 in Amazon New Releases for Western Horrors. She is also the author of the short story collection *Shrouded Horror: Tales of the Uncanny* (Dragon's Roost Press, 2024) and *Melinda West and the Gremlin Queen* (Brigids Gate Press, 2025). In addition to writing, she is the co-chair and founder of the Horror Writers

Association San Diego chapter, co-creator of Monsters Gunslingers The Game, and member of numerous writing organizations, including the Science Fiction and Fantasy Writers Association.

KC can be found at
www.KCGrifant.com
Social media at: @KCGrifant

Samuel McQuail is an autistic author with both a flair for the dramatic and a background in psychology, both of which see frequent use in his work. Best tempted to parties with the promise of cheesecake and cats.

Fred Furtado is a biologist, journalist and science communicator in Rio de Janeiro. He writes science fiction, fantasy and horror, but has a particular fascination for stories that feature superbeings or superpowers. Fred also writes for roleplaying games and produces the *Superseeds* column on Patreon.

Fred can be found at:
http://patchlord.com
Twitter and Instagram at @patchlord

Anna Fitzgerald Healy grew up on a small island in Maine. Her writing is largely informed by her childhood in rural New England and cold winter nights curled up watching black-and-white movies. Today, she lives in a dilapidated castle in the Hollywood Hills, formerly home to Clara Bow in the 1920's. Anna studied at Emerson College. Her writing has been featured in literary magazines and short story anthologies. Her debut mystery novel *Etiquette for Lovers and Killers* is forthcoming from Putnam Press (US) and Fleet (UK) in 2025.

Samantha Lokai is originally from the Caribbean and currently resides in England where she writes dark fiction, incorporating elements of neo-noir, gothic, folklore and horror. Her work has appeared in *Strand Magazine*, *Dangerous Waters: Deadly Women of the Sea* (Brigids Gate Press) *Crimson Bones* (Brigids Gate Press) and The Horror Tree. When not writing, Samantha can be found indulging in her love for books, nature, and her curiosity for the strange and unusual.

Samantha can be found on Twitter at: @samanthaslk1

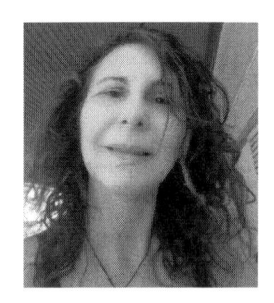

Christine Lucas is a Greek author, a retired Air Force officer (disabled) and mostly self-taught in English. Her work appears in several print and online magazines, including Future SF Digest, Pseudopod and Strange Horizons. She was a finalist for the 2017 WSFA award and the 2021 Emeka Walter Dinjos Memorial Award For Disability In Speculative Fiction. Her collection of short stories, titled *Fates and Furies* was published in late 2019 by Candlemark & Gleam.

Hiro Finn Hoshino is an Australian author. With a background in contemporary performing arts, he loves to weave surrealism into his uncanny, fantastical worlds. His short stories have found homes in publications across Australia and the USA, with "The Visitor" earning an Honorable Mention at the Writer's Digest 90th Annual Writing Competition. He is currently working with a watercolor artist on a children's novella *Dream Bear and the Teardrop Acorn* while researching native Ainu mythology in Hokkaido, Japan.

Christopher O'Halloran (he/him) is the factory-working, Canadian, actor-turned-author of *Pushing Daisy*, his upcoming debut novel from Lethe Press (2025). His shorter work has been published by Kaleidotrope, NoSleep Podcast, *Cosmic Horror Monthly*, Dark Moon Books, and others. He is editor of the anthology, *Howls from the Wreckage*. Visit COauthor.ca for stories, reviews, and updates on upcoming novels.

Simo Srinivas is a writer of all things weird and queer. They were named 2023's Brave New Weird Breakout Author by Tenebrous Press, and their work has appeared in several magazines and anthologies, including *Fantasy*, *Strange Horizons*, and *Archive of the Odd*, among others.

Simo can be found at:
http://srinivassimo.com
Twitter/Bluesky/Instagram @srinivassimo.

Jen Mierisch's dream job is to write Twilight Zone episodes, but until then, she's a website administrator by day and a writer of odd stories by night. Jen's work can be found in *The Arcanist*, NoSleep Podcast, Scare Street, and numerous anthologies. Jen can be found haunting her local library near Chicago, USA.

Ray Pantle writes horror and other dark fiction, largely focused on internal character transformations, loners and outcasts, flawed protagonists, and the raw yet sympathetic depictions of mental illness. He has been published in *That Which Cannot Be Undone: An Ohio Horror Anthology*. You can find him in Columbus, Ohio, with his wife and their many spoiled cats.

Micah Castle is a weird fiction and horror writer. His stories have appeared in various magazines, websites, and anthologies, and he's the author of *The World He Once Knew* (Fedowar Press), *A Home in the Darkness* (DEMAIN Publishing), and *Reconstructing a Relationship* (D&T Publishing).

While away from the keyboard, he enjoys spending time with his wife, playing with his animals, spending hours in the woods, and can typically be found reading a book somewhere in his Pennsylvania home.

Patricia Miller is a member of SFWA and writes science fiction, fantasy, and horror. Publications include short fiction in numerous anthologies, *Metastellar, Zooscape, Stupefying Stories,* and *Cinnabar Moth Literary Collections*. Her most current publications include stories in *99 Fleeting Fantasies* edited by Jennifer Brozek and *Dastardly Damsels* coming in Fall 2024 by Crystal Lake Publishing.

Sheila Massie is a speculative fiction writer of fantasy and horror, both dark and hopeful, (though not always in the same story). She holds a 3rd degree black belt in TaeKwon-Do and, when away from her writing desk, trains empowerment self-defense instructors internationally. She enjoys a good sipping tequila, can't live a day without cheese or tea, and doesn't like mornings. She lives with her husband and her brat of a Miniature Rottweiler in Victoria, BC, Canada. Her fiction has appeared *in Flash Fiction Online, Daily Science Fiction, Augur Magazine* and elsewhere.

Sheila can be found at:
sheilamassie.com

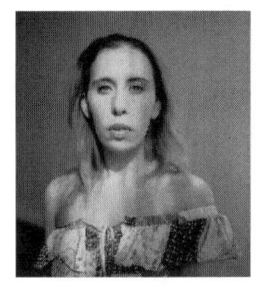

Stephanie Parent is a writer of dark fiction and poetry. After many years in Los Angeles, she now resides in her hometown of Baltimore, Maryland. Her debut horror novel *The Briars* was published by Cemetery Gates Media.

Bebe Bayliss is a California-born Canadian author writing mystery & suspense, science fiction, fantasy, paranormal, weird west, and horror, with stories featured in anthologies from Zombies Need Brains, Flame Tree Publishing, Brigids Gate Press, and Air and Nothingness Press. She co-writes mystery novels with Gini Koch, including *Fall's Girl* and upcoming *Something Wicked*. Bebe lives in British Columbia with a very tall husband and a very small dog.

Bebe can be found at:
www.bebebayliss.com

Linda D. Addison, award-winning author of five collections, including *How To Recognize A Demon Has Become Your Friend*, the first African-American recipient of the HWA Bram Stoker Award®, received the HWA Mentor of the Year Award, the HWA Lifetime Achievement Award and SFPA Grand Master of Fantastic Poetry.

Photo courtesy of Courtney Hartley.

Linda can be found at:
www.LindaAddisonWriter.com

About the Editor

S.D. Vassallo is a co-founder and editor for Brigids Gate Press. He's also a writer who loves horror, fantasy, science fiction and crime fiction. He was born and raised in New Orleans, but currently lives in the Midwest with his wife, son, and two black cats who refuse to admit that coyotes exist. When not reading, writing or editing, he can be found gazing at the endless skies of the wide-open prairie. He often spends the night outdoors when the full moon is in sway.

About the Artist

Alison Flannery is a slightly feral artist who lives and works in Denver, Colorado. Her work is inspired by nature and she works primarily in oil paint and paper collage, sometimes both at the same time. Alison's work can be seen on her website: www.AlisonFlannery.com

More From Brigids Gate Press

Scissor Sisters

Ed. Rae Knowles & April Yates

21 tales of sapphic villains, curated by April Yates and Rae Knowles. Featuring the work of:

Hatteras Mange, Anastasia Dziekan, Ariel Marken Jack, Maerwynn Blackwood, Avra Margariti, Grace R. Reynolds, Evelyn Freeling, Hailey Piper, T.O. King, M.S. Dean, Chloe Spencer, Mae Murray, L.R. Stuart, Alex Luceli Jiménez, Cheyanne Brabo, Luc Diamant, Alyssa Lennander, Anya Leigh Josephs, Lindz McLeod, Caitlin Marceau, Shelly Lavigne.

And a bonus tale from Eric Raglin!

Seers and Sybls

Ed. MJ Pankey

Oracles.
Prophets.
Sibyls.
Seers.
Fortune tellers.

These, and many other names were given to those who had the sight, who could look into the future and see what awaits us. Sometimes, those glimpses come unbidden and unasked for. Sometimes they are given for a fee. Sometimes they drive the recipient mad with the knowledge of what the future holds.

Others view those so gifted with suspicion, doubt, envy, and occasionally anger. Rarely are prophets thanked for their predictions. They bear the curse of knowing what's coming along with the scorn and fear shown them by the rest of society.

Seers and Sibyls is a collection of 30 stories and poems about those who have the power to see the future. Will you open the book and read their prophecies?

Featuring the stories and poems of: David Marino, Beth O'Brien, Victoria Brun, Rose Strickman, Zachary Rosenberg, Erin L. Swann, Nico Penaranda, A.L. Munson, Caroline Johnson, Marshall John Moore, N.R. Lambert, Susan Jordan, Jeremy Megargee, Nwejesu Ekpenisi, Jennifer Bushroe, Laura Marden, Joseph Mathias, Stephanie Ellis, Bettina Theissen, Misty Urban, Gerri Leen, Kayla Whittle, Ivy L. James, Matthew Yap, Cormack Baldwin, Shannon Connor Winward, Jacqueline Kate Goldblatt, Devan Barlow, Jay McKenzie, Sam Muller

WERE TALES: A SHAPESHIFTER ANTHOLOGY

Ed. S.D. Vassallo and Steven M. Long

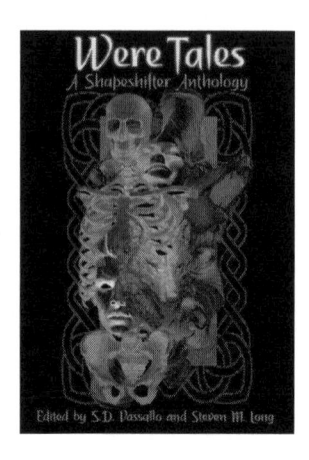

Werewolves. Berserkers. Kitsune. From the most ancient times, tales have been told of people who transform into beasts. Sometimes they're friendly and helpful. Sometimes they're tricksters. And sometimes, they're terrifying.

Were Tales is a collection of scary, thrilling, dark, mysterious, and even humorous short stories and poems of shapeshifters, from the talented minds of Jonathan Maberry, Stephanie Ellis, Gabino Iglesias, Laurel Hightower, Eric J. Guignard, Michelle Garza and Melissa Lason, Shane Douglas Keene, Clara Madrigano, Kev Harrison, Beverley Lee, S.H. Cooper, Elle Turpitt, Catherine McCarthy, Alyson Faye, Theresa Derwin, Ruschelle Dillon, Baba Jide Low, H.R. Boldwood, Ben Monroe, Cynthia Pelayo, Cindy O'Quinn, Sara Tantlinger, Stephanie M. Wytovich, Linda Addison, Villimey Mist, Tabatha Wood, and Christina Sng.

Dangerous Waters: Deadly Women of the Sea

Ed. Julia C. Lewis

Malevolent mermaids.

Sinister sirens.

Scary selkies.

And other dangerous women of the deep blue sea.

Dangerous waters takes us deep beneath the ocean waves and shows us once more why we need to be cautious about venturing out into the water.

Featuring stories, drabbles and poems by Sandra Ljubjanović, John Higgins, Patrick Rutigliano, Candace Robinson, Emmanuel Williams, Desirée M. Niccoli, L. Marie Wood, Samantha Lokai, Christina Henneman, Gully Novaro, Christine Lukas, Alice Austin, Dawn Vogel, Victoria Nations, Mark Towse, Kristin Cleaveland, Ben Monroe, Kurt Newton, E.M. Linden, Eva Papasoulioti, Ann Wuehler, Rachel Dib, A.R. Fredericksen, Daniel Pyle, Megan Hart, Ef Deal, Katherine Traylor, Juliegh Howard-Hobson, Simon Kewin, Elana Gomel, Lauren E. Reynolds, Grace R. Reynolds, René Galván, Marshall J. Moore, Ngo Binh Anh Khoa, Roxie Vorhees, April Yates, Kaitlin Tremblay, T.K. Howell,

BRIGIDS GATE PRESS

Kayla Whittle, Emily Y. Teng, Briana McGuckin, Tom Farr, Cassandra Taylor, Steven-Elliot Altman, Paul M. Feeney, Lucy Collins, Marianne Halbert, Rosie Arcane, Antonia Rachel Ward, Steven Lord, and Jessica Peter.

Visit our website at: www.brigidsgatepress.com

Made in the USA
Middletown, DE
24 April 2025

74662406R00156